P9-DNE-380

## Meet the Cutter Force Initiative

**COLONEL R. A. "RAGS" CUTTER:** A career military man, Cutter left the GU Army when he ran afoul of Army politics. At large, Cutter realized that there was a need for his kind of expertise and created a fighting force for specialized, smaller-scale actions.

**JO SIMS:** A former PsyOps lieutenant in the GU Navy, Sims is drop-dead gorgeous and as adept with small arms as she is with her mind.

**TOMAS "DOC" WINK:** A former ER doctor, Wink is an adrenaline junkie who doesn't feel alive unless he is on the razor's edge defying death.

**ROY "GRAMPS" DEMONDE:** Previously the PR director for a major corporation, Gramps lost his family in the revolution and is always looking for a way to stick it to the GU.

**FORMENTARA:** A *mahu* and cybernetics whiz adept at installing and maintaining all kinds of bioengineered implants.

**MEGAN "GUNNY" SAYEED:** A master weaponsmith and expert shooter. If it throws any kind of missile or a particle beam, Gunny can use it, upside down and over her shoulder.

**_KLUTH_FEM "KAY":** A Vastalimi who can kill using only her bare hands, feet, or fangs—even though at heart she is a pacifist.

**Praise for the novels of Steve Perry**

"A crackling good story. I enjoyed it immensely!"
—Chris Claremont

"Heroic . . . Perry builds his protagonist into a mythical figure without losing his human dimension. It's refreshing."
—*Newsday*

"Perry provides plenty of action [and] expertise about weapons and combat."
—*Booklist*

"Noteworthy."
—*Fantasy and Science Fiction*

"Another sci-fi winner . . . Cleanly written . . . The story accelerates smoothly at an adventurous clip, bristling with martial arts feats and as many pop-out weapons as a Swiss Army knife."
—*The Oregonian*

"Plenty of blood, guts, and wild fight scenes."
—*VOYA*

"Excellent reading."
—*Science Fiction Review*

"Action and adventure flow cleanly from Perry's pen."
—*Pulp and Celluloid*

# THE RAMAL EXTRACTION

## CUTTER'S WARS

# STEVE PERRY

ACE BOOKS, NEW YORK

**THE BERKLEY PUBLISHING GROUP**
**Published by the Penguin Group**
**Penguin Group (USA) Inc.**
**375 Hudson Street, New York, New York 10014, USA**

Penguin Group (Canada), 90 Eglinton Avenue East, Suite 700, Toronto, Ontario M4P 2Y3, Canada (a division of Pearson Penguin Canada Inc.) • Penguin Books Ltd., 80 Strand, London WC2R 0RL, England • Penguin Ireland, 25 St. Stephen's Green, Dublin 2, Ireland (a division of Penguin Books Ltd.) • Penguin Group (Australia), 707 Collins Street, Melbourne, Victoria 3008, Australia (a division of Pearson Australia Group Pty. Ltd.) • Penguin Books India Pvt. Ltd., 11 Community Centre, Panchsheel Park, New Delhi—110 017, India • Penguin Group (NZ), 67 Apollo Drive, Rosedale, Auckland 0632, New Zealand (a division of Pearson New Zealand Ltd.) • Penguin Books Rosebank Office Park, 181 Jan Smuts Avenue, Parktown North 2193, South Africa • Penguin China, B7 Jaiming Center, 27 East Third Ring Road North, Chaoyang District, Beijing 100020, China

Penguin Books Ltd., Registered Offices: 80 Strand, London WC2R 0RL, England

This is a work of fiction. Names, characters, places, and incidents either are the product of the author's imagination or are used fictitiously, and any resemblance to actual persons, living or dead, business establishments, events, or locales is entirely coincidental. The publisher does not have any control over and does not assume any responsibility for author or third-party websites or their content.

THE RAMAL EXTRACTION: CUTTER'S WARS

An Ace Book / published by arrangement with the author

PUBLISHING HISTORY
Ace mass-market edition / January 2013

Copyright © 2012 by Steve Perry.
Cover art by Kris Keller.
Cover design by Lesley Worrell.
Interior text design by Laura K. Corless.

All rights reserved.
No part of this book may be reproduced, scanned, or distributed in any printed or electronic form without permission. Please do not participate in or encourage piracy of copyrighted materials in violation of the author's rights. Purchase only authorized editions. For information, address: The Berkley Publishing Group, a division of Penguin Group (USA) Inc., 375 Hudson Street, New York, New York 10014.

ISBN: 978-0-425-25662-6

ACE
Ace Books are published by The Berkley Publishing Group, a division of Penguin Group (USA) Inc., 375 Hudson Street, New York, New York 10014.
ACE and the "A" design are trademarks of Penguin Group (USA) Inc.

PRINTED IN THE UNITED STATES OF AMERICA

10  9  8  7  6  5  4  3  2  1

If you purchased this book without a cover, you should be aware that this book is stolen property. It was reported as "unsold and destroyed" to the publisher, and neither the author nor the publisher has received any payment for this "stripped book."

**ALWAYS LEARNING**          **PEARSON**

*This book is for Dianne,*
*and how could anybody who knows me think otherwise?*

*And for the musical jam groups the NFUs and the CMs,*
*where I finally began learning how to play nicely—*
*more or less—with others . . .*

# ACKNOWLEDGMENTS

Thanks go this time:

To Ginjer Buchanan and her team at Ace/Berkley/Putnam/Penguin, with whom I've had a long and lucrative relationship, spanning several decades.

To the adept crew at the Jean Naggar Literary Agency.

To the Thursday gang in Cotten's garage, who bang shins and thump ribs in an effort to learn *Maha Guru* Stevan Plinck's improvement of the Javanese-based knife system *Pukulan Pentjak Silat Sera Plinck*, which continues to be the centerpiece of my martial arts training.

To master bladesmith Chuck Pippin, for the knife that Doc Tomas Wink carries for chores other than healing surgery.

To artist Ubin Li, who gave me a working image of Kay.

To the faithful readers of my two weblogs: the general one, at www.themanwhonevermissed.blogspot.com, and the more martial one, silatseraplinck.blogspot.com. You're in the neighborhood? Drop by and sit a spell.

And to my space opera fans who have stuck with me all these years, a special thanks for your loyalty. Couldn't have done it without you, folks.

Fog, like moonlight, obscures and distorts an army's vision, causing things to appear other than they actually are.

—CARL VON CLAUSEWITZ
(*FILTREPROPRE*, V3)

# ONE

Quasi-serious death blew past Cutter's helmet, the sharp and hard whistle of a hypersonic rifle round.

The shiftsuit's tacticals IDed and tracked the bullet, backwalked the angle, and a red enemy-sig lit on Cutter's heads-up display.

Red, because the suit's computer was programmed to assume that anybody shooting at you was an enemy.

Must have taken the programmer a while to come up with that rationale.

Colonel R. A. "Rags" Cutter knew exactly where the sniper was—that old resiplex, third floor, two windows south of the corner, 104 meters *that* way. If he wanted, he could get the shooter's height and weight from the suit's pradar, but . . . why bother?

Cutter ducked behind a recycle bin, a stacked-everplast tub full of enough garbage to provide cover and not just concealment. There were several of these bins on the curb, and the suit's filters didn't cut out all the odor of rotting organics.

Obviously, it was trash-pickup day.

The suit's computer ran a quick scan on the composition of the wall and spotted up a chart for what it would take to breach it: Their sidearms would be a waste of needles. Their AW explosive rounds would need a few hits in the same spot—the material's Rockwell showed that it was apparently a local stone equivalent to marble, and fairly thick. The AP rockets would punch right through, of course, but at 1196 New Dollars each, those were better reserved for hard targets—spend one on a tank or a juggernaut, that was a good deal; piss one away on a sniper? Bad for the bottom line. Wasn't like it had been in the real army, where you shot whatever you wanted and piss on the cost, Mama Terra had plenty more where those came from.

"Y'all all right over there, Colonel?" That was Gunny Megan Sayeed's droll SoTerran vox in his sonicware. She was behind the next recycle bin, ten meters to local south.

She was aware that the sniper's weapon was no real threat to the suits Cutter and the rest of the pent wore. As long as that was all the sniper had to throw.

If he could afford them, Cutter would use Fully-Augmented-Shiftsuits for every trooper on every stand-up-shoot-back mission. Best technology available here in the late twenty-fourth century, they were. Unfortunately, those leases also cost a small fortune, and his operating budget usually only allowed for a few unless the customer had really deep pockets. FAS's were outstanding tactical wear. The soft and breathable fabric would harden to Class VI personal armor two milliseconds after any missile impact, and bullets would bounce right off. It would defuse charged-particle-beam pulses up to eighty watts, and lasers and masers would take all day to raise the temperature inside the suit five degrees. Well, it would take most of a minute, which was practically all day. Plus the chameleon shift could make you virtually invisible to anybody seeing in the human visual spectrum . . .

"I'd be a lot happier if one of my loyal and efficient troops would lob a boomer into that window and shut down that sniper, you know, just in case he's waiting for us to get overconfident before he starts shooting serious AP. And not to put too fine a point on it, why hasn't somebody already done it?"

Boomers only ran about fifty noodle apiece. They could afford that.

There was a short pause, and Gunny said, "Well, actually, Kay was gettin' kind of antsy, so Ah let her off the leash."

Cutter shook his head. "You know we aren't getting paid by the hour?"

"You just got here, so Ah got to choose. 'Sides, aren't you the one always tellin' us to accommodate the talents when we can? That's old school up there, Rags, he's usin' a *gunpowder* hunting rifle, for chrissake. And besides, Ah don't think it will—"

There came a horrific scream; despite the adrenaline dampers circulating in his blood, the hair on Cutter's neck stirred as his flesh goose-bumped.

The terrified yell stopped as if cut off by a knife.

*Or by a set of really sharp, diamond-hard, alien claws delivered across a throat at inhumanly fast speed.*

"—take all that long," Gunny finished.

Cutter could almost feel her smile. "Nobody likes a smart-ass, Gunny. That's the last one, right?"

"Yessuh, Colonel, suh, ten for ten, and mission accomplished."

Cutter stood. Gunny was already on her feet, and the two troopers also rising behind her.

All things considered, this hadn't been a bad operation. They'd been hired to find and take out a bandit cell that had been hijacking TotalMart's hovervans, when the local police proved ineffective. That turned out to be because the local police were part of the cell—at least two of the KIAs were for sure, maybe more, the b.g. checker hadn't run them all down, what with a couple of them being no more than small and bloody bits scattered over half a klick. What they got for riding in a piss-poor armored vehicle and eating an AP rocket.

An expensive rocket . . .

Cheop was a backlane planet, part of the three-habitable-worlds Filay System, and a van full of high-end augmentation gear, exotic foodstuffs, pharmaceuticals, or just semi-intelligent robotics could be worth a million or two ND, easy. TotalMart rural vans were the size of two-family houses, and packed tight, to maximize delivery-to-cost ratios. The bandits had hit three of them over a period of a few weeks. One had been destroyed, and they were holding the other two for ransom. Lot of balls to do that, the bandits; steal and clean the vans out, then charge the company to get the empties back. Since the vans were spendy hardware, the hijackers could have all retired rich—except they got greedy.

Smart crooks knew when it was time to leave the party. Always better a little early than too late. Stupid crooks stayed too long.

Enter Cutter Force Initiative, because the GU's Army hated having to space to the middle of nowhere to protect the galaxy's largest corporation's bottom line. They would do it, because big money talks loud enough, so everybody has to listen, but they didn't like it. And after the most recent revolution, they were stretched thin.

The fucking GU Army . . .

*Don't go down that corridor, Cutter. Living well is the best revenge, remember?*

*Yeah, I remember being booted out of the Detached Guerrilla Forces by the fucking GU Army, too.*

Yeah. It was his gain, and since they were underwritten by TotalMart, it didn't hurt to kick ass and have the veeps in Security nodding and smiling. And TM even paid on time, another plus.

TM would send people to collect the stolen trucks and a

fair amount of the cargo would be retrieved. No, it wasn't a bad op at all . . .

The purple flash on his HUD made Cutter glance toward the building. *Kluth*fem ambled out from the place and loped toward where he and Gunny stood. She was suitless but had a transponder. The tactical always purpled a Vastalimi's sig, not that anybody with eyes would mistake one of them for human. They were about shoulder high to an average man and looked like a cross among a tiger, an ape, and a praying mantis. Bipeds, with a short, thick, orangish fur and almost humanlike arms and legs, but with tapering, wedge-shaped heads and big eyes, Vastalimi were as deadly a soldier as you'd want.

Too bad more of them weren't big on leaving their home-world. Cutter would hire a whole platoon if he could. Some ops, when the enemy found out he had *one* Vastalimi working for him, they'd quit right then.

"Kay," he said, as the Vastalimi arrived. Her real name was difficult for a human to pronounce properly, and *Kluth*-fem was a generic that didn't really translate exactly into Trade. The troops called her Kay, and she was good with that.

"Colonel."

"Any problems?" It was a joke, but he kept his face serious.

She gave him a look, kind of like when a puppy hears a strange noise and turns her head this way and that to regard it. "No," she said. "No problems." Her Trade was clean, if somewhat inhumanly accented. A lot better than his Vasta-limi. He could produce maybe fifteen or twenty words in their main dialect that a native speaker might understand: *Well met*; *Farewell*; *Require a healer*; interrogatives for *toi-let, food, drink*; *Stop! Okay*; and the insult *Your sister for-nicates with prey*. It was a throat-busting language for humans, who weren't rigged with some kind of vocalware.

One of his favorite war stories was about when a GU

Army Recon Kill Team did a sortie on New Java a few years back. Recon KTs were badasses, they sported combatware augs out the ass—hormone pumps, auditories, ophthalmics, nerve boosters, viral/molecular tacticals. They were trained to razor sharpness, carrying major firepower and ready to wreck or die.

According to the tale, the KT octet, after a terrorist cell, had kicked the wrong door and charged inside.

Instead of terrorists, there had been a Vastalimi family on a vacation, having dinner. Male, female, a couple of half-grown children. Forty-five seconds after the RKT booted the door, they were all dead, and the Vastalimi family didn't have a scratch on any of them. According to the most extreme version of the tale, they took out the Recon team, then sat back down and finished supper . . .

Gave a whole new spin on the term "top predator."

Probably apocryphal, that story. But he had seen Kay move, and while she was as adept with small arms as most in the unit, she preferred her claws when it came to close combat. Retracted, you could barely see them, they looked like not-particularly-long dark nails. Extended, they were four-centimeter curved needles, and she could tear her way through an isotet or wooden wall as fast as a strong man flailing with a pair of smatchets.

And Vastalimi didn't mount—or need—cybernetic augmentation to outdo humans in much of anything, either . . .

"Colonel?"

Opchan Three, that was Sims, back at the field command vehicle.

"Go ahead, Jo."

"We about done here?"

"Haven't you been watching the feed?"

"What, and miss Chef Flambé on the Cooking Channel? We're doing chocolate soufflés today."

He chuckled. "Yeah, we're done." Jo had been PsyOps,

when she'd been in the Army, a first looie. She liked to pull chains, and she was good at it.

"Gramps just called, and we have an offer for a gig on Ananda, an extraction."

"Kidnapping?"

"Haven't seen all the details yet, but looks like it."

Cutter considered that. Extractions were sometimes iffy—badly timed, the kidnappers would, often as not, just kill the victim and run. On the other hand, the pay was good, and the risks to the unit minimal compared to chasing pirates or dealing with rebellions, warlords, or other private militaries.

"We're on the way in. Get the details."

"Don't slam the door when you get here, I don't want my soufflé to fall."

# TWO

The Forward Command Vehicle was about the size of a double-wide pubtrans floatbus, and the medical suite aft was large enough to squeeze six gurneys into it in an emergency though it had only three that could make full use of the suite's D&T units. With the diagnose-and-treat systems lit, a medic didn't need to do much hands-on work, just monitor and stand by for problems the dins couldn't manage, which, frankly, were apt to be beyond any but the sharpest combat docs.

Tomas Wink liked to consider himself among the sharpest, and he'd had enough time in grade to make the claim.

The UV lights kept the air free of most nasty pathogens though it gave the place a slightly scorched smell.

The trooper on the table was a question. He'd been hit by the blast of an IED shear that blew him into a tree four meters away from where he'd been walking. The suit had absorbed and deflected the explosion and the impact somewhat, but they weren't magic, those suits. It was like the old joke about the problem with jumping out of a hopper at altitude: It wasn't the fall that killed you, it was the sudden stop.

Physically, the trooper—his name was Fletcher—looked mostly okay. Some bruises, contusions, nothing broken or majorly torn. But his vitals were off—pulse, respiration, BP were all too fast. His hormones were whacked, and his chem scans a-jumble. Adrenaline and testosterone were sky-high.

Easy enough to calm down, but better that he could find a cause.

Wink knew what it was generally—something in his combatware augmentation was malfunctioning. But the C-scans had come up clean, the myoneurals showed the effect but not the cause, and everything on Fletcher's implant or viral-molecular nanocircuitry list checked out as within normal parameters. He had the standard galactic-military issue: hormone reservoir and pump; auditory and optical sets; nerve enhancers. Nothing else listed.

Might have to get Formentara in here. Zhe would figure it out in a hurry, but he hated to give up that easily.

Wink looked at the naked man sitting on the exam table. He had a thought.

"My chart says your sexual preferences are hetero."

"Yeah, so?"

"You ever see Captain Sims in the buff?"

Fletcher grinned. "I might have passed her in the shower a few times."

As Wink watched, the soldier sported a sudden rampant erection. Jo Sims was drop-dead gorgeous, and a lust magnet among those attracted to women. But to pop a boner with a doctor looking right at you?

Wink grinned. "Dickware," he said. "You're running dickware."

Fletcher's carnal grin vanished.

It wasn't against regs to sport nonissue military augs, if you could afford them. Most couldn't, and those who could paid for it in more ways than one. First, they weren't cheap. A good high-end combat-rated aug could run six months' pay, and the top-of-the-line stuff? If you had to ask what they cost, you couldn't afford them.

Second, the more augs you wore, the more they chewed on your physiology. The old heuristic was, every general-system aug you got cost you five years of life span. At 150 standard years, ten or twelve augs would lop five or six decades off the end. Wink had known rich aug-hogs who ran twenty systems. Live fast, die young, and leave an absolutely hideous corpse, and that didn't even speak to the psychological problems. Now and then, an aug-hog would unbalance and go amok, and those who sported military- or assassin-ware could wipe out a lot of people before they got taken down.

Double-edged sword, that.

"It's not illegal," Fletcher said.

"Not for the Cutters, though you got it while you were in the Army didn't you?"

The kid nodded. "Yeah."

The Army didn't care for pornware. It made you a better killer? Hey, they were all for that. It made you a better fucker? They didn't want the troops distracted going to, or in the middle of, a firefight. Make war, not love.

"I don't care about exercising your willie. I'm your medic, son, and I need to know these things if I am going to keep you alive and fit. It's piggybacked, isn't it?"

"Yeah."

"Where?"

"On the myostim adjunct."

Wink nodded. That's why he hadn't spotted it. Kid had been hiding it from the Army docs, some of whom might have noticed but most of whom wouldn't have if they'd even bothered to look. He'd have found it eventually. That wasn't the first place he'd have looked.

"Lie down."

The kid did, and Wink went to adjust the D&T. The aug had been damaged from the impact with the tree. It was easy enough to fix once you knew what the problem was, and if he was in a good mood, Wink could repair it so it was better than before, just a matter of inserting the right virus and nanosires into the right gene and spinning it. If he was in a bad mood, he could shut it down, or even reverse it. Fix it so Fletcher couldn't get it up with a crane and a roomful of pornoproj stars paid only if they got him off . . .

That would be cruel, and he wouldn't do that. The troops needed to blow off steam, sex was as good a way as any, and better than a lot of other options. As he well knew personally.

Wink grinned. Formentara would still get a kick out of this story. It was hir kind of thing. Zhe knew way more about cybernetic biologicals than he did. Maybe more than *any*-body did. If Wink wanted wetware of any kind, Formentara was who he'd want installing and tweaking it.

The D&T hummed away, and Wink stood there watching. He was bored. He was usually bored. He needed to do something active. Preferably with some risk to life or limb. Sex was way safer, mostly. Unless you decided you wanted to do it with the wrong person in the wrong place at the wrong time, just to juice it up. Once, he had picked up a miner's woman in a downlow pub near the big iridium mine on Far Bundaloh. Taken her into a stall in the public toilet and had noisy intercourse there. The miners were hard-asses and they would have casually killed him for all kinds of reasons just because they felt like it, but that one, screwing one of their fems? That would have put him high up the to-do list.

It had given the activity a certain spice . . .

# THREE

In the comshack, Jo Sims did a quick, personal radiopathic scan—one of her most useful augs, what with the subcell neuron implants, she had all kinds of available frequencies—and admitted the ophthalmic flit from Formentara: *Time for a tune-up,* scrolled across her field of vision. And if that's what Formentara said, Jo was good with that.

Formentara was a *mahu,* a human androgyne whose gender wasn't readily apparent at first glance. Nor on second, third, nor however many glances. Nobody in the unit claimed to know whether Formentara was a "he," a "she," or "other," but Jo didn't care. Zhe was the best hands-on cybernetist around, the kind of diagnostician who could run hir fingers over your body and intuit what was wrong with your onboard systems, then fix them while zhe ate a sandwich and read a novel. Hir expertise was beyond science and well into art.

Why zhe wasn't under contract to some giant university or corporate cybernetics unit was a mystery—zhe could make five times what CFI paid anywhere in the civilized galaxy, no questions asked.

Jo had more implants than anybody she knew who wasn't dead. They gave her power and ability beyond most humans', but, she had been told going in, at a cost: They would kill her eventually, and sooner rather than later.

She had made her choices, for her own reasons, and she was willing to live—and die—with those. She had never expected to see seventy or eighty standard years—until she met Formentara.

"Camel cark!" Formentara had said. "If systems are balanced and maintained right? If you repair wear-and-tear biodamage and gross injuries properly? No reason you can't live out a normal span, you don't burn the lamps overtime."

"How many technomedics can do that?" Jo had asked. "Keep systems that perfectly balanced?"

Formentara grinned. "Counting myself? Two. Maybe three."

Jo laughed. "I expect they have a long waiting list."

Zhe shrugged. "If they spouted off and *told* people they can do it, sure."

"You just told me."

"And that's the deal: I'll keep you running, but you keep it to yourself."

Jo didn't take long to answer: "I'm good with that."

Zhe grinned. "I figured."

Jo shook the fugue and got back to the project at hand. A kidnapping, and an op she'd be running. Rags liked fieldwork, but his time was better spent running big strategy, not little tacticals. He was the colonel and she the captain, but he knew he was too valuable to risk in too many dustups, so his forays into the field were limited. Now and then, he had to get out and shoot something, but she was careful to keep those to scrapes where the risk was minimal. He didn't like it, but he did it. He'd sit back at the mobile HQ and drum his fingers, unless the shit really hit the fan.

Or he got really bored.

At least, she'd get a chance to get out of this fucking

form-chair and back into action where she belonged. A chance to stretch.

Better get the b.g. stuff collected so she could do the briefing. In extraction work, time was the biggest enemy. If the kidnapped victim wasn't killed immediately, there was usually a period when they might be recovered alive. But after a few weeks, the longer the elapsed time, the fewer chances of a live recovery.

## FOUR

On the *GS Frag*, a Class III Leapship that could haul eighty people and all their gear in relative comfort eighty light-years at a Leap, and twice that many people in a pinch, Jo Sims stood at the head of the conference room table. Seated around the table were Gunny, Gramps, Doc, Formentara, and *Kluth*fem. Colonel Cutter leaned against the carbon-fiber inner wall near the room's primary hatch.

"All right, folks, listen up. We are on our way to Ananda, half of a binary system with Om, planets circling a class G2V star, FHND 31-Epsilon—that's Flamsteed-Halley New Designation for those of you not planning a second career as an astronomer.

"Informally, the system is called Lance. Mid-rim, Orion Arm, turn left at the Dagger Nebula and straight on 'til morning.

"Ananda is an E-type world in the ninety-eighth percentile for atmosphere and gravity, a little more oxy, a little less nitrogen. Your circulating antibacterials and antivirals have been updated to deal with the local bugs.

"Twenty-two-hour days, 369-day years, climate range Within Terran Standard Limits, but shading more into tropical, save toward the poles.

"Activate your sunblocks and drink a lot of replenishment fluid.

"There are no indigenous intelligent species. Eight-tenths of the place consists of saline seas, landmasses clustered mostly around the equator, with small-continent-sized islands farther north or south.

"The usual—trees, mountains, lakes, plains, like that. Lots of trees where we are going, so expect to see a lot of wood construction.

"Population nine hundred million, originally settled by wealthy immigrants from TerraIndia, the local businesses are chiefly agro- and aquacultural, mining, and assorted light industry. Largely self-sufficient, their unique exports are medical-grade Rhodopsin, a visual-purple substance extracted from a local fish, used in military vessel viral-molecular computer-memory systems, and Heavenspice."

"Ooh," Gunny said, "Heavenspice. Doubles the cost of a good meal for one sprinkle of that. Worth it, though."

"Good meal?" Gramps said. "When's the last time you ate anything other than field rats or vat-grown mysteryburger burned to a crisp? Dusting those with Heavenspice would be a crime against nature."

"You'd know *all* about crimes against nature, wouldn't you, old man?" Gunny said. She smiled.

Jo ignored them. "The reason we got this job is because TotalMart has a couple of big stores on the world, plus being an exporter. They work long-term contracts with both the Rhodopsin fish processors and the Heavenspice Growers Union, and they want to keep the Rajah happy, so they recommended us. We need to move somewhat cautiously, so as not to—"

She stopped. "Am I boring you, Doctor?"

Wink looked at Jo. He faked a big yawn.

"Truth, fem? I confess, I am pretty much somnambulant."

She lit her Stress Analyzer aug, just because she could. Always useful for PsyOps to know when somebody was lying. She scanned the heads-up display—another direct send to her optic nerves.

Heartbeat. Respiration. Blood pressure. Myotonus. Perspiration. Conductivity. Eye movement . . .

Given his stats, the yawn wasn't fake. He was pretty much relaxed enough to be on the edge of nodding off.

The fucker—

"And that's different than usual *how*, Doc?" Gramps said. "You the only man I ever knew could go to sleep sucking a bulb of hot soup while falling down a flight of stairs."

There was a soft whicker from Kay. They didn't laugh loud, the Vastalimi, but they did laugh a lot, and they seemed to understand human humor just fine, even if they didn't always agree with it. A typical Vastalimi joke would feature a punch line in which half a dozen people might be dismembered in a particularly hideous fashion, with the resulting gore put to some use that would make humans go pale and excuse themselves from the room while the Vastalimi whickered themselves silly laughing.

*And he slipped in the blood and smashed his nose against the wall, then fell and cracked his skull, and his sister said, "That will teach you!"*

*Whicker, whicker, whicker . . .*

Different species, different ideas of what was funny.

Next to Kay, Formentara. Jo thought hir expression was slightly amused, but with hir, it was, like most everything else about Formentara, hard to tell.

Cutter did like disparate characters on his teams as long as they were competent.

She shook her head. Yes, there probably wasn't any real need to learn about stellar classes and where the planet stood in relation to the galaxy, but you never knew what might be useful, so she was thorough in her coverage of new operations. Better to have it and not need it than the other way around.

Nobody ever bitched about having too much ammo in a shoot-out.

"If I might continue?"

Wink offered a theatrical shrug and a shit-eating grin. *Don't mind me.*

"Our client is named Ramal, he's the Rajah of New Mumbai. His daughter, Indira, has apparently been kidnapped by a person or persons undetermined. Our mission is get her back, preferably alive. Which means we'll have to figure out who took her first."

"Ransom demand?" That from Gunny.

"Not thus far. The political situation is mostly fine, but at a continental level is apparently less than copacetic. There are several . . . rajahnates? rajahdoms? that run most of what goes on on-planet. They don't all get along. Plus the usual malcontent insurgents, who would seem to be the obvious suspects.

"Indira is engaged to be wed in the next month, they are big on single-partner, different-sex coupling locally, a major celebration attached, and this has put a crimp in those plans."

"We sure she didn't just run off?" Gunny asked. "No ransom demand, how do we know she was kidnapped? Some of these old-style societies still go in for arranged marriages and such. Maybe she didn't want to connect with her mate-to-be?"

"That has to be considered," Jo said. "We haven't seen all their data yet."

*Kluth*fem made a sharp tongue-click sound.

"Kay? Something?"

The Vastalimi said, "If the female's departure was voluntary, are we obligated to return her if we locate her?"

"No. She is an adult by local and GU standards. If she left on her own and we find her, we report that to our client. Up to them to work that out."

Kay chirred. There came a pleasant, faint musky odor, a pheromone that Vastalimi females sometimes emitted when they were pleased.

They had had some interesting moral codes, the Vastalimi. Apparently on Kay's homeworld, females had been held more or less in thrall until the last hundred years or so. The females finally got tired of it. There had been a short and fairly bloodless revolution. Females refused en masse to have sex with the males. Any male who attempted rape was hunted down by cadres of females and castrated.

At some point, the males saw the light. Which probably made them a little smarter than human males, she figured, who still tended to think of themselves as God's gift to women . . .

The female Vastalimi were still touchy about such things. If Indira had left on her own, and somebody wanted to make her come back, Kay wouldn't have any part of that. Or maybe she'd get in somebody's way, a not-inconsiderable obstacle. It was good to have a Vastalimi as your friend, bad to have one as an enemy.

Jo glanced at Cutter. "Colonel?"

Rags said, "Jo has pretty much covered it, but my contact inside TotalMart has let me know that local biz folk tend to be insular and suspicious of outsiders. Oh—and the GU Army's Ex-Tee-J-Corps has a base in New Mumbai, just outside the capital city."

There came a chorus of groans at that. XTJC fielded some good officers and troops, but in Jo's experience, they also always had more than their share of total assholes. Most GU military didn't have any use for mercenary cadres, but Jaycore *really* didn't like them. She'd never met anybody in any of those units who called the Cutters anything other than "cutthroats."

A couple of times, she had come close to pulling a blade, and offering, "You mean like this?"

"You know the drill, people. Live with it," Rags said.

"With any good luck, we'll be in and out of there in a hurry, and spending our bonuses during a nice thirty-day liberty."

Jo nodded at this, but the truth was, she wasn't much on liberty. Too much trouble she could get into in the civilian world without even trying.

She picked it up: "Rest of it is in your downlinks, read over it, we'll hit n-vac at 0800 ST and arrive in the vicinity in seventy-two hours. Back to full gee once we finish the Leap, so better hit the myostim. If you are wheezing and dragging two minutes after we exit the ship, you can stay here and collect base pay while the rest of us divvy up your bonus."

Gunny laughed. "You hear that, Gramps? I'm gonna be spending your bonus NDs on my spa vacation in Bali."

"Sheeit, Chocolatte, I'll give you a two-minute head start in a four-minute race and still run your skinny brown butt into the ground."

"What, you went and got jet augs installed in your ass?

"Come by my cabin, I'll show you what I got augmented."

"You *wish*."

"Nah, it's *your* loss."

Jo shook her head. Gramps was the oldest guy in the room, but he was only fifty-one SYs, beating Rags by six months. Still, that made him fifteen or so years older than Gunny, and eighteen older than Jo. They liked to razz him about being an old fart, but truth was, he was in pretty good shape for a man his age. And given the back-and-forth with Gunny, Jo wouldn't be at all surprised to see them wind up in the sleepsack together. Military foreplay was often combative. Gunny could shoot the nuts off a minifly at five meters, and Gramps could have them weighed, measured, and sold for a profit before the fly's nads hit the ground. She'd seen stranger pairings.

"That's it, we're done. Try to stay out of trouble."

# FIVE

*Kluth*fem sniffed the alien air at the spaceport as she stepped into the hard sunshine from the ship's dinghy, seeking the scents of predators and prey. Mostly what she got were the stinks of lube and fuel and hot plastcrete, and the body odors of the humans waiting there. With humans, you sometimes got prey, sometimes predator, and sometimes both from the same individual mixed together. Ever fascinating, that identity shift. Even dying Vastalimi never smelled like prey.

They were on the outskirts of the largest city in the country, also named "Ramal," a seaport on the west coast. There was a slight tang of ocean in the atmosphere. There was also a faint hint of Rel, the amphibious aliens sometimes seen from Out the Arm, but she couldn't spot Rel among the humans standing in the heat of the day, nor any on the crews bustling about the port's parked vessels. Interesting. She made a mental note to follow that up: Prey could be useful at times.

There were a dozen humans waiting, all males, under the shade of a portable canopy. She cataloged the twelve: four dignitaries, armed with what appeared to be gem-encrusted, forearm-length, slightly curved, ceremonial knives in gilded sheathes.

Eight guards, each bearing slung carbines and sidearms. They also had sheathed knives, but in plain scabbards, sans decorative stones on the handles. Working blades.

These men were obviously fit and alert for any signs of danger. Their eyes were hidden by polarized glasses, but her vision was enough to dimly see past the plastic.

One of the guards flicked a sharp glance at her, eyes only, a predator's look, and she felt her claws start to reflexively extend. She quickly retracted them. In her culture, a hunting glance was a challenge, and had to be answered: *You see me as prey? Behold my claws and reconsider.*

The glancer would be the first of her targets if those guns lifted to point in their direction. Then the one to his left, who was larger and thus likely to be slower; then the one on the right, next to the youngest human. After that, they would have moved, and she would have to see how they had shifted position to choose the next target. She knew they were unaugmented, but she could smell the increased hormonal flux from here, and on the possibility they could read Vastalimi scent, she exuded contentment pheromones. Let them think she was no threat.

Always best to have an enemy underestimate you and be surprised, if need be.

She couldn't see them, but she expected there were other guards at a remove, hundreds, maybe thousands of meters away, armed with long-range weapons.

Humans did love their guns.

Cutter Colonel, dressed in a uniform custom-made for such meetings, with ribbons and medals agleam on the chest, took the lead. As he approached the contingent, the eldest of the humans, a tall man with a thin gray beard and a blood-colored turban, stepped forward to greet him, palms pressed together in front of his torso. His silks were thin, bright, and draped to cover his more than ample girth, flowing in shifting shades of red and purple. This would be, she guessed, the Rajah for whom they'd be working

She could hear the greeting easily enough; most humans would not be able to do so at this distance.

Yes, the Rajah. And the younger man next to him?

Many among the Vastalimi didn't bother to tell one human from another visually, and some of them offered that all humans not only looked the same, they stank the same. Kay considered it a useful skill to differentiate them by sight as well as smell, and she had devoted the time and effort necessary to learn both. It had been useful more than a few times. One did not need to ask *Who goes there?* in the night if one could recognize one's own team by their odors.

Thus she was sure that the younger man was not a close relation, based on his dissimilarity of features.

She caught a name: *Rama Jadak*.

Ah. The husband-to-be? Or was it a common name here?

There was a transport parked not far away, a shaded awning from the canopy leading to it. This was a bus-sized vehicle, sufficient to contain them all; however, Cutter had arranged for other transports, and those smaller vehicles were parked past the largest one. Once aground on a planet that might be hostile, it was best to avoid giving a potential enemy a single and mayhaps easy target, and since they weren't here to guard the Rajah, he was not their primary concern.

To avoid giving offense, none of the humans in her party stood armed, at least not visibly so. There would be serious weapons in their transports, vehicles manned by their own people; as soon as they got there, they would arm themselves better.

Even though her preference was for claw-to-claw, that wasn't always the best option. She had known some on her homeworld, martial-arts masters, who'd thought themselves invincible; swaggerers who believed that no one could lay a blade or beam on them because they were so adept. And some were experts, walking murder.

Too, some of those masters had been killed by Vastalimi with less than a tenth of their skill but who brought better deathware to the fight. At ten meters, the sharpest claw or tooth was a poor tool against a gun firing a dozen fléchettes a second. Only a fool thought otherwise.

Yes, one felt the need to test one's self, to push her limits and see; however, there were times to fight claw-to-claw, and times to shoot an enemy from a distance, and it was a idiot who didn't try to learn which was which. Pride in one's skill was fine, as long as it did not blind one to reality.

The greeting ceremonies over—humans had many variations of this one, most of them a waste of time as far as Kay was concerned—they headed for the transports.

The world was hotter than she liked; double-coat fur was great for keeping cold out but also equally good at keeping the heat in, and while she could lower her blood pressure and trigger an autonomic cooling response in emergencies, that was not the case here. Uncomfortable was not an emergency. And she might as well get used to it since they might be on this planet for weeks.

As they neared the rented transports, Kay felt her nape fur bristle. She glanced around, didn't see any obvious new threats—no fanatics waving long knives, no incoming vehicles heading for them, no signs of small aircraft focused in their direction. But there was something, and she had long ago learned to trust that atavistic danger signal.

Jo drifted toward her. Before she could speak, Kay said, "I feel it. Do you detect a source?"

"No. But there are twelve armed men over there by that roller, eight of whom are carrying projectile weapons.

"Yes."

A human with a gun might be your friend, but he was still a human with a gun. If you didn't know and trust him, you kept tabs on him. And even then, trusting most humans with or without guns was problematical. You only had to fail once badly, and you would be dead.

Vastalimi could, of course, lie, but no known race in the galaxy could begin to compete with humans in that arena. Humans would often lie unthinkingly, almost reflexively, about things large or small. And they even qualified the term with degrees: White lies. Fibs. Whoppers. Prevarications, lies of omission. It was fascinating how many ways they could dress up or dress down the notion of deliberate untruths.

The nearest guard was twenty-two meters from Kay, the farthest twenty-eight, with the Rajah, his potential son-in-law? and the other two between them.

The radiopathic button clicked in Kay's ear as Sims subvocalized into the comtac unit: "Colonel, Kay confirms my impression."

The com was set for short range and encoded, so if anybody chanced to hear it, they wouldn't know what was being said.

"Copy," the colonel said. "You heard the fems, people, whatever shooters you have hidden, loosen 'em up, and not all at once. Watch the Rajah's people. Anybody points killware in our direction, hose them. And since the Rajah is our client, best if we keep him alive until we get paid, too."

There came a cricket chorus of acknowledgment clicks.

"Can't see the Rajah or his mucky-mucks going into slaughter-spree," Jo said to Kay. "Rich people seldom run amok; they hire somebody to do that for them. Likely it will be one of the guards or their driver."

"Agreed." Their transports were manned by CFI's own people, and while it was not impossible that one of them could be compromised, it was less likely than the alternatives. They didn't know the Rajah's guards nor his driver.

Sims Captain triggered an aug. Kay felt the human's temperature rise slightly, accompanied by a flush of her fair skin. Jo was in combat mode and would be able to move 39 percent faster with an 80 percent usable increase in her normal strength; additionally, her vision, hearing, and senses of touch would also be enhanced. She would be almost as fast and strong as Kay though her vision and hearing would still be somewhat less. And the human would burn much more energy much quicker.

"Let's hear the arms report," Cutter said. "Helm?"

"Port ceepee turret locked on the bus, Colonel. Say it, I'll light it up."

Cutter said, "So we don't sweat the bus. I've got my flat-pack deuce."

"Same here," Jo said. "Plus the biozapper."

The flat-pack pistol was gas-operated, small and flat enough to be slipped into a pocket, the magazine held twenty 2mm poisoned fléchettes. It had an effective range of thirty meters. Sufficient for unarmored soft targets.

The augware bio-capacitor in Sims would fire a single electrical bolt eight meters; however, it would take half an hour to recharge for another shot.

"T&T," Kay said. *Teeth and talons.*

Kay listened as the others in their party rattled off their concealed weaponry:

"Pulse wand." That from Dr. Wink.

"Willis four-point-four," Gunny said. "Also a thermex mini and a Rilke knife."

"Where the hell are you hiding all that?" Gramps said.

"Wouldn't you like to know?"

A Willis 4.4mm pistol was only slightly smaller than a standard service sidearm. Its double-stack electric magazine held thirty rounds of explosive pellets and on full auto would chop a large human in half with five hits in a line. A thermex minigrenade would cook unprotected soft targets in a five-meter radius of the detonation. A sharp Rilke knife would pierce softweave and flex-ceramic armor with little effort.

Gunny Sayeed was well armed for somebody supposedly not in that mode. Of course, she always was well armed.

"All right," Cutter said, "let's stay on track for the vehicles—"

Kay sensed the guard's intent to move. Before he had his carbine unslung, she sprang; by the time he had both hands on the stock, she was only eight meters away. As he lifted the weapon and began to bring it to bear on the Rajah, she was five meters, still increasing her speed.

Almost close enough to leap—

Jo had also moved; she was two meters back and two to Kay's right, and in slow-vision-predator mode, Kay saw two more guards unshipping their weapons.

Were they intending to protect the Rajah? Simply copying their fellows? Or part of an assassination attempt?

The guards appeared focused on the Rajah and not each other, and as Kay leaped and snapped her claws out, she hoped Jo could see that the other two were part of the problem—

She hit the guard just as he triggered his weapon, knocking him and the firing carbine flying. Projectiles splashed off the plastcrete, sparking as they hit, but it did not appear any of them struck the Rajah—

Kay tore out the guard's throat with her right hand and pushed him away with her right foot, already past him and arcing into a long forward roll—she was going too fast to stop—

She heard the second guard scream as Jo bowled into him, and became aware of the third guard's head exploding into a spew of blood and bone and brains as she rolled up and half turned to face the rest of the Rajah's party—

One of the guards swung his weapon in her direction—

"Tell your guards to stand down!" Cutter yelled. "It's over!"

The Rajah yelled at the guards: "Do not shoot!"

She was already sidling to her right, putting the Rajah between herself and the guard tracking her—

The guard with the gun pointing toward her froze as he covered the Rajah. He jerked the muzzle away.

Not an assassin, then. Or one who thought it better not to try now.

The Rajah yelled again. "Do *not* shoot! Guns down!"

The guards lowered their weapons.

Still in a crouch and ready to move, Kay took in the scene.

Her target was down, already mostly bled out; Jo's target lay on his back, his arm obviously broken. The third guard, missing the top half of his skull, was sprawled boneless, certainly dead.

Twenty meters away, Gunny Sayeed stood holding her pistol with two hands, muzzle pointing skyward, alert for more threats.

"Head shot," Gramps said. "What a fucking show-off."

Gunny grinned. "Those who can, do, old man."

The colonel was wrong, though. It wasn't quite over. The driver of the bus stepped out of the vehicle's door with a short rifle and swung it up to point at the Rajah—

Jo, who was closest, pointed her right forefinger at him, and said, "Stop!"

She didn't wait to see if the driver would obey. A crackling green bolt shot from her fingertip and struck him. He jittered, dropped his weapon, and fell, spasming and twitching as his nervous system burned out.

Sims shook her hand. "Ow. Ow! I keep forgetting how much that stings!" She stuck the tip of her finger into her mouth.

*Now* it was over. Except for what would no doubt be a major investigation into the Rajah's guards, to see who was apt to cut loose at him again and who'd step in front of those guns to save him . . .

# SIX

The head of the Rajah's Security Unit was a massive, swarthy man, two meters tall and maybe 130 kilos; he had a thick, black beard but a shaved head, and he looked as if he could chew nails and piss needles. His curved knife had a plain, well-worn grip-scales, and the sidearm he wore was a massive, gray-handled thing in a beat-up leather holster. No silks, he was in a blue flexsuit and traction boots.

Nothing ceremonial here; this was a man who used his weapons a lot and was geared to move in a hurry.

Wink wondered if his pulse wand would even slow the giant down if he decided to give him grief. Be interesting to find out . . .

The security man, introduced as Ganesh, stood at the head of a long, oval table made of wood with a beautiful, close-grained flame pattern in it, light against dark.

Behind him on the wall, a hologram flowered, and Ganesh nodded at the recording.

Cool air flowed over them, a welcome relief to the heat outside. Wink had never liked hard tropics. Give him a temperate world with mountains and a lot of liquid water, that was his kind of planet. Deserts and jungles? Leave those for lizards and apes.

There weren't any other locals here except the Rajah's prospective son-in-law, Rama, whose father, if Wink remembered his briefing, was the son of the rajah next door. Jadak? Something like that?

For their part, they numbered half a dozen: the colonel, Jo, Gramps, Gunny, Kay, and himself. All of them carried holstered sidearms now, and there were a pair of CFI troopers outside the conference-room door with assault rifles watching their backs, with two quads more at the transports.

The half-size holoproj showed a courtyard, viewed from maybe four meters above. The courtyard was full of colorful tropical plants, a small bubbling pool of water with orange-and-white hand-sized fish darting about in it, and a walk of what appeared to be dark cobblestones or a pretty good imitation of them.

After a few seconds, a woman appeared, walking from the right side of the frame toward the left. The woman wore a sari-style garment in what looked to be a pale blue silk, with matching slippers. A slight breeze molded the cloth to the front of her body. From the drape of the cloth, she was obviously female, a bit thin, but curvy. Her hair was dark, parted in the middle, and worn in a long braid that hung midway down her back, and she carried a cage of bamboo, containing a scarlet bird the size of a small parrot, but with a straw-yellow-colored, toucanlike bill.

"The Rajah's daughter, Indira," Ganesh said. His voice was high, girlish, and Wink had trouble reconciling that soprano with the man's appearance. There was something spicy on his breath, a pleasant, mintlike odor.

As they watched the recording, a figure approached the woman from directly underneath the security cam. He was taller than she was by a head, wearing a gray coverall with a hood, and she turned to face him as he drew nearer. Only his back was visible.

There was no audio, but the woman said something.

"She asks, 'Who are you?' " Ganesh said.

Indira frowned.

The man—perhaps a large woman?—pulled a small pistol from a coverall pocket. The figure wore thin gloves.

Indira tried to run, but the gunner fired before she could take even one step. She dropped the bird's cage, clutched at her belly, and doubled over—but stayed on her feet, swaying.

The cage hit the cobblestones and broke apart.

The bird freed itself from the wreck and took to the air. Three meters high, four, level with the camera—

The shooter thrust the gun at the bird and fired again.

The bird dropped like a brick. Hit the cobblestones, bounced once, lay still.

Gunny said, "That's a good shot with a stubby handgun, to hit a bird in flight point shooting. He's some kind of pro."

The shooter pocketed the weapon, caught the wobbly woman, and hoisted her over his shoulder in a rescue worker's carry.

*A man. He moved like a man,* Wink thought.

The kidnapper hurried away, in the direction the woman had been heading. He disappeared.

Ganesh waved one hand. The projection shut off.

Jo said, "Was the bird some kind of messenger? Apt to bring help?"

"No," Rama said. "It was a warbler, trained to sing traditional songs. My gift to her."

"Apparently the shooter was not a music lover," Gramps said, but his voice was quiet, so Wink barely heard it. Probably just as well the Rajah and his people didn't hear it.

"We believe the bird was shot to tell us something," Ganesh said.

"What would that be?" That from Kay.

Ganesh ignored her. He looked instead at Cutter. "We recovered the projectile from the bird and examined the missile. A low-velocity anesthetic dart. Sufficient to kill the bird, but only potent enough to make a human semiconscious for a short time. They meant us to know they had not killed her. They would know the garden was covered by cameras. With the bird, that would be sufficient for us to know."

Wink caught a whiff of Vastalimi hormone. Kay was angry, at least a little.

Ganesh caught it, too. He turned and gave Kay a cold glare. He said something almost under his breath, and Wink heard it—*Karāhiyat*—but didn't recognize the term.

Kay's claws popped out, and she grinned at Ganesh, angled her head to one side.

Not a pleasant expression, that—

"At ease, Kay," Cutter said.

After a moment, Kay's claws vanished. She kept watching Ganesh.

Ganesh sneered. He tried to stare Kay down, but he was wasting his time. Vastalimi had nictitating membranes that protected their eyes. She could hold that expression unblinking all day if she wanted. Humans didn't win staring contests with Vastalimi. Plus, if the Vastalimi got tired of it, he or she could always just claw the offending eyes out . . .

After a bit, Ganesh glanced away.

"And there has been no call for ransom?" Jo asked.

Rama shook his head. "We have had no demands of any kind from those who took her. They are allowing us to twist in the wind."

Jo said, "If they wanted her dead, they could have killed her right there."

That mirrored Wink's thought. Shoot her with something harder and leave the body.

"Unless they had worse than a clean and quick death in mind," Ganesh said. He kept staring at Kay.

Rama hissed something at the big man, who quickly looked down at the floor.

"Your pardon, sah."

"She is *not* dead," Rama said to the others. "I would *know*. But those who took her will wish their parents had never met before they die!"

Jo said, "And you have no idea who might have done this?"

Ganesh shook his head. "We do not. The Rajah has enemies. Some insurgents who would change the world to suit themselves. Foolish, but enemies."

"As do I have enemies," Rama added. "And I will address them." His fury was barely suppressed.

"We'll want a list," Jo said.

"Of course."

After they left, headed back to their transports, Gunny walked next to Wink. She said, "That ole boy Ganesh don't know how close he just came to leavin' this plane."

Wink looked at her.

"He called Kay an abomination in Hindi. Apparently she knows that tongue."

Wink shook his head. "A xenophobe. Great."

"Yep. He gives her any shit when Rags ain't around? Ah wouldn't want to be him."

*Me, neither.* Around Vastalimi, it wasn't a good idea to say such things, especially to the females. They didn't put up with much crap. They were always willing to go to the end, win, lose, die, all the same.

Jo stepped up closer to them.

Wink had never bothered to get much in the way of augmentation, and he wasn't running stressware, though he knew Jo was. "Was the bald asshole lying?"

Jo shook her head. "Not that I could tell. Unless he's got better autonomic control than he does of his emotions, I didn't get stress tweaks except when he looked at Kay. He doesn't seem to know who took the girl by the indirect questions we asked."

Wink said, "What of the intended? He telling the truth?"

"He hopes she's alive, though he can't be sure—I'm a little leery of folks who claim ESP. She could be dead. He certainly seems pissed off about it."

"But like you said," Wink added, "if that was the intent, they could have easily killed her. Do we know how the kidnapper got past her guards?"

"Nobody follows them around inside the palace," Jo said. "How they got inside? Nobody seems to know that, either. There are blind spots where the cams don't go. Didn't see him come in, didn't see them leave."

"Knew what he was doin'," Gunny said.

"Obviously."

"So it would seem they had other plans for her," Jo said.

"Which could mean she is still breathing," Wink said.

"Anything is possible."

They caught up to the others.

Cutter said, "Well, I'm going back to the ship. Might take a little nap. Get the FCV set up, put together an investigative plan. Give me a briefing when I wake up."

Jo nodded. "Yes, sir."

# SEVEN

When they got the FCV rolled out and were halfway through the checklist, Jo got a call from the outlying sentry on the north road.

"Captain, we got company. J-Corps, a looie, sergeant, and four troopers, inbound in an AT roller. Should we let them pass?"

He sounded hopeful, but Jo didn't want trouble with the GU. "Wave 'em through and smile politely. I'll handle it."

"Yes, Cap." He sounded disappointed. There was little love lost between regular and corporate military—until the regular guys came looking for a job, of course.

Kay was already outside, standing in the hard-edged shade offered by the FCV, looking at the roller coming up the road.

"GU Army vehicle approaching," Kay said.

"I heard. Why don't you stand there and sharpen your claws or something while I speak to them. I know it's against your nature, but try and look dangerous." She grinned.

Kay whickered.

The roller arrived three seconds later, top up and a cold pump blasting—Jo could feel the cool draft from three meters away when it stopped and the doors opened. The soldiers exited.

The lieutenant, a tall woman with a military buzz, slipped her compact helmet on, adjusted the lid, and gave Jo a long, cool stare before she and the sergeant ambled over.

The sergeant was male, shorter, shaped rather like a brick, and had a face that had known too many fists and maybe a few boots over too many years. Both wore tropical greens, the camo unlit, and both sported issue 12mm Hauser pistols.

*There is no need to fear, the Galactic Union Army is here . . .*

The other troops stayed by the roller, rifles slung, in parade rest. Wouldn't take long to heat their uniforms up to the sweat point. Military-issue garb was not nearly as breathable and fashionable as the Cutters' own boilersuits.

"Who's in charge here?" the lieutenant said.

"For the moment, the XO would be me," Jo said. "Captain Sims, CFI."

The sergeant grinned but the lieutenant kept her expression flat. "Captain. I'm Lieutenant Dodd, XTJC. I was given to understand that Cutter was here."

"*Colonel* Cutter is unavailable at the moment, *Lieutenant*."

The sergeant looked as if he was about to speak when something caught his attention. That would be Kay, stepping out of the deep shadow into the sunshine. Her orange fur gleamed enough so Jo could see it reflected on the sergeant's scarred face.

Nice. Perfect timing.

He had missed her. A mistake, and he knew it.

The sergeant drifted his right hand nearer the butt of his pistol.

"Lay that hand on your weapon, Sergeant, and you won't like what it gets you."

He looked away from Kay and at Jo's face. "Oh, really?"

"Hosep. At ease," Dodd said.

"We don't have to stand here and listen to this cutthroat make idle threats, ma'am—"

Dodd said, "Seal it, Sergeant. The captain here is running more augs than all of us put together, and that's a *Vastalimi* less than four meters away, in case you lost your memory of how fast they can move. There are only six of us."

He considered that. Outgunned, and he knew it. He nodded.

"We didn't come to tussle," Dodd said. "Only to deliver a message from Colonel Hatachi. We know why you are here. As long as you obey GU laws, we won't have any problems. Step over the line, we come down on you like the thunderbolts of Zeus."

Jo smiled. "Nobody is looking for trouble, Lieutenant; we're just here to do our job."

"Your job." Hosep said. "That's funny."

Jo kept her smile in place. "Yeah, it is, kinda. Because if you'd been doing *your* job, probably we wouldn't be here at all."

Not true, it wasn't their responsibility, but it was a good cheap shot. XTJC brought that out in her.

Whatever he might have said to that, Dodd cut him off: "That's it. We're done. Let's go."

She nodded at Jo. "Captain."

"Lieutenant."

They headed back to the roller, loaded in, and drove off.

Gunny drifted over from behind a stack of water barrels. "Been a while since Ah got to shoot any GU Army guys. Too bad he didn't pull that Hauser. Time he got that tank out the holster, we could have been back in the FCV having a beer. If that old fart Gramps hasn't drunk it all up."

"What, you think I'm deaf in here?" came Gramps's vox from the com.

"Why not? You blind. Let's not even go down the road to 'stupid.'"

He laughed.

Gunny said, "But that looie isn't stupid, is she, Cap? She knew who you were, unless she has some way of seeing how many augs you have on board."

Jo nodded. "Yeah. They did their homework. But as long as they stay out of our hair? No problem."

"You think they will? Stay out of our hair?" Gunny said.

She sighed. "Do they ever?"

— — — — — —

Cutter was still setting up his field office in the still-drying ferrofoam structure. Great stuff, ferrofoam. Put up a plastic mesh frame, spray it on, it hardened to a stonelike solidity in an hour. Three or four centimeters of it would stop most small-arms missiles. First thirty or forty minutes, it was pliable, easy to shape or cut. It had a harsh chemical stink until it dried, smelled like hot gun lube. A halfway decent engineer could make it into anything you needed for field ops. Unless you double-walled it, it wasn't that good for insulation once it set, but that's what heaters and coolers were for. It was cheap and easy to transport, and you could break it down with a chemical spray when you were done, leaving nothing but a little goo that didn't even harm the environment all that much.

If he had any money, he'd invest in the company that made it. Beat the alternatives all to hell and gone.

Gramps stuck his head in the door. "Colonel, we got an incoming call from the kidnappers." Before he could ask, Gramps said, "Rajah's security hasn't reported it to us, but we have a tap on his pipe."

That was SOP. "Let's hear it."

Gramps waved a finger at his handheld.

"We have your daughter. If you wish to see her alive again, you will follow our instructions. We know about your mercenaries, and if you speak of this to them, the girl dies. We will call you again soon. Sorry about the songbird."

The voice was synthesized, a voxbot, probably generated from text.

"I don't suppose we got a backwalk?"

"Nossir, it's planetweb, bounced from all over the world. They ain't entirely foolish."

Cutter nodded. "So they are testing to see if the Rajah is going to tell us."

"Be my guess. Have to wonder why he'd bother hiring us if he isn't, but you know how the clients get."

He knew. Once the threats began, there were families that swallowed and rethought their decisions to hire recovery forces.

Gramps said, "The bit about the bird is to let us know for sure they were in the garden."

"Yes. Or had access to the security recording."

His com buzzed. Cutter held up one hand to caution Gramps to be quiet.

"Cutter."

The call was on speaker: "Colonel, it is Rama here. The kidnappers have contacted us. The Rajah would like to see you when it is convenient."

Gramps raised an eyebrow.

"On my way. Out."

Once the connection was cut, Gramps said, "Well, I guess that answers that."

"So it would seem. I'll go and have a chat with him."

# EIGHT

Nearly an a hour after Rags left, Gunny drifted over to the op center and nodded at Gramps. "So, the colonel's gone to see the Rajah about the kidnapper's message?"

"Christus, this place is full of spies! How'd you know that?"

She shrugged and smiled. "Soldiers' grapevine, Gramps, you know how it works."

"Sure, I was there when it was invented, wasn't I?"

"You said it, not me."

"You were thinking it."

"Can't hang a woman for what she's thinking."

"Good thing."

"Anything new and interesting?"

"Funny you should ask. Want to see a vid?"

"Not if it's porn. That's mostly what you look at, isn't it?"

He grinned. "It *is* porn, sort of. But you'll like it. Trust me."

He waved his hand over the viewer. The holographic projection lit.

"Hot off our spyweb, came in a few minutes after Rags left. It's a recording from one of our birdshit cams. In an area called Rat's Nest, that's a bad section of town, just east of the Rajah's compound."

The view was from about four meters high. The alley was empty, save for some boxes stacked near one of the garbage intakes. The manhole-sized cover on the intake was up, the lid propped in place by what looked like a short mop. The buildings bordering the alley looked like thetic-stone overlay, probably slapped onto local wood.

After a few seconds, *Kluth*fem ambled into the shot.

Gunny looked at Gramps, then back at the image. Birdshit cams, so-called because of how they were deployed, angle-dropped from small robotic flappers to stick on contact, were sharp enough to gather fairly clean intel. One of the first things CFI did when it landed on a new planet was deploy "birds" to sow cams. They were motion-detecting and tracking, and this one autofocused on Kay, centering her in the view.

"You know how Kay likes to go and get the lay of the land," Gramps said.

Gunny nodded.

Two seconds later, a large human arrived from behind Kay. He had a shaved head and a thick beard.

"Why, look at that, it's that ole boy Ganesh. Oh, my."

Gramps nodded.

There was no audio, and that was too bad—Gunny would love to hear what the Anandan was saying.

Kay inclined her head to the left, then the right, and the angle was such that they could see she didn't seem to be speaking, only listening.

Kay shrugged, a gesture that meant more or less what it would done by a human.

She turned, as if to leave.

The Rajah's security man whipped his knife out and chopped down, as if trying to split Kay's head—

*Ho—!*

Kay blurred, moving too fast for Gunny to follow her moves—

—Ganesh toppled like his bones had suddenly dissolved.

"Holy shit," Gunny said.

Kay turned and walked off. Ganesh lay unmoving on the alley floor.

"He dead?"

"Wishful thinking. Watch it again in slomo." He waved his hand, wiggled a finger a couple of times. "One-third speed."

This time, when the knife came out, Gunny could see that Kay had anticipated his attack and was already in motion. She jinked to the outside of Ganesh's arm, blocked the downward cut with her right hand, shoved his arm down, then smashed the side of his head with her left-palm heel. She slid a hair to her left, shot a strike to his throat with her right hand, catching him with a V between her thumb and other fingers. Then she stepped in, smacked his ribs with a left elbow, her right knee thudded into his groin, and she followed up with a right elbow to his nose.

*Bap-bap-bap-bap-bap!*

Gunny looked at the timer inset.

Just about a second from the time the knife appeared. Impressive, as always, watching Kay move.

But was what *more* interesting?

"No claws," Gunny said.

"Yep. You know that's considered major contempt for an opponent on her world."

"Yeah. Cub play."

"I just downloaded the local medic's report. Fool-boy Ganesh there has a concussion, a broken hyoid, two cracked ribs, a badly bruised testicle, and a broken nose. I'd guess he'll be taking a few days off."

"And he's lucky that's all he's got. You think he'll try her again?"

"Would you?"

"Ah'd never have tried her in the first place. Ah wouldn't want to risk shooting her from across the room."

"Me, neither."

"Probably wouldn't hurt for us to keep an eye on ole Ganesh if we are still around when he gets back up to snuff."

"Yes." He shook his head.

"What?"

"That expression. 'Up to snuff.' What does that mean?"

She smiled. "Well, you know me, Ah'm just a poor ignorant gunnery sergeant trying to get by, not any kind of his-tori-an, but Ah do believe it has to do with an ancient stimulant made from powdered tobacco that was inhaled nasally. The sudden influx of nicotine into the mucosa caused a sharpening of one's thoughts and feelings, thus the phrase originally meant that. Over time, it came to mean 'meeting a required standard.' "

He looked at her as if she'd turned into a big spider.

"Who the fuck are you? What have you done with Gunny?"

She laughed. Had to give a man who could make her laugh points for that. "Thanks for the show."

"My pleasure. Make you hot?"

"It purely did. Too bad there aren't any men around to take advantage of it."

"Get the fuck out of my office."

She laughed.

– – – – – –

Cutter sat across from Ramal and his perhaps-future son-in-law. He noticed that the head of security wasn't there.

"Where is Ganesh?"

"He had an accident," Rama said. He waved one hand, dismissing it. "Not important. We know who sent the message."

Cutter said, "Was there more to it than what you played for me?"

"No."

"Then I don't see how you know who sent it. I didn't hear any identification. Were you able to source it?"

Rama said, "There is no need! The tone of the words identify him as if he had spoken his name aloud!"

Cutter nodded. "I see. Maybe you could explain?"

Rama looked at Ramal. The older man offered a slight nod.

The younger man said. "The land that abuts My Most Honored Rajah Ramal's kingdom of New Mumbai to the east is Balaji, ruled by the Thakore Ilmay Luzor, a vile and despicable man begat by thieves and murderers and desecrators. His line has for a century frothed and foamed like mad *freaux* kits, yapping and trying to nip at the heels of his betters. He is a backstabber, a scoundrel without principles, an eater of scat who would stab himself if he could but bleed on our shirts by the deed."

Cutter kept his face impassive. "I see."

"It is the phrase 'Sorry about the bird' that reveals him. It is exactly the kind of thing he would say. My beloved Indira is assaulted, kidnapped, spirited away, and this piece of filth apologizes for killing a songbird! It could be none other!"

Rama paused, appeared to gather himself a little, tamping down his anger. "The thakoredom has harried us—and I include my own father's realm of Pahal in this, for we are bordered to Luzor's territory to the north—for many years. Small insults, stings, disputes over the demarcator through the Inland Sea—never quite worthy of full-scale retaliation, but constant and irritating. This time, he has crossed too far the line. This time, he will pay with his blood in the dust!"

Cutter said nothing, but if there was going to be a war, he wanted to renegotiate their contract if they were going to stick around and be part of it. Kidnapping was one thing; war rates were much steeper.

"We could crush him," the Rajah said. "Our combined

armies outnumber his by three or four to one; however, a precipitous attack might cause the death of my daughter. We would win, but I and Rama would lose." He paused a moment. "And war is expensive."

Cutter almost grinned but held it. The old man had orbited the local sun a few times.

"Perhaps, a smaller incursion," the Rajah said. "A surgical strike that cuts through to where my daughter is . . ." He paused. "Once we locate her."

Rama said, "Now that we know who is responsible, my agents will find her. And once she is recovered, we will deal with Luzor once and for all."

Cutter said, "With the proper intel, we can make such a foray."

He sensed that the meeting was done. He nodded and stood. Rama also came to his feet. Rama said, "Honored Rajah, I will go immediately to harry my spies to greater action."

The Rajah waved one hand toward the door as he, too, stood.

Rama headed out. Cutter made to follow him.

"Colonel, bide a moment, if you would?"

Cutter paused.

Once Rama was gone, the Rajah spoke. "My future son-in-law is young and full of himself. His blood runs hot, and he is quick to righteous anger. His feelings for my daughter and his sense of outraged trespass might . . . cloud his judgment."

Cutter nodded.

The Rajah stared past him for a moment, then pulled his focus back to Cutter. "The primary goal here is the safe return of my daughter, who has always been the jewel of my heart. That Rama would wade through rivers of blood to slaughter her killers in a white-hot rage would be of little comfort to me."

"I understand."

"You have children?"

"I had a son." *Had.*

"Ah. So you do understand. Rama is a good boy and his intentions honorable, but I engaged you because I want a cool and experienced hand guiding this affair. Please do not hesitate to do whatever you think is necessary to achieve the goal. Accept Rama's help or not, that's up to you. If he gets in your way, be as diplomatic as you can be to go around him, but . . ." He trailed off.

Cutter got that, too. "We will do our best, sir."

"Who can ask for more? Thank you, Colonel."

# NINE

In the still-chemical-smelly conference room:

The colonel looked around the room at his core team. "So that's it. Questions? Comments?"

Gunny said, "So we are standing by to see what Rama finds out?"

Cutter glanced at Jo. She said, "No, we are gathering our own intelligence. No offense to the locals, but they have axes to grind and might be a bit on the subjective side in that arena."

There were a few chuckles at that.

"You all know how this game is played," Jo continued. "Wink can talk to the medicos; Formentara will check with the augmentors—"

"On *this* planet?" Formentara said. "They have augmentors?" Zhe offered an expression of mock amazement. "Using what? Abacuses and pickaxes?"

Jo shook her head, grinning. "Gramps, go find the money. Gunny, there are bound to be working-class pubs. Buy somebody a drink, get the view from the street."

"There are other nonhuman species here," Kay said. "Perhaps they might have information. I will seek them out."

"See if you can do that without killing too many of the locals," Jo said.

"I have killed none of them yet, save that guard."

That was good for a few more laughs. They'd seen the vid starring Ganesh the Incredibly Stupid. And that tag: *yet* . . .

Part of the standard CFI contract was immunity from local laws. And more than a few times, that had been tested to the limits. It had been rescinded once, and they'd had to shoot their way out of the port. Bad for business, when you had to square off with your clients. People got pissy about the littlest things, too. On that operation, they'd probably taken out thirty people on the field, wounded a couple dozen more. What the locals wanted to hang them for? It had to do with being out and about on a local religious holiday. Hey, you can pile the bodies anywhere you want, but don't show your heathen faces on the Sacred Anniversary of Zanu's Holy Ascension!

"Fan out and find out," Jo said. "Time is money. Quicker we clear this, the bigger our bonuses."

After the room had emptied, save for herself and Cutter, Jo said, "You think Rama is going to be part of the solution or part of the problem?"

He shrugged. "Can't say. The Rajah seems to think more hindrance than help, if I read him right, and the kid seems to have a major hard-on for the Thakore next door."

"I'm on that," she said. "I'll have a file for you to look at in a few minutes."

"Good. I think I might tool on over to the range and shoot a target or three; the rust is starting to thicken on my trigger finger."

"Hell getting old," she said.

"Yeah. Come back and see me when you're my age."

"If you are still around."

He smiled. "There's that."

------

Gramps knew all about money, credit, banking, and the shades of marketing: white, gray, and black. Somebody was always looking to get a bigger slice of whatever pie was available and always looking for easier ways to do it. It didn't take him an hour playing on the local nets to figure out where the serious players were in the money games on Ananda. Legal, quasi-legal, criminal, these tended to blend together most places. A step this way, and you were above-board and clean as a new needle. A step the other way, and you were into the gray, where some things were fine as long as you didn't look too closely, and others might get you lock-time if you got caught doing them.

Another step or so, it was shoot-first-and-don't-bother-to-ask-the-corpse questions.

Dealing with the mostly honest and clean shoes was usually the safest way to start poking around. If you couldn't find out what you wanted to know there, you could always head for the crap-boot slums.

Thus he found himself in the foyer of the Anandan version of the Orders of Patrons of Agriculture, the local growers association. It was a new building, high-tech, cold, and sterile, with art and architecture that showcased how much everything had cost. New money liked to flaunt itself; old money tended to be a little lower key.

Fifteen stories tall, a lot of glass plate and exposed stress-plast girders, the headquarters, and paid for by, the exportation of Heavenspice, nearly all of which grown here was controlled by the association who owned this building.

"Captain Demonde?"

Gramps smiled at the sweet young man who had come to fetch him.

"If you'll follow me, Director Sergal will see you now."

Sergal was a tall, fit woman, probably forty or so, with carefully upswept and statically held jet-colored hair that made her look as if she were standing over an air grate. She wore silk cling in a shimmery silver and had a smile that would cut emeralds.

Fine-looking woman, she was.

She stood behind a desk carved from what looked to be a single piece of granite. There was a window behind her that offered a view of the city. The perks of power.

"Captain Demonde. How nice to meet you. Please, sit. How may I be of assistance?"

Gramps sat on the angular and ugly couch, which was every bit as uncomfortable as it looked. Sergal seated herself in her custom form-chair, which would be infinitely more pleasant an experience. He had to look up, since the couch was at least fifteen centimeters shorter than her chair.

There were a number of ways he could go about this, but straightforward was the easiest. She would have had him checked out, as much as possible, and there was nothing to be gained from being devious.

Well. Not yet.

"As you are no doubt aware, Director, the Rajah's daughter Indira has been kidnapped."

"I have heard, yes."

"I am with CFI, and the Rajah has employed us to aid in his daughter's return."

"Of course."

First the carrot: "The Rajah has placed his full confidence in CFI and would be most appreciative of those who help us achieve the safety and freedom of his daughter."

"Naturally, we wish to be of any help in this matter that we can," she said.

"To that end, I need some information."

She waited, that hard smile set in place.

"Who benefits the most financially as a result of this kidnapping?"

"I beg your pardon?"

He leaned back as if the couch were the most comfortable seat he'd ever ridden. "Come, come, fem, it's not that difficult a query. I'm not talking about some criminal collecting a ransom. Who benefits if the Rajah is distracted thus?"

She frowned, and the smile disappeared. He could almost hear her mind working.

"I'm not sure I would be comfortable discussing this."

So much for the carrot.

So, the stick:

"It is my understanding that the Rajah can raise the export tax on your products 100 percent with a wave of one hand, is this not so?"

"He could. But he wouldn't do that."

"Want to bet? Want to be the person who caused it to happen? Because I can guarantee you that everybody and her old fembot Milly will know who was responsible for that because they stood in the way of Indira's safe return."

That got him a small smile—a real one, he thought— mostly in the eyes. "My. A soldier who knows how to play smashball. How interesting. What exactly do you need, Captain Demonde?"

"Call me 'Gramps,' all my friends do."

"And you think we are going to be friends?"

"Why not? Smart, successful, handsome fem such as yourself? A relationship could be mutually beneficial. Never can tell when you might need a soldier who knows how to play smashball. One hand washes the other."

She laughed. "Nicely done. I'll get you a list of players and companies who might find a way to take advantage of the Rajah's agitation."

"I would appreciate that."

"A word of advice. We here in the city are civilized—or what passes for it on this world. Out in the countryside, the growers and overseers and workers are, ah, somewhat more . . . primitive and direct. Step off the path in the wrong place, and you'll get your ass handed to you, and nobody will ever find it, nor you."

"Good to know, Fem Director."

"You must call me 'Lareece.'" She paused for a moment. "Gramps."

They both smiled.

It was always a pleasure to do business with a real professional in the field.

– – – – – –

"You can *do* that? Really?"

Formentara gave the man a small shrug. "It's not that hard."

The building was cheap castplast and the fittings and furniture new, but tacky. Bottom-of-the-line hardware, and the couches were plush but really ugly. The place smelled of vapor-nebulized hemp. *I worked in this dump, I'd stay stoned, too.*

The man shook his head. "Not that hard? There isn't anybody on this entire *planet* who can tune that aug that fine."

The comment was what it was, but it also offered hir a challenge: *I don't believe you.*

Formentara said, "If I may use your board?"

"By all means."

The local had been doing a preop tune, no patient attached, only the aug itself, adjusting the factory presets to the specific patient's scan record. You could do it once the 'plant was over because you still had to do touch-ups anyhow, but it was easier to do the nuts-and-bolts stuff at this stage.

Zhe sat, donned her own temple frame, and ran hir fingers over the board's sensor. Zhe queried, then logged onto the system, found the patient's sig, and his aug-scan, and ran a quick call-and-response. For a good augmentor, this would take a minute. It took hir eighteen seconds. Green, green, and green.

The local augmentor's voice was quiet, nearly a hiss: "Shiva!"

"You get faster with practice," Formentara said.

Then zhe was into the flow, the sensoria of hands-on, mind-on VR that programmers and benders used to access the complexity of augmentation.

Time went away. There was only the *now* . . .

Zhe glanced at the timer's inset automatically as the fugue ended. Preop done. Six minutes. Not bad. Not hir best, but it was a borrowed board and a scan zhe'd never seen before. And crappy gear. One had to allow for that.

Behind her, the local man stood as if he'd been punched in the gut. "Sweet Durga's Taut Titties," he said. "I've never seen anything like that. Who the fuck are you?"

"I have a little skill," Formentara said. Hir smile was as sweet as zhe could make it. Had the hook been set?

"Can you show me how to do what you just did?"

"I can."

"How much? I'll sell my house if I have to."

"I just want to ask a few questions, is all."

"Questions? Shit, ask. If I don't have the answers, I'll find somebody who does."

"Sit," Formentara said. "Watch, and learn . . ."

------

Gunny had changed into civilian threads, not that anybody who'd ever spent any time in the military would be fooled by that. She knew she had the look, but she softened it a little. If somebody thought she was GU military? She could make that work in her favor.

The gray-on-black synthetics draped in the right places to showcase her body—muting the musculature and accentuating the feminine curves, such that they were. Tight here, loose enough there to hide her SOB-carry, a small precharged air pistol. She wore calf-length boots of faux ostrich leather, with a dagger in the right and a hand wand in the left. She'd like a little more hardware, but she was going to a pub, and if things got spewey, she was going to retreat, and all she needed was enough to clear a path. A bunch of pub patrons was not the Chinese Army . . .

Not some kind of drop-dead gorgeous fem they'd be lining up to get at, but not so ugly they'd turn away in disgust. Especially after a few ales or hits of herb.

The first pub she'd picked was near the port, but a little off the tourist lanes. Mostly locals, she figured, but the odd soldier or businessperson who went for the booze and food. A good representative place.

She arrived around 2100. The pub, called Lakshmi's Lair, was moderately crowded. Room for eighty or so, maybe sixty-five there, all humans that she could tell. The place was two cuts above poor, four below rich, a working soul's watering hole. There were small oval tables and seats, a long bar of what looked to be flame-grained, dark wood, with a line of stools, and rows of bottles, bulbs, nebulizers, and vaporizers behind the three tenders working the bar. Lot of wood construction, what with all the forests on this world.

It smelled like dopesmoke, a pleasant, burning-leaves scent.

Gunny made her way to the bar, ordered one of the tap ales, and turned to look at the room while she sipped on her drink.

Ventilators sucked out much of the smoke from those who indulged in lit hemp or other herbals. There was a mostly happy walla from the patrons, noisy, but not overly so, people having a good time. In her experience, the drunken brawls, if there were going to be any, would generally start later in the evening.

There were two bouncers working the floor, easy to spot from how they moved around, watching for trouble. One of them was short and built like he had molded armor on under his shirt—thick, heavy, but light on his feet.

The other bouncer was taller, muscular, but lithe, and very smooth as he drifted this way and that, making a circuit through the tables and patrons, looking for possible trouble.

Both men had zappers in palm-lock pockets on their right hips.

Good bouncers would get to trouble and shut it down before it cranked up far. A smile, a word, a free drink, and failing those? Fast and economical violence and hustle the offending party out the door.

Gunny sipped at her ale again. Well. Another planet, another pub. Might as well get to work.

She started sizing up the patrons, looking for one she could get into a conversation with. It would be easier as the night wore on; drink loosened a lot of tongues, and the thing was to pick the right talker.

There were official channels but the vox populi was hard to beat for a lot of things. Not always the most accurate information but a feel for what people believed, that was important. What the woman-on-the-street thought went past statistics and got to applied sociology. *What do I think? Hey, sister, let me tell you what I think . . .*

There was a trio of soldiers near the back, in street clothes, but obviously military. Not them, she decided. If they mistook her as one of them, it wouldn't take long to get over that notion—she didn't know the local postings well enough to fool them. And they'd want more answers than they'd supply.

*Hey, you with the cutthroats? What are you really doing here—?*

*Hey, I hear you are supposed to be hard-asses, is that right? Let's see how tough you are—*

*Hey, I never screwed a cutthroat before, want to give it a go—?*

Beating the crap out of or shooting three XTJC troopers would be fun, but it wouldn't get the job done, would it?

There were a few loners at the bar, looking for pickups.

Two women, four men, and none of them hitting on each other, so that probably meant either they'd tried and struck out, or they knew each other and weren't interested. Might be something there.

Lot of couples or trios of various compositions around the room. Possible, but more complicated and probably not worth the effort.

But before she could decide who looked like the best possibility, somebody eased up behind her at the bar. She felt them more than saw them, and she slowly adjusted her position to have a peripheral look.

It was the tall bouncer.

"Evening, fem," he said.

She smiled. "That it is." She raised her glass a hair in his direction.

"First time in the Lair?"

"As it happens. How'd you guess?"

"I would have remembered seeing you before."

She nodded. It was a compliment. She returned it. "I believe you would."

That got a tight smile. "You on shore leave?"

She looked at him. Nice-looking kid, midtwenties, and either he'd marked her as possible trouble, or maybe somebody he wanted to get to know better.

Hey. There was no rule said you couldn't talk to the bouncer, right? And as a local working a pub, maybe he was as good a source as any; plus, he wasn't hard on the eyes.

"In a manner of speaking."

He waited.

Sometimes the truth worked as well as anything else. What the hell. "I'm with CFI."

He nodded. "The Rajah's daughter."

"Not exactly a secret, is it?"

He smiled. Good teeth. Really was a nice-looking kid.

"Big news, small planet. People talk."

"Working a pub, you probably hear a lot of that."

"More than a little, yeah."

"You ex-military?"

"No. Ex-police."

Young, for ex-police. She waited.

"Admin and I had our differences. I quit a step ahead of being fired."

She nodded. "Happens. I'm Megan Sayeed. My friends call me Gunny."

"Stavo Parjanya. Mine call me Slick."

Both of them grinned.

"I don't want to keep your from work," she said.

"Rudy's got it, he'll call me if something interesting happens. So, what do you need, Gunny?"

"We're gathering intel. More we know, better our chances of getting the girl back. She well thought of around here?"

"Far as I know. Does charity work, smiles at the camera. I haven't heard anything bad about her. Father is pretty popular. Nobody's taken a shot at him in years until you got here. There are radicals who don't like the way things work, but they tend to stay out in the weeds and throw rocks from there."

"What about the betrothed?"

"Rama," he said. "Well, he's something of a dickhead from what I hear. Ambitious, and the scat is, he likes to kick people who aren't allowed to hit back. The kingdoms are at peace, the marriage will probably help keep it that way."

"The marriage arranged, or for love?"

"Traditionally at that level, they are arranged for political reasons. They seem to get along okay, nothing I've heard says otherwise. She's rich and pretty, he's rich and handsome, those kind of people aren't like you and me. They have other options. They don't have to love each other, they just have to look as if they do. Word is, she actually likes the guy. Bad boys always have women."

"I can see that you are going to be very helpful. So, what

time does your shift end, Slick? Got anybody waiting at home?"

He grinned big at that.

She gave the grin back. Well, there were a lot worse ways to spend her time, hey?

And really, it *was* work . . .

# TEN

Wink did his research on a stretch of river east of the city, where the average windspeed during the day in this season was 50 kph, and his main informant was a kiter who was also a medic.

Well, she *had* been a practicing medic. He had done a background on her.

The woman had been board-certified in microthoracic surgery, an expert cutter who could make the lasers dance well enough to carve her initials onto a white blood cell if she wanted. But she'd discovered kiting, and it took her over. She sold her practice, bought an industrial fabber, set up shop next to the river in a small town, and began making rides and gossamers. She was good at detail work, her gear was first-rate, and pretty soon, she was earning twice the money running the shop as she'd been fixing vessels and nerves. This spoke well of following one's passion.

Vanyu was her name, and also the name of her windrunning product line. Boards, gossamers, the best this world had to offer.

Wink had fallen in love with kiting ten years back, and any world that had enough wind and water, he usually found a way to get into the air there.

Kiting was a combination of surfing, parasailing, gymnastics, and cliff diving. How a run worked was, you got your board up to speed, using a gossamer kite, sailing before the wind. The lift, you left the board and went up. You ascended to whatever height you could handle, popped the kite loose, and then finished with a dive that could range from a pure swan to a nine-trick tumbling fall. After you were done, the autopilot would home in on your beacon and deliver the board to where you came up, using a small inboard capacitor motor, charged by solar. An autocompactor would close your kite and let it fall not too far away—though sometimes the wind would take even a gossamer ball the size of your head some distance, so you had to use the locator to find it.

It was dangerous. Mistime it, and you could smack the water crooked from forty meters up and break half your bones, drown if your emergency floats didn't inflate properly. It was right up there with underwater cave spelunking and netless high-wire racing for serious injury and death. Which, Wink knew, was part of the appeal for him.

He wasn't galactic-class at it, but he was better than average. He didn't see it as a competitive thing but as a personal challenge. Mostly, he was a feetfirster, but he had a few head-down entries.

When he saw Vanyu do her first pass, he realized she was as good as he was and then some. She had the body for it—she was slim, short, and tight—and she did a triple front with a half twist, a branny, and hit the water nicely. A little angle on the slosh, not much.

Wink waited his turn and, on his run, did his mount, got thirty meters up, and did a quadruple flyaway ending in a feetfirst entry. Not the greatest routine, but solid, and he lucked out on the entry, going straight in and not making much splash.

When he got back to the shore, he got some nods of approval, including one from Vanyu. He drifted over close to her as they waited for their turns.

"Haven't seen you before," she said.

"Just got here, from offworld. I'm Tomas Wink."

"Vanyu."

He nodded. "Yeah, I know. I'm using your gear."

She smiled.

"We have something else in common," he said.

She raised an eyebrow.

"I'm a medic. Working with CFI."

"CFI?"

"Private military. Here on a contract."

"The Rajah's missing daughter?"

"Yep."

"Huh. Well, that was a pretty good run. Great entry."

"Thanks."

"What are you doing next?"

"Front one-and-a-half in a layout."

"Height?"

"Forty."

"Really? That's a tricky height for it."

"Guy who taught it to me had it down pretty good. Won the SC with it."

"Graffinger? *Graffinger* taught you?"

It was shameless name-dropping. Hego Graffinger was a three-time champ in Open Class Kiting, who retired after an unbeaten final season. He was a Terran and he stuck close to home, didn't like to travel, but skill-wise? He was to Wink as Wink was to an asymmetrical brick. Anybody who knew squat about kiting knew who Hego was.

"I patched him up once after he broke an arm. He said he owed me one."

She looked at him. "He won his last Systems Championship with a bonded arm, if I recall correctly. Upper-right humerus."

"Yep. Just distal to the deltoid tuberosity. My orthostat glue." He mimed using an injector.

"Wow."

"So, I'm a stranger here. Mind if I pick your brain about local stuff?"

"Go ahead. But if you land that front sommie-and-a-half clean? I will want you to teach it to me."

"Deal . . ."

------

Kay checked, but there were no other Vastalimi in the Rajah's realm. That would have been her preference, to find her own kind, but her own kind tended to stay home. Galactic civilization had so many rules about the smallest things, it was difficult to avoid running afoul of them. Swat a pest, and it died? Humans sometimes got all excited.

Failing that, she went looking for Rel, and it didn't take her long to find them.

Rel were pear-shaped herbivores, bipeds about the height of an average human, but half again as heavy. They were hairless, had a spongelike grayish flesh, and they liked to decorate themselves with assorted paints or dyes, ranging across the visible spectrum. They were clever, did a brisk trade business, and when they came into contact with a Vastalimi, they became prey, an instinctive reaction that made them want to run away. They could control it, but they couldn't hide it, and when one of her kind met one of theirs, she owned that Rel, body and spirit.

Rel preferred to gather in dark, cool places, since their homeworld was dark and cool through much of their habitable territory.

It was but a matter of a few moments for a hunter of her skill to locate her prey.

The public house was dim, and the air inside it moist and considerably cooler than outside. Both were to Kay's liking.

There were a dozen or so of the aliens in the place,

gathered together in the back, and when she entered the room, she heard their collective intakes of breath:

*Carnivore! Freeze!*

Kay smiled and walked directly to the nearest table of Rel.

Nobody got in her way.

She sat, uninvited, and smiled at the Rel nearest her, a male with his skin colored in a rainbow of shimmering, pulsing colors, faintly phosphorescent in the dim lighting.

She spoke her True Name aloud, a sound neither Rel nor humans were particularly adept at reproducing. "And you are?"

The male shivered but managed to control his voice.

"I am Zeth, of the Hallows. My lineage—"

"—is, I am sure, replete with deed-doers and appropriately famous kin," she said. "But I have no need of that information."

"Wh-wh-what is it you want from m-m-me?"

She smiled.

– – – – – –

Time for a strategy-and-tactics meeting.

Cutter stood near the doorway in the temp HQ, leaning against the wall. There was a story to that, Jo was sure, why he liked to stand, and by the door, but he'd never told it. Just like there was one about why he was called Rags. Gramps knew that one, supposedly, but he wouldn't tell it, he'd just laugh and shake his head.

The place still had a faint chemical odor the air coolers hadn't filtered out, and the air was too dry, but it was comfortable enough.

It was her show, and she nodded at the core group. "Okay. What you found out, what you think it means. Gramps?"

Gramps said, "There are people whose pockets fill with NDs if the Rajah is occupied. I got a list and ran checks on them, but I don't see anybody who leaps out. The Rajah is apparently an easygoing sort, but not when it comes to his family. If he finds who is responsible for his daughter's being grabbed, they are dead, their families are going to forfeit any property they own in his kingdom, and their asses will be kicked across the continent. You'd need to make a shit-load of money to make that risk worthwhile.

"Meanwhile, I got some stuff on the Thakore Ilmay Luzor. While Rama might consider him vile and despicable, he doesn't seem to be much worse or better than any of the rulers on this world. Prince of a fellow or scum of the galaxy, depends on who's telling the story and their connection to it.

"Luzor has several palaces in his country, and a couple of them are far enough out of the way that he could stash somebody there without the locals catching it. Pretty much it."

Jo nodded. "Formentara?"

"The state of augmentation on this world is primitive. Most of the locals don't hold with it—manly men and wom-anly women consider it a crutch they'd rather not use. If Brahma had wanted them to see into the infrared, then he would have given them different eyes, blatha-blatha, that kind of crap."

Zhe smiled. "What this means is that Luzor's Army is basic stock, and save for a few bodyguards, whose identities are kept secret, the chance of running into somebody faster or stronger than we are is small.

"However, Luzor, it is rumored, has had some modifica-tion of his sexual gear, so that he is somewhat larger and more potent than once he was."

"Still hope for you, Gramps."

Gramps looked at Gunny and shook his head. "I can give you testimonials, kid."

"From your *paid* companions?" Her smile was sweet as it could be.

Gramps laughed.

Point to Gunny.

Jo said, "Gunny. You're talking. Keep going."

Gunny nodded. "My contact allows as how the marriage between Rama and Indira is political. If it follows custom, they will smile and hold hands in public, wave at parade-goers and festival attendees, produce a couple of heirs, but have private lives behind closed doors if they want. She seems to like him more than she needs to, though Ah can't tell how he feels. Word is, he's a bad boy, and the fems line up to fall under him."

"Yep, us bad boys, we get the women," Gramps said.

It was Gunny's turn to laugh.

"Makes you wonder if Rama's rage against her kidnappers is anything other than his ego being stepped on." That from Wink. "How dare somebody insult me thus!"

"Something to consider," Jo said.

Gunny continued: "Rama is apparently a bully, hides behind his rank.

"Luzor has a couple of favorite watering holes, one of which is next to his summer palace in the highlands. Somebody spotted him there day before yesterday."

"Could mean Indira is nearby if he has her," Gramps ventured.

"Or that she's across the country, and he's giving us something to look at," Jo said. "Table that, we'll get back to it.

"Doc?"

"Luzor seems to be in good health. His vices are mostly those of heteromale adults. Has three wives and four mistresses, ten kids. No animals, aliens, nor children in his bed. He drinks a little, tokes some, eats well enough so he's carrying a few kilos padding. Like to gamble, bets on windskiff races, and has a distillery where he likes to tinker with liquor, mostly blended whiskey. "

Jo waited, but Wink was done. She turned to look at Kay.

Kay said, "The kidnapped girl is supposedly being held at a hunting lodge in the foothills of the Rudra mountain range along this country's borders with Pahal and Balaji. I do not have the PPS coordinates, but I have the name of a nearby body of water, Lake Om."

*"What?"* That from Rags.

It was followed by a chorus of overlapping fuck-me and aw-shit comments from the rest of the group.

"You couldn't have just *said* that before we all prattled on?" Wink said.

"It was not my turn to speak," she said.

Jo chuckled, and most of the rest of them did the same, or at least grinned. Good that the deadliest being on the planet was so polite, hey?

"How did you get this?"

"There are Rel here. I asked one of them, and he told me."

"You believe him?"

"Yes. Rel are prey."

"Oh, well, sure, I guess that explains it," Gramps said.

"Prey cannot help themselves. They will give up anything to avoid being killed and eaten. The Rel knew that had I caught him in a lie, he would be in trouble."

"Would you have done that?" Jo asked.

"I would not have eaten him. I do not care for the taste of Rel."

Jo didn't ask the obvious question: How Kay knew what Rel tasted like.

Some of the others exchanged amused looks. Yeah. They heard what she said, and understood the implications. Must have eaten at least part of one . . .

"Any information about who is holding her?"

"The Rel did not have details. He had the basic information from a fellow Rel who got it somewhere unknown. That one is no longer in the area, else I would have questioned him."

*I bet you would have.* "Well, then," Jo said. "We have a focus. Let's find out everything we can about this hunting lodge."

# ELEVEN

One of the things that a small private military force needs to know how to do is gather intel, and CFI was as good at it as anybody. It didn't take long to find out what was available on the area; they had tapped into weathersats, the local computer nets, and now they were gathered around a projected map of that part of the world.

The overview was enough for them to see the green of giant forests and of an inland sea and several large lakes and rivers.

"All right," Jo said, "here's the place. This is the spysat feed from twenty thousand klicks. That is Lake Om, on the border with New Mumbai, Pahal, and Balaji. These are the Rudra Mountains, and it's in the northern reach of the Sanvi Forest—or the southern arm of the Kadam Forest, depending on how you want to look at it.

"There is apparently some disagreement as to whether Lake Om is in Pahal or Balaji—the Pahali claim it, so do the Balajians. It has apparently changed hands a couple of times in the last thirty years.

Jo nodded at the map. "Zoom, one centimeter to one thousand meters."

The map expanded to a closer view.

"It's rugged territory. Hilly, old-growth forest, only one road along the shore of the lake, and only a couple linking that to anywhere. Military border guards on both sides keep a fragile peace at the moment, and they have been known to throw stuff at each other every now and then."

"Border duty sucks," Gunny said. "Easy to get killed by a bored sniper."

"Zoom, one centimeter to three hundred meters.

"There is the only structure deemed a hunting lodge on the lake's southern shore. There are five fishing lodges, and several summer homes, but because of the dispute, none of these are supposed to be in use, so if somebody is there, either they sneaked in, or they have somebody's approval."

The others nodded. Sure. They knew how that worked.

"Air traffic is restricted, and with the roads guarded, that means—"

"Crap," Gramps said. "We'll have to hike in."

"If you get tired, Ah can carry you," Gunny said.

"You think?"

"Sure, dried-up old husk like you? No problem."

He smiled at her. "On your back?"

"Never mind, Ah rescind my offer."

"Zoom, one centimeter to five meters.

"No vehicles parked where we can see them at the lodge, and there doesn't seem to be any heat sig when we peep at it with IR, but if you look closely at that dirt road—full zoom—you'll see that there is fan splash to the sides, see? And wheel tracks, too. Weather history says it rained there six days ago, four centimeters total, which is enough to have washed away fan or tire marks, so somebody drove to or from the place on that road since it rained."

She looked around. "Anybody want to offer any suggestions on our approach?"

Nobody did; they knew how it had to go: Treetop-hugging flight to a spot far enough away to avoid being detected but close enough to get there on foot. Stay in the forest as much as possible to keep from being spotted visually by surveillance flights, some kind of bollixer to screw up DLIR or MS gear on aircraft sensors or ground sensornet, for however long it took to hike to the place. Avoid the soldiers on either side, figure out a way to breach the lodge, find the girl, and collect her without getting her or themselves killed.

Oh, and stay off the XTJC's scopes, while they were at it. Because they sure as shit would meddle with it, just in case CFI *might* possibly break some law, and there were some going to be bent and busted on an operation like this, so they had a point.

They'd need a local, a guide who knew the terrain. Maps were fine, but never the territory, and what looked like an easy walk from a spycam might be a complete impossibility for a soldier on foot.

Still, this was what they did, and they were good at it. Set it up properly and turn it loose, and they could make it run.

"So, let's lay it out," Jo said.

– – – – – –

"This here is Singh," Gunny said, "a private in the Rajah's Army who grew up near the border where we are going. The Rajah has lent him to us for a while."

Wink guessed that Singh was about nineteen, if that. Either he was using depil, or didn't need it, because he didn't have any facial hair, as most of the older troops here seemed to have. Fresh. Still wet from the morning's dew, but the Rajah sent him.

Jo said, "Welcome aboard, Singh. You know the territory around Lake Om?"

"Yes, Captain, sah, I was born in Vishnu Village, in the North Reach. I lived there until I joined the Honored Rajah's Army six months ago."

"Combat experience?" Jo asked.

"No, Captain, sah, not as yet. Eighty-eight hours sim-training."

"Well, with any luck, we won't see any action on this mission. In and out fast and clean."

The boy's smile seemed to falter a hair, and Wink figured the kid would love to see it blow up so he could shoot some enemies. Young soldiers had a lot of expectations and fantasies about how it would be and what they would do and feel. Invariably wrong, those expectations.

"We will be fielding a small strike team," Jo continued. "Half a dozen plus yourself. We'll be hiking, and we will want to get as close as we can by air without being detected, and stay out of sight until we achieve our objective. We need your knowledge to make this go like we want."

"I understand, Captain, sah."

Jo grinned. "Just call me Jo, it will make things easier. We are less formal than regular military."

"Yes, Jo, sah."

Wink grinned at that one.

Jo said, "You'll stay with Gunny until we take off, she'll acquaint you with our procedures, which might be a little different than what you are used to."

Wink smiled bigger at that. There was an understatement. If the kid got used to how they did things, it would ruin him for any kind of regular army. And, of course, the real reason he had to stay with Gunny was for security. The Rajah might have vetted him, but once he got the particulars, they didn't want him wandering off where he might be tempted to tell somebody about his glorious new assignment. Lot of ops had been busted because somebody bragged too soon.

Wink was going even though he wasn't the best combatant. If somebody got tagged, or the girl was injured, they needed a medic who could function in the middle of a crapstorm, and he could do that. He could shoot well enough to hit man-sized targets nearby.

Kay appeared, as she often seemed to, from out of nowhere.

"Something?" Jo asked her.

"We are being spied upon."

"Sure," Jo said, "that goes without saying. Lot of eyes pointed in our direction, probably birdshit cams all over the place, sats footprinting us every hour. Fart, and an electronic ear will hear it, and an e-nose sniff it and catalog the odor."

"These eyes are organic, and belong to the XTJC sergeant we met shortly after we began to set up camp."

"Our friend Hothead Hosep? Really? Where is he?"

"Three kilometers to the southwest, on the roof of a temple, atop a small rise. High enough to allow him to see our buildings. He has a scope on the camp."

Wink said, "How did you spot him?"

"I caught his scent on my patrol."

Wink shook his head. Hard to hide from somebody who could ID you by your body odor fifty meters away.

"We could put up a balloon wall," Gunny allowed. "Block the sucker's view."

"And let him know we know he is there," Jo said, "so he can move or bring in a different watcher. No, better the devil we know than the devil we don't." She paused. "Might be good to give him something to wonder about."

"If you are captured by the enemy, don't let them give you to PsyOps," Wink said.

"I hear that," Gramps said.

"I think *The Man in the Iron Mask*," Jo said. "Gunny, see if we have somebody who is close to a somatic match."

"Got it."

- - - - - -

Singh, who seemed to be a likable sort, wondered what they were taking about, and Gramps elected to tell him while Gunny was off running her errand—Singh wasn't going anywhere, and maybe they could teach the kid enough to help him stay alive in the sometimes-tricky world of the private military.

As he led the younger man to his temporary quarters, Gramps filled him in.

"Here's the deal, Singh. When you have a spy watching, and you know it, you have an advantage if he doesn't know that *you* know he's there. So you can put on a show and he'll buy it because he thinks he's watching something real."

Singh nodded. "I understand. And this . . . masked man?"

"*L'Homme au Masque de Fer*, an old Terran story. There are several versions, but the most well-known one concerns a French king who had his twin brother imprisoned, to protect his rule. He did not want to kill his sibling, but it was important that nobody knew who he was, and the tale goes that he had an iron mask made to hide his brother's identity, and he kept him in the mask and imprisoned for life."

"That sounds cruel."

"It was Terra, son, cruel goes with the territory. In any event, there were people who suspected that *Le Roi*—the King—had done this thing, and they tried to find and reveal the prisoner's identity.

"In one version, this happened, and the brothers were made to trade places—the King was masked and jailed and his twin freed to become the ruler, with only a few men the wiser."

"Karma. But what has that to do with this situation?"

"Suppose, just for the sake of argument, that our spy hiding in the temple up on the hill happens to see a security detail moving a prisoner into a vehicle? This prisoner is, say, wearing a hood so facial features are hidden, but also suppose that a somatotype scan of this action comes up with a female of a height, weight, and physique that is not too different from that of the Rajah's daughter, Indira?"

Singh considered that for a moment. The concentration on his face faded as he got it: "A spy might think that CFI had found Indira but was keeping her for some purpose. Extortion, perhaps."

Gramps grinned. "Good. What else?"

The young man blinked and thought about that. He was not slow: "So if the vehicle carrying this decoy were to drive away, the spy would likely have it followed?"

"Exactly."

"But—to what end? What would be the point?"

"Couple-three things: to keep J-Corps busy watching the left hand while our right hand does something else. To screw with them—to waste the XTJC's money and manpower in payment for spying on us. That can mount up fast, troops, vehicles, spysat time.

"And maybe to anger them enough do something foolish that might give us an advantage in dealing with them."

"Anger them?"

"We lead them on a merry chase to a location a couple of hundred klicks away where our people can slip out a back way. Leave J-Corps a note stapled to a wall when they kick in the door looking for the kidnapped woman: 'Gotcha, assholes!' "

Singh liked that. He grinned. Then he frowned, and said, "Is this not dangerous?"

"Some. But if the OIC of the local garrison, Colonel Hatachi, is any kind of old hand, he or she will know we outmaneuvered 'em and will take a lesson from it. Enemy outsmarts you, you give him credit."

"And if Colonel Hatachi is vindictive?"

Gramps shrugged. "We deal with that if it happens."

"Surely they have more than one watcher?"

"Oh, yeah. But if they think they have something worth taking down, they might well go after the red herring big-time."

"Red herring?"

"Herring is a type of cold-water fish, and 'red' refers to

a way of curing it that gives it a pungent, strong odor. On Earth, people used to use certain kinds of canines to track escaped prisoners. The old story is that these fish were used to distract the tracking dogs."

"Crushed rosa pepper is better," Singh said. "We have hounds on Ananda, used for the same tasks. A dusting of pepper behind one makes them sneeze and impairs their ability."

Gramps grinned.

"So we will be leaving on the mission soon?"

"Yes. We have a plan, and the longer we wait, the more variables can creep in. There is virtue in patience, but sometimes, quicker works better. Gunny will see that you get the kit you need when she gets back. Welcome to CFI, Singh."

## TWELVE

Jo would have loved to see the expressions on the J-Corps dickwads' faces when they kicked in the door of the building where they thought they were going to catch cutthroats doing something majorly illegal. She had printed out the hardcopy alliterative note herself: "Hey, Hosep—how's it hanging?"

Yes, it was petty, but sometimes, that's what you did. Never pass up a chance to fuck over an enemy . . .

By the time Hosep and the J-Corps guys calmed down, Jo and her strike team would be long gone . . .

— — — — — —

Gunny didn't like being saddled with the kid; it had been a while since she'd had to take care of a total noob—Rags liked his people seasoned, and while CFI recruits weren't always perfect, they had track records, it was a requirement. Been a long time since she'd had to show somebody which end of the gun to hold and which to point . . .

She would have preferred to have a combat ranger with

ten years in war zones under his belt walking point, but it happened that the best guy available as a guide for this sortie was Singh, and that was what they had to work with. They had to make do.

Still, she had babysat enough unscuffed boots when she'd been in the regular army, and it came back even after a long time away from it: Do what I tell you, do it right fucking now and don't ask fucking questions . . .

As they sat in the hopper, zipping along seventy meters up, just over the tops of the tallest trees in one of the major forests that were thick all over this country, she could see how eager Singh was to get into it. He looked the part—the shift-suit and pack, the carbine, the nervous half smile and shifting gaze. Her quick assessment of his skills allowed that he knew how to fire his weapon well enough, and his response to commands was decent. He had basic military training, but he was untested, and when the line went hot, it was never the same as training. Some of it might survive first contact with the enemy, assuming he lived through it.

Well. With any luck, there wouldn't be any contact with the enemy until they got to the hunting lodge, and once he helped them get there? He was expendable.

Gunny didn't feel any guilt at the thought, she was long past that. Once there was an engagement, once the boomware cranked, shit happened. Best plans ever, people still got zapped, that was the nature of the activity. If you survived, that was good. If not, too bad. If you wanted to die in bed, you should never leave home, and you better be careful stepping out the shower—shit happened everywhere.

She had only to keep him alive until they got where they were going, though she'd try to keep him that way until they were done. He seemed like a nice enough kid.

Her com button popped: "That's the Avril River we are crossing, portside," Jo said. "Means we are nearly through the Sanvi Forest, about a hundred kilometers from our landing site. We arrive in the vicinity in fifteen minutes, people."

It was a big stretch of woods—there was as much of it north of the border in Pahal and Balaji as on the New Mumbai side. It had different names to the north and east, but it was the same old-growth firlike trees in an unbroken swath more than four hundred klicks long, as much as a hundred klicks wide in places.

Lot of green, and there were seven or eight other major forests on this continent, not quite as big, but big enough. Plenty of building material, animal and plant habitat, and nobody would freeze on this planet for lack of something to burn for a long damn time.

Thick trees, dense canopy, not much undergrowth, relatively speaking, that was good for them. It would keep them from being seen from the air and allow them to do a fast forced march.

Fifteen minutes? She could lean back and drop off for a quick snooze . . .

— — — — — —

Wink missed the fluttery belly and anal pucker, the need to go pee when his bladder was empty, the speedy surges, the smell of his own sweat. Once upon a time, he had those every time he anticipated another dance with Dame Death.

Not so much lately.

He smiled. It was something one of his med-school teachers liked to say, back in the day. Dr. Morse had been a short, heavyset, bald man for whom the treatment for alopecia hadn't worked; he was forever making passes at the students and rarely scoring, and he considered himself a philosopher of sorts.

"Once you dance with Dame Death? No other partner will do."

Wink knew he liked to say it because he had heard him

repeat that at least twenty times during his rotation through
Morse's class. How he meant it was not how Wink thought
of it, but it was a nice line.

He was also self-aware enough to know that he was
addicted to it, dancing with Death.

The feeling was easy enough to fix. There were chems or
augs that would damp the adrenaline surges, the fight-or-flight
reflex that lived in the cave at the back of a man's mind. Pop
a pill, stick a derm, trigger an implant, you could smooth the
jagged rushes considerably. Do it in the middle of a firefight,
darts and missiles singing into your ears as they zipped past,
bodies dropping all around you, you could be as calm as a
vacuum, heart rate slow, blood pressure low, no more excitement than somebody checking the time of day. As it was, he
was getting there on his own.

Or you could reverse the process and make your body
feel all the symptoms of about-to-die, with no real threat
at all.

He could do either of those. But he wouldn't. Tricking
his system into or out of it wasn't the same. It had to be real.
There had to be that knowledge that each encounter with
Dame Death might be his last.

He lived for those moments.

It had always been his secret, from the time he'd been a
teenager. He had known even then that he shouldn't tell
anybody how he felt, and he'd learned the way to pass a
psych test by skirting questions that were designed to ferret
out such things.

It wasn't a death wish. It was a see-how-close-you-can-
get-and-live wish.

Go to a kite contest, hang out with free climbers, cave
divers, speed racers, you met your fellow defiers. They knew
each other, and they knew why they were there. Brothers and
sisters under the skin, hormone junkies, thrillwalkers . . .

He'd be carrying guns on this op, carbine and a sidearm.
It wasn't the regular military, and even though he was a

medic, he had no problems with shooting somebody trying to kill him. Not that he was gonna win awards for his marksmanship, but at close range, you pulled the trigger and waved the gun like a hose's nozzle, you'd hit something. He'd done it before, and if he made it past this time, he'd do it again.

Maybe he'd get a chance to use his knife.

– – – – – –

"Wake up, Gramps, time to go to work."

He opened one eye and regarded Gunny. "Says the woman who has been snoring like a bone saw grinding on a steel plate."

She gave him a little grin. "I just hope you don't fall back asleep once we are on the ground."

"Not a problem, given how entertaining it is to watch you stumble through anything thicker than a new-mowed lawn. I keep the recording, hell, I can sell tickets to it later: 'Behold! The Bumbling Buffoons. Critics agree, it's the funniest thing on the galaxyweb!'"

Gunny gave him the finger to go with the smile.

He would be riding the command chair here in the hopper once they landed, and observing. He could have stayed at the base camp—he was not foremost a foot soldier but a desk jockey, and that's where he'd be able to do the most good. But he wanted to be closer to the action than hundreds of klicks away, and able to do something should the need arise. And he wasn't too old to get sore feet marching if it came to that.

Normally, in a hot op, the team would be wired, full telemetrics and audviz, so he'd be able to see and hear what they saw and heard, assuming the fucking casters worked like they were supposed to, which was never a given. Truth is the first casualty in war, but communications is the second. In this case, however, they were running silent, no transmissions other than LOS lasercom to each other in the field.

Sometimes, even encrypted was no good—you didn't

want to give anybody a heads-up by having them come across a transmission where there wasn't supposed to be any—they might be disposed to go see what was making it. Unseen but known was not the same as invisible.

In the middle of a battlefield, not a problem. Out in the briars, where there might not be much electromagnetic traffic? Not so good.

If the team needed a ride in a hurry, they could break sig-silence and holler. The hopper was better than walking, and it had enough hardware to make an enemy keep his head down or risk getting it blown off. There were enough scramblers and sig-suppressors on board to keep most robotic smart stuff off them; enough sheathing to keep them blurry on sensor scopes; enough armor to stop small-arms fire if somebody eyeballed them. The pilot was good at the job. Wouldn't be the Air Cav coming to the rescue if everything went into the toilet, but it would give an enemy something to think about maybe long enough for the team to get their asses in gear and the hell away.

"Use a bigger hammer!" had its place, but sometimes a laser scalpel was better than a maul.

"On approach," the pilot said over their coms. Her name was Magil, but for some reason, everybody called her Nancy. "Hang on, it's a little tight."

The hopper began to settle. Demonde looked through the thick porthole plastic, but it was dark and even with his spookeyes lit, nothing to see but trees, trees, and more trees, the tops of which were getting really close . . .

Abruptly, there was a clearing, and the hopper dropped into it with a stomach-lurching suddenness, slowing as it neared the ground.

Gramps noticed that there wasn't that much empty space around them as they settled into the landing.

"We're down," Nancy said. "And thank you for flying Cutter Transport. We hope you enjoy your destination, and do come back, if it isn't final . . ."

The engine sounds faded, and it got quiet.

"My grandfather cleared this spot forty years ago," Singh said. "He used to plant a couple of acres of Heavenspice each year. He figured that was small enough and far away enough from the town so poachers would have to work to find and steal his crop. He installed a retractable live-camouflage net over the clearing, so it was invisible from a few hundred meters up."

"Did that work?"

"Mostly. He never talked about it to me. It's a tightly regulated business. As I understand it, he didn't have the proper permits and licenses, so it wasn't legal for him to grow it. But I heard my father talking to my uncle once about what happened to a team of thieves who somehow found the crop."

Gunny said, "And . . . ?"

"There were four armed men who supposedly arrived here to steal the harvest. My uncle said that my grandfather hid and caught them unawares. They were never seen again."

"Sounds like my kind of man," Gramps said.

"What—old and sneaky?"

"Exactly right, Gunny. And don't forget 'deadly.' And 'handsome.' "

That brought smiles all around.

"Okay," Jo said, "let's get this show on the road. We have six hours of darkness and a hard three-hour march to get to the lodge. Singh?"

"This way, sah," he said.

Kay was at the door before Singh. She couldn't wait to get outside.

- - - - -

The Sanvi Forest straddled the borders where New Mumbai, Pahal, and Balaji came together, in the foothills of the Rudra Mountains. Most of the mountain range was in Pahal, but there were fair-sized peaks in all three countries, and the march was uphill almost from the moment they started. Singh and Gunny took point, Wink and Jo behind them, with Kay ranging behind and to the sides. Normally, Kay would have been out front, but Singh knew the territory.

It wasn't easy going, given the pace, but it wasn't like a jungle you had to machete your way through; the tree canopy blocked much of the sun, and the needles lay thick and probably acidic upon the ground, so underbrush wasn't a problem. The biggest trees were two-and-a-half to three meters in diameter, substantial suckers. So it was asses and elbows on a quick march, the FAS's heavy enough to make it work. There was enough light for the spookeyes to work so they could see, the computers in those giving a faux-visual color, albeit the color was somewhat dim. And sometimes, the computer's speculation at what color a thing was tended to be off. She'd had to make a mental shift when something she'd seen at night through spookeyes as dark blue turned out to be crimson when viewed in daylight.

－ － － － －

Kay moved through the forest much quieter than her human companions, picked soft spots and almost instinctively avoided things that would crack under her feet. Hunters who made noises frightened prey, and in the days when that was how her people fed themselves, prey faster than you who ran meant you didn't eat.

There were animals here, she could smell them, occasionally hear them, and now and then, catch a glimpse of one as it froze or moved away from the team as it advanced. No predators of any significant size she sensed, but her research had mentioned that there were some in the forests that might be dangerous. That could be an adventure, but they couldn't afford the noise. She'd have to shoo it off or kill it quietly.

In the dark, she relied more on her nose than her eyes,

but she could see well enough; her vision went deeper into the red and violet than unaugmented humans'.

She didn't like being at the rear though she understood the need. The local human leading them knew the way, and stealth and speed were both necessary. Should there be any enemies about, they would not be sneaking up on the team from behind, could Kay help it.

The pace was quick for humans, if slow for her, and she ranged back and forth, stopping frequently to look and listen, to sniff the warm night air, alert for any signs of other humans in the woods. Unless they were much more adept than most of their species, there weren't any others here. Yet.

- - - - - -

Jo didn't need an external timer since she had a heads-up aug for time and distance, though she was pretty good at guessing, then checking herself. The PPS, which was receive-only, said they had gotten to where they needed to be.

Singh confirmed it. "We are a kilometer from the lodge," he said.

The five of them moved in close. Kay kept her back to the group, scanning the area. Even clumped together, any DLIR overflights wouldn't pick them up in the FAS's. Kay was the only one of the five not in an FAS, and she'd probably register as an animal.

Kay would wear armor, old-fashioned Dragonskin sheath or ultralight flexifoam-ceramic, if they made her, but since the suit's sensors were only marginally better than her own senses, she didn't see the point in slowing herself down with a suit, and her argument was simple: If she could dodge faster than somebody targeting her, was that not better than depending on the suit to stop the missile?

It was hard to argue with that, especially given the Vastalimi record in pretty much any kind of combatsit when compared to humans. If it ain't broke, don't break it.

"All right. Just like the scenario we ran, by the numbers. Let's move out."

Everybody nodded. They all looked ready; even Singh, who was obviously nervous. Jo glanced at Gunny, who gave her an almost imperceptible nod. *Yeah, I got him.*

They moved out.

# THIRTEEN

The Rajah was polite. He made small talk while the servants brought tea and some kind of nut-cluster snack that was quite tasty. But Cutter had been in enough meetings with clients and higher-ups to know there was a point and that he would get to it sooner or later.

"These are good," he said. He nodded at the dish of nutty things. The dish looked as if it had been carved from artificial emerald by somebody with great artistic skills.

"I shall tell my chef you enjoyed them, she will be pleased."

There was a pause. Then: "I am given to understand that members of your group have . . . gone into the field."

*Yep, probably halfway to their objective by now.* He said, "I am flattered that you noticed, sir."

Both men grinned at what was said and left unsaid:

*Spying on us?*

*To be certain.*

The Rajah shrugged. "One picks up bits and pieces of this and that."

He was waiting for Cutter to be more forthcoming, and since he was the client, it wasn't politic to tell him to go piss up a tree. But Cutter had also learned a long time ago not to tell anybody who didn't have a *need to know* anything that might come back to bite him on the ass. It only took once to drive that lesson home.

"We are following leads."

"One of which would be in the vicinity of our border with Pahal and Balaji, in the foothills of the Rudras?"

Cutter grinned. Of course he'd know that much; they had borrowed one of his soldiers for a guide, and the Rajah would know who, and he'd have to be slow if he couldn't figure out why. He wasn't slow. Cutter would bet last year's income against a bent hard curry noodle that the Rajah's people had seen the hopper with the team when it took off and knew how many passengers it carried. They wouldn't be able to track it, not with the stealth gear working. Might have had eyes on it until the pilot went into her evasives, after which their trackers would have had to be magicians to stay with it.

And the scout? Cutter would also bet big that he'd been told to keep track of things and to be ready to talk about it if the Rajah asked. But that would be later.

"It's a promising lead, sir, but I didn't want to be precipitous. Strategic and tactical information is best kept close to the chest. It is hard to let something accidentally slip if a man has no knowledge of it."

The Rajah sipped his tea. "I understand. But you feel that this is a promising lead."

"There are a lot of promises in the recycle bins of history, sir. There seems to be little point in waving them around unless they deliver."

The Rajah nodded. He put his teacup down and looked directly at Cutter. "She is my daughter, Colonel. You would not be here if I was not greatly concerned for her safety."

"I understand, sir. And you would not have hired us if

we didn't have a reputation for doing everything possible to address your concerns properly."

The Rajah sighed. Yes. He knew that Cutter wasn't going to tell him the details. Perhaps the walls here had ears that belonged to somebody not as concerned with the missing girl's safety. There was no benefit in risking that. The Rajah was canny enough to know that even if he didn't like it.

"We will keep you informed of any significant progress, sir."

"Thank you, Colonel."

— — — — — —

On his way back to his compound, Cutter got a call. He grinned at the caller's ID.

"Cutter here."

"Colonel, this is Colonel Hatachi."

"Good evening to you, sir."

"Not really. You have any idea how much your little stunt cost me in man- and machine-hours?"

Cutter grinned. He was good with numbers. He could probably come up with a pretty decent estimate. And he could have pretended he didn't know what Hatachi was talking about, but that would have been insulting, and there was no need for that.

"Sorry, sir, but our job wasn't being made any easier with your people standing so close. You stick your nose up somebody's butt, you might not like what you smell."

Hatachi chuckled. "Point taken, Colonel. My sergeant wants to line you all up and shoot you, but he got suckered, so he has to live with it. But be advised, we won't be so easy to gully again."

"Understood, sir. I appreciate your position and only ask that you try to appreciate ours."

"As long as you don't make too much noise or burn anything down, we'll stand back a ways. But if you step crooked, we will come down on you like a ton of rock."

"I wouldn't expect anything else, Colonel."

"Good evening."

"And to you."

— — — — —

"Stand by," Jo subvocalized.

They had spread out and arrived at a small rise in the vicinity of the lodge, and to outward appearance, there was nothing to indicate any problems.

With the lights from the main building damping the spookeyes, Jo couldn't see the others though she knew where they were supposed to be.

The lodge was constructed of logs stripped of bark, laser-planed to a consistent size, and trimmed and finished with some kind of wood preserver. Large enough to house thirty people in private rooms, the interior belied the exterior—the appliances, communications, and comforts were as modern as any to be found in the planet's cities. There were half a dozen fireplaces, but they were for show; the heating and cooling plants were state-of-the-art. There were lights that could be made to flicker and look like candles, but they ran off solar batteries. It was fake rustic, animal heads mounted on the walls, designed to offer the illusion of a bygone time, to make visitors think they were roughing it.

The team had memorized the floor plans, seen the computer sims, knew the layout.

There were enough exterior lights to show the trimmed lawn surrounding the lodge. There were two guards patrolling the lawn, men with carbines. They weren't in any kind of uniform but dressed for the weather, which was chilly, given the altitude. The guards ambled back and forth, one to the north, the other to the south, staying close to the building. Neither moved like a man expecting trouble.

"Let's hear it," Jo said.

Her suit's com clicked.

"Ah got two guards with slung eight-millimeter Centuros crushing crickets. Nothin' else."

"Ditto. My suit's heads-up says the yard is clear except for those two," Wink said.

Singh said, "I confirm that."

"Kay?"

There was a short pause, a couple of seconds. "Something is not right," she said.

Jo extended her senses to the limits of her augmentation, seeking a sight or sound or smell or something on the electromagnetic spectrum that offered any danger.

Nothing.

"Got a specific, Kay?"

"No."

"Stand by."

Between the suit's sensors and her implants, Jo was about as sharp as a human could get. She made it eight warm bodies inside the lodge, and the placement of those, when she called up the simview, had one of them in a small, windowless utility room, with another in the hallway outside that room's door. The rest were in various places fanned away from those two.

It seemed pretty obvious to Jo what the situation was: Indira was locked in the utility room, a guard posted on the door. The rest only mattered if they got in the way.

The plan was flexible, but simple: They would go in via the least congested entrance. She and Gunny and Kay would take out the opposition while Wink fetched the girl. Singh would stay outside and cover their backs. Assuming the girl was fit or could be made so, Wink would bring her out, and they'd haul ass. Once they were back in the woods, they'd call Gramps and arrange the pickup point. With luck running their way, they'd be back at the Rajah's by dawn.

But Jo had learned that Kay was sometimes more

sensitive than the suit and her augs put together, so she hesitated. Did another scan and still came up dry.

She had to make a choice.

"We're a go," Jo said. "But stay edgy. Gunny?"

"Lined up."

"On my 'now.' "

Jo glanced at her carbine, to make sure the selector was on silent. The suppressed mode was pretty quiet, but it did cut down on the velocity of the bullet. The computer sights supposedly took that into account, but it was 150 meters to her target, and she needed a cold-bore head shot, so she liked to calculate that kind of trajectory herself to be sure it matched.

She lined the virtual scope up on the guard to the north side of the lodge. The scope's optics were good enough to let her see in darkness, which was where she wanted to take the shot, but the transition from light to shadow was tricky. The scope's adjustment for that took a quarter second, and she needed to allow for that, plus the timing with Gunny.

Range: 148 meters. Wind velocity: two klicks per hour from the south-southwest. Suppressed velocity: 812 meters per second. Local gravity, Coriolis effect, humidity . . .

The guard was about to walk past the corner of the building, and there was a post that partially blocked the outside spotlight, just there. Her aug gave her the count and she spoke it aloud: "In three . . . two . . . one—now."

Jo pressed the trigger.

The scope gave her the image of the guard's head jerking and spraying fluid as he collapsed, dead before he hit the lawn.

"Down," she and Gunny said simultaneously.

"Crank up your bollixers. Southwest entrance, go!"

Jo came up and ran. Their suit's bollixers put out pulses that should confuse, for a short while, all but the best military-grade motion detectors, heat-sig sensors, and pradar pulses. Not for long, but enough so somebody sitting on a scope would frown and wonder what she was seeing, which should be enough time to get inside. After that, it didn't matter, the party would be on.

Jo came up and sprinted, carbine held ready to fire if necessary, but there weren't any targets popping up.

Kay reached the door first, and had the old-style mechanical lock open before Gunny arrived, a hair ahead of Jo. She heard Wink coming up behind her, double-checked with a quick glance. The suit, good as it was, sometimes had trouble on the ID circuit when the bollixers lit—

Then they were inside. Jo killed her bollixers, looked at the heads-up for targets, and saw the muzzle flashes and heard the shots incoming almost instantly.

So much for surprise—

Kay said, "Wait—"

A round blew past Jo, missing by centimeters—

Her suit flashed a red warning sig: AP—!

*Shit—!*

She spotted a man aiming a J&S Rail Rifle at her and hit him with a triplet from her own carbine, two center of mass, one to the head. He went down—

In the heat of it, with her augs and the suit spewing info at her, Jo knew one thing:

*It was a trap!*

"Wink!"

"Not her," his voice came through the com, as if he was offering an opinion on the weather, no excitement at all. "It's a guy with a gun—hold on—*ow*—mother*fucker*!"

"Disengage!" Jo said. "Out, out, out, right fucking now!"

Kay bounded past, paused a half second to shoot somebody Jo saw peripherally, and was gone. Kay had known a hair before the first round went off—

Jo was followed by the Vastalimi—

Gunny was at the door, firing past Jo at targets behind her—

AP bullets smacked into the thick log walls next to Gunny and punched through thirty centimeters of wood and into the night. Those would hole their suits.

*They* knew *we were coming*—

"Evasive action, rendezvous point Alpha," Jo said. "Go!"

The sound of an airborne troop transport rumbled over her. She felt the repeller charge make her hair stand up.

Jo glanced up to see rounds spangle and spark off the transport's hull, every tenth one a tracer.

Singh, in the bushes—

"*Move*, Singh!"

An antipersonnel rocket lanced down from the carrier at the source of the rifle fire—

"Singh!"

"I'm clear," he said. "Hold on—"

There was a small *whump!* to her left, and she saw the IR sig of a rifle grenade as Singh fired his launcher. It went off level with, but to the port side of, the transport, and was close enough to cloud the pilot's armored window with shrapnel.

The carrier sheared off to avoid taking more fire but dropped fast.

Even as she ran, Jo saw the transport land and troops start pouring out.

"We got company, people, get gone!"

She cranked it up, moving much faster than an unaugmented human, the suit notwithstanding.

*Fuck*—!

— — — — — —

Kay would have preferred to stop and use her claws on the human who stepped out to block her intended path; her rage was hot, but the transport had alighted and there were thirty more heavily armed troops on the ground, and she couldn't afford the time. She shot the carbine, no sights, indexed the angle—

The bullet went through the man's eye and exited the back of his skull.

Her way was clear. The rendezvous was a kilometer into the forest, off the approach line they had taken coming in. She didn't wear a suit, but she could sense the others of her team. So far, they were all still alive and moving.

It had been a gull. The kidnapped female had not been in the building. She hadn't been able to tell for sure until she was inside, and by then, the attack had begun. They were lucky none of them had been killed.

She was going to speak to a certain Rel about this—

— — — — — —

Wink ran, feeling as alive as he ever had. A firefight. Unexpected, dangerous, they might still die, but so far, they had survived.

He had a small problem: One of the armor-piercing rounds had skewered his suit. It hadn't done any real damage—it had hit just under his left arm, halfway down the lat, punched through the muscle, and exited the suit's back. Kiting gave you good lats. The suit's rudimentary medcomp stiffened a patch over the wound, a memory-foam pad that applied enough pressure to mostly stop the bleeding. The suit asked him if he wanted a local or a systemic painkiller, and he opted for neither—better to feel the injury and avoid doing more harm to it than to deaden it and risk fucking it up more. He'd hurt himself worse and lived with it, he could live with this.

Unless, of course, he got killed heading for Alpha point.

Getting shot was his own fault. He had expected to find the girl after he iced the "guard" and opened the door to the storage room. Instead, there had been a shooter who got a round off before Wink took him down.

He didn't enjoy that part of it particularly, the shooting, but that was what you had to live with if you chose to carry a gun. Fucker shot him? Served him right.

He *really* didn't like the *getting-shot* part—

- - - - - -

Gunny knew a clusterfuck when she saw one, and this had been that. Yeah, she'd gone three for three inside the lodge, but when that fucking transport landed, there was no way they were gonna beat thirty-some soldiers, and that is sure as shit what they were—combat troops, not some raggedy-ass bandits who didn't know their asses from holes in the ground. They weren't in any kind of uniform she recognized, but they were moving right, they were *some*body's army, and that put a new spin on this whole affair.

Somebody had known that they were coming; it had been a setup.

The question was, who?

There was *no* question what they were gonna do about it when they found out, least not in her mind. Assuming, of course, they lived to tell anybody.

Speaking of which, she hoped Jo was calling Gramps and getting his ass lifted. They were gonna need a ride pretty damn quick, or they were gonna get spiked.

- - - - - -

"I'm here," Gramps said. "How's tricks?"

"Got a situation," Jo said. "The lodge was a trap. No Indira. We shot our way out, but there's a shitload of real infantry fanning out after us. We are going to rendezvous at Alpha. Be nice if you could get into the air and stand by for our go-to after that."

"Copy, Jo. Anybody hurt?"

"Wink says he got a minor wound; nobody else reporting any injuries."

Gramps felt a flush of relief. He waved at Nancy, gave her the hand-swoop up-jive for get-it-in-the-air.

The engines had been on standby, they came online and whined up to full power.

"Pick a spot," Gramps said. "We'll meet you there."

"Acknowledged. Tell Nancy to keep her eyes open—they got a transport with a platoon, and they are carrying J&S Rails, they can probably afford ground-to-air or a warbird. If you get shot down, we have to walk all the way home."

"Well, we wouldn't want that, would we? Stay edgy, Jo."

"You bet your ass I will. Might want to pass it along to Rags, JIC. Off-line."

Gramps sighed. A trap? How was that possible? They hadn't told anybody but the colonel where they were going, and he wouldn't have said anything to anybody. Which meant somebody knew where they were going *before* they ever lifted.

There was an ugly can of worms.

Well. Worry about that later.

He opened a secure pipe and hailed the colonel.

"What's the situation?" Cool, but alert.

"Lodge was a trap, no girl. Team got out okay and are running through the woods, but there's a platoon of what Jo calls 'real infantry' chasing them. They'll decide on an extraction site once they see what's what, and I'll collect them."

There was a short silence. "How did they know we were coming?"

"That's the question, isn't it? Nobody but you and us knew that, we didn't tell anybody and I'm guessing you didn't, either, so . . ."

". . . so they threw out a lure, and we bit on it."

"Looks like, yeah."

"And they knew we were there to go for it."

"You need help?"

"Nah, Nancy and I got it."

Another short silence. "Collect them and come back to base. We'll work the rest out when you get here. Off-line."

"Off-line," Gramps said.

To Nancy, he said, "Keep it low and keep the scopes on high. Might be some smoke and fire coming our way. Shall we rise?"

The hopper lifted.

# FOURTEEN

Kay was there when Jo got to the site. Singh and Gunny were the last to arrive, a minute after Wink. It was dark, the tree canopy particularly thick. No smell of other humans in the air.

"Everybody okay?" Jo asked.

Everybody nodded.

Gunny looked at Wink. "Doc, you let somebody put a *hole* in that suit? Rags will have your ass, much as these things cost."

"Yeah, well, these suckers aren't as great as they are supposed to be, are they? They are supposed to stop bullets! I might sue 'em for the puncture in my lat."

They all laughed, save for Singh. He was still running on adrenaline, Jo realized; you could see he had a tremor. Best give him something to occupy his mind.

"Okay, Singh, what's our best way to a place where the hopper can land for our evac? Be nice it was close, the bad guys are on their way to find us."

Singh took a deep breath and blew most of it out. "There

is a gold placer site two kilometers from here, to the south-west. Abandoned and mostly overgrown, but a clearing next to the stream is flat, bare rock. I don't think it shows on a map. You could land a small VTOL craft there."

"Kay, take point with Singh. Gunny and I will cover our asses. Doc, you ride in the pocket. Anybody see anybody not us, spike them, but keep moving. We don't have time to stop and play around. Go."

As they dropped back, Gunny said it aloud: "They knew we were coming, Jo. And they knew enough to carry J&S's."

"That thought crossed my mind. We'll suss it out once we get back to base."

"You have Gramps call it in?"

"Yep. But Rags won't send help unless we ask for it."

"We'd never hear the end of how much that costs if we do that."

Jo grinned. "Don't I know it. We just need to outrun 'em, and we have a head start. You want left or right?"

"Right. Mah good side."

They both smiled.

— — — — — —

They were most of a klick along when Kay smelled the enemy. She stopped, held up one hand for Singh to do the same. "We have humans ahead," she said.

"How many?" Jo.

Kay sniffed, inhaling deeply, swiveling her head from left to right, then back again. "A dozen. A picket line."

"They must know about the placer site," Singh said. "I don't have them on my suit's sensor."

"Bollixed," Jo said. "Can we go around them?"

Doc Wink arrived.

Kay looked at Singh.

"Maybe to the north," Singh said. "There's a ravine to the south that's deep enough to be a problem. It can be traversed, but the going will be very slow."

Jo and Gunny got there. Gunny said, "Our pursuers are five minutes behind us. They know about the pickets, got to figure they know about the ravine. Bet your bonus they'll be angling to the north to cut us off."

"So you are saying we are fucked?" Singh said.

"Nah, Ah'm saying we don't have a lot of time to break through and hope Gramps and Nancy don't get lost coming to pick us up. How far away are we from the site?"

"A little over a kilometer."

Jo said, "I got it." She switched to the tactical channel. "Gramps?"

"Here."

"You got our PPS sig?"

"Of course."

"We are heading for a clearing approximately one kilometer southwest of our location. Next to a stream, an old gold mine. We have an obstacle, so it might be a few minutes before we get there. Be nice if you were on the ground with the door open when we show up. We'll need to be leaving in a hurry. And come in quick and quiet, somebody might be looking for you."

"I'll see what I can manage."

"Off-line."

Jo looked at Kay. "How far apart are they?"

"Twenty-five meters."

"Okay. Right up the middle."

Singh said, "What are we doing?"

Jo looked at him. "We are in a closing pincer, between the pickets and the pursuers. If we are going to get to where the hopper can land, we have to get out of it. Terrain says we can't go south, and if we try going around, to the north, it will take too long. So we punch right through the line and move as fast as we can. Speed is of the essence, we are run-and-gun. Lose the suits."

Singh stared at her as if she had just turned into a giant lizard. "What?"

Jo continued. "The pickets have gear that messes with our sensors, so we will have to use visual. The suits won't stop what they are throwing, and they'll hose, spray-and-pray, so the camo won't help. And they will slow us down.

"They are using capacitor-driven railguns, so our spook-eyes will work, there won't be any muzzle flash. But if somebody chain-fires photonics, the strobes will screw the 'eyes."

"Will they do that?"

"Maybe, but *we* will for sure. So their nightsight won't work, either. Kay and I will know where they are, and we will be firing at them. Fire only if you are *certain* you have a valid target. It's going to be just like a strobe scenario, only they'll be using live ammo instead of taggers.

He nodded. "A-All r-r-ight."

"Everybody ready? Wink?"

"What? I'm trying to take a nap over here."

"Get a pressure patch ready and get out the FAS, we are going jogging."

"Man," Wink said. "You know Rags is going to shit a square brick when we show up without these suits. They aren't covered by insurance."

They stripped to their skivvies, black polyprop sheaths that covered them from neck to ankles. "Put your boots back on," Jo ordered.

She looked at Wink. "How is your wound?"

"Nothing I can't plug with some dermastat."

"Plug it. And Wink? Stay behind Gunny."

Jo glanced at Gunny, then at Kay, then pointed her nose at Singh. He was putting his boots back on, he didn't catch it.

Gunny and Kay nodded at Jo in return. They would let Singh get a step or two ahead of them when they moved. It wouldn't matter to anybody shooting in their direction from the picket line if he was a meter ahead or behind, but that way, he wouldn't accidentally shoot one of them in the back. Even a combat veteran could get excited in the middle of a firefight, and Singh wasn't that.

"Ready?"

They all nodded.

"Let's do it."

- - - - - -

"Well, looky here," Nancy said. "It must be a celebration—somebody is shooting off fireworks."

She had already zigged to port by the time Gramps spotted the ground-to-air missile heading their way. Not that the evasive move was necessary: the hopper's tactical computer had tagged the missile, painted it with a laser, and launched a counterrocket that hit it five hundred meters away from the vessel. It made a bright splash against the polarized portholes.

The viewscreen was a full-sheet starlight sandwich, and the night was as a somewhat-faded day looking through it. It cut the glare as the missile blew up.

They had gained some altitude to look for the clearing, which was why the GTA.

"There it is," he said.

"You sure? Doesn't look big enough."

"I get that a lot. Trust me, it'll look bigger in a minute."

The hopper dropped, and his belly roiled at the sudden lack of gravity.

- - - - - -

Kay set the photonic grenade bar for a three-second delay and a sequential quarter-second strobe. She threw the PGB into the air ahead of her in a high arc, mentally timing it. She heard the *pop!* as the globes separated from each other, six of them, each the size of a walnut. No matter which way they landed, some portion of the globe would flash, unless it was completely buried, only they'd mostly go off in the air—

"Eyes!" she said. She shut her own as the first of the globes ignited, and it was bright even against her lids. To somebody looking right at it, it would be blinding. Spookeyes would cut out and protect the circuits and a user's vision, but a quarter second later, and for a total of a second-and-a-half, the night-vision gear would be cutting in and out as the grenades lit.

*Strobe. Strobe. Strobe—*

Kay had marked her path, and she opened her other senses, listening, smelling, feeling the ground under her feet, and ran. The nearest enemy was fifty meters away—

She heard the railguns go off—they were shooting blind—and pointed her own weapon at the source of the sound. She could smell the human's fear-sweat.

Kay fired. Was rewarded with a scream.

*—Strobe. Strobe—*

Kay opened her eyes, picked up the second target to her left.

Fired—

— — — — — —

Jo saw the man angling in from her right, his weapon on full auto. Stupid—the J&S fired a heavy projectile at high velocity, and the recoil was stout. Even as she watched with her augmented sight amped to full, she saw the muzzle of his weapon rising, so by the eighth or ninth shot, the guy was shooting at the stars. She gave him a pair of three-round bursts, pointing high. The first burst hit him in the neck armor, the second blew through his helmet's face bubble—

Two more angled in from her left, but Gunny had them, that was four? no, five down, and they had a big hole in the line.

Just ahead of her a step, Singh waved his carbine back and forth, also on full auto, and chipped bark from several trees. There wasn't anybody in his line of sight.

So much for don't shoot unless you are sure of your target—

*—Wait, there was an enemy!*

She swung her weapon over to cover him, but Singh's

rapid hose found the solider and stitched across his belly. The man went down—

– – – – – –

Gunny didn't follow the two she'd spiked as they fell, that was a beginner's mistake she hadn't made in a long time. She looked for more targets, could hear railguns, but their shooters weren't visible. There were at least seven more troops out there, but they didn't seem in a hurry to get here.

They'd punched through the line and were past it. She moved her finger off the weapon's trigger and kept running—

– – – – – –

Wink didn't see anybody ahead of him except Gunny. To his left, Kay ran, with Singh a couple of meters ahead of her.

*Now* he was up! His heart raced, his blood sang with ancient songs of life and death, his breath was too loud in the night. The pain in his lat was gone, the glue would either hold or it wouldn't, but that wasn't important.

There was a body on the ground just ahead. Gunny leaped over it.

"Watch your step!" she called out.

"Got it!" Wink yelled back.

He leaped over the downed body. Was he dead? That didn't matter, either. Wink wasn't dead. That's what mattered—

– – – – – –

Three hundred meters past the line, Jo stopped, turned, and using every one of her sensory augs, scanned the woods behind them.

Nothing.

"Kay?"

Eight meters away, Kay said, "We are clear."

"But we won't be for long." *Click.* "Gramps?"

"Nancy and I are having a picnic by the water here," he

said. "Why don't you all come on by and join us? I'll save you a sandwich."

"Three minutes," Jo said.

"Don't put any mustard on mine," Gunny said.

"Chocolatte, I've got some special sauce I've been saving for you."

"Ah bet," Gunny said. "You just keep right on savin' it."

# FIFTEEN

Once the hopper was airborne and fifteen klicks away, they all felt better.

Gramps shook his head. "Children, children, what have you done with your dress clothes? Your father is going to be sooo unhappy with you."

"It was such a nice night," Gunny said. "And those suits were so hot."

"Yeah, he can take it out of our allowances," Wink said. He was regluing the hole in his muscle shut; it had leaked a little.

Singh stared at them. He was still shaking. "How—how can you make jokes?"

The kid was rattled. All the crap he'd been told about combat, whatever simulacra he had run, none of it applied the way the real deal did. He was one step away from losing it, shaky, his skin pale, sweat beaded on his face. In shock.

Wink said, "Not like you expected, was it?"

Singh shook his head. "No."

Wink looked around at the others. "We've all been where you are."

Singh looked at him.

"If you are a soldier, you train for battle. It's them or you, and that's the choice. If you can't wrap your mind around that, you can't stay in this line of work.

"Oh, you can get a posting behind the lines, run a desk, repair rollers, shuffle supplies, stay out of the field, but when you put on the uniform, you are on call to pull the trigger if it comes to that.

"Enemy kicks in the door of the air-conditioned office you are in, even if you are a photon-pushing clerk, it's kill or die. That's what soldiers do."

"You are a *medic*."

"And I have killed men. More than a few."

"I never shot anybody before. It all happened so fast. There he was, and I shot him!" He paused. "I was afraid," Singh said.

"We were all afraid," Jo said.

That wasn't strictly true, Wink knew. In combat, people got moving fast, and they tended not to notice. Jo had been too busy. Gunny had ice water in her veins. Kay? Nothing frightened her he had ever seen.

And Wink *enjoyed* it too much. The fear was the spice. But the kid didn't need to hear any of that right now.

Singh stared at his boots, shaking his head.

Wink said, "We've all been where you are, Singh. We all killed somebody the first time. It isn't an easy thing."

The young man looked at him.

"It will be a while before we get back to the base," Wink said. "You want to hear a story?"

"About what?"

"About the first man I killed."

Singh looked up.

------

"I was at India General, on Terra, a megaplex teaching hospital we called Panda, short for 'pandemonium,' which means, 'House of Demons.' Which is pretty much what it seemed like.

"Seventeen thousand patients, ten floors, place half a klick by half a klick, every kind of illness and injury you can think of and a bunch you wouldn't ever imagine. Huge place, and half the time, PPS didn't work, and you had to resort to hard-copy maps to find your way around.

"I was an intern, four months in, one of five covering our resident, who was overworked but sharp. Our rotation was through the burn unit, and among two hundred others, there were some soldiers with bad plasma injuries from a training accident at the GA base just outside the city. An AP carrier's capacitor overloaded and sheeted. Killed fifty-odd outright, injured thirty others. Enough so the Army's hospital was overwhelmed.

"Panda got the worst of them, and when I say 'worst,' if you've ever been around plasma burns, you know what I'm talking about."

Most of the crew nodded. Yeah. They'd been to war.

"We had five with deep charring, third-degree, lot of soft tissue and bone destruction. They were there when I started my rotation, and they'd be there long after I was gone.

"There was one guy, Benton, who'd caught the flash full on. Burned out his eyes, took most of his face down to the skull, ears gone, half his voluntary muscular system destroyed outright. Charred off his penis and testicles, melted both knees, stripped his hands palmar sides to the skeleton. He was swathed in artificial skin and biodenics, and his CNS and peripheral pain receptors mostly pulse-blocked so he wasn't screaming in agony, but he was feeling constant disquiet, six on a one-to-ten scale, and he knew what had happened to him and what it meant.

"He was looking at at least two more years in the skin-tent, daily debriding, waiting for the muscles and skin to be cloned and regrown, multiple surgeries to replace arteries, veins, his eyes and optical nerves, a cloned face transplant, plus rehab physical and emotional therapy that would probably take him three more years after he was ambulatory. Been much cheaper to let him die, but bad for troop morale.

"He was a teaching case, Benton, destined to be poked and prodded and cut upon by a legion of student doctors and techs for a long time, so there was that, too.

"At best, with everything working exactly as it should, in five years, he'd be 50–60 percent of what he'd been—and his own mother wouldn't recognize him.

"He couldn't talk out loud—his mouth and half his tongue were gone. The surgeons had done implants so he could hear and see after a fashion—computer-augmented cam vision—but he had a com aug he could subvocalize enough so pickups could deliver speech. Plus he had an EEG aug so he could run a computer, could read and create messages.

"People have survived worse, but barely.

"Benton was in the depths of major depression. He had every kind of neurochem circulating that the neurologists and psychiatrists could throw at it, but his mood wasn't what you'd call elevated. He had a certain amount of control over the dosages, within safe limits, a demand-switch, but mostly, he wasn't keeping himself zoned out.

"He'd had a lot of time to think about things. Pretty much all he had.

"Even with a new dick and balls cloned, any chances of fathering his own germ-cell children anytime soon were iffy because his life partner had bailed, and nobody was coming round to visit: He had no immediate family, and all the members of his squad had been killed in the blast that maimed him.

"I could not even imagine myself in his situation. It was overwhelmingly horrifying. I'd rather be dead.

"One night, as I was checking his tubing and tentware, Benton lit his computer:

" *'Should have died with my unit.'*

"Yeah, I thought, he was right.

"But I had read his chart, and I knew he had been raised in a traditional religion, and I said what they'd taught me to say in med-school psych to people of faith. 'But you didn't, so there must be a reason.'

" *'What possible reason?'*

"I shrugged. 'I don't know. Maybe someday, you save the galaxy. Maybe you discover a cure for death.'

" *'Maybe I go through years of shit and fall over dead from complications. I want to leave now and save myself the grief. God let this happen, fuck God.'*

"I was with him. I knew the stats for long-term prognosis in this kind of case, and it wasn't good. Suicide was the second leading cause of death, after immune-system dysfunction, either or both as likely as not.

"He had a point. At some juncture, living is not better than dying.

"Here we were, spending millions on keeping this kid alive, and to what end?

"I hurt for Benton. He was essentially an overcooked soypro roast, and the best he could look forward to after years of misery and pain was to be half the man he had been, and probably a short and unhappy life after that."

He looked around at the others. They were attentive, waiting.

They would know where he was going, except, maybe, for Singh.

"The burn-unit recorders caught our conversation, of course, and there were cams set to watch the patients, as well as all the telemetry gear. I said all the right things, didn't do anything that could have been construed as malpractice or worse. 'I wish I could help you,' I said."

Wink stopped talking. There was a long pause.

"I was an okay programmer," he finally said. "Good enough to get into the central medical system and out again without being caught. I built a program for Benton's chem-demand switch. It was on a timer. For six hours, he would have the ability to administer more of the chem to himself than was allowed. A lethal amount. After which, the program would shut off and eat itself, and only an expert looking for it would be able to spot that it had been there, and even then, not what it had been."

Gunny nodded. "Uh-huh."

"I went to see Benton. Asked how he was feeling. *'The same.'*

" 'Maybe if you allowed yourself more antidepressants, that might do the trick.'

" *'Yeah. Maybe.'*

"Two hours later, Benton died."

"I'm not sure that qualifies as your first one," Gramps said. "You didn't actually kill him."

"I gave him a gun, cocked it, put it in his hand, and pressed the barrel against his head," Wink said. "And if I could have pulled the trigger and gotten away with it, I would have saved him that, too. It qualifies."

"Qualifies as mercy, too," Gunny said.

"Obviously, they didn't catch you," Jo said.

"They knew. My resident pulled me aside, and said, 'The official cause of death here was a hypersensitivity to Pacem-Myotica. That's what goes into my report. But I heard the recording, kid, and I know what you did. I understand why, and I don't even blame you, but it better not happen on my watch again, 'prehendo?'

"Yeah. I understood.

"And that was that."

He looked at Singh. The boy nodded.

Did it make a difference to him? Sometimes it helped just to know you weren't the only passenger on the ship.

And sometimes it didn't . . .

# SIXTEEN

Cutter leaned against the wall and looked at his staff. "Jo, you want to start?"

She nodded. Mostly for Formentara's benefit, she ran through the particulars of the mission. And while it was patently obvious to everybody, she restated it:

"It was a trap. They knew we were coming."

Cutter played devil's advocate: "You sure? Isn't it possible they set up the lodge as a decoy and just happened to catch us?"

"I don't think so. Couple reasons: First, we're the Rajah's main recovery team, and there's no secret about us, so if somebody was going to find the lodge, we should have been at the top of the worry list.

"Second, whoever is running the opposition here has a shitload of money and some serious personpower to have that much gear and boots ready to spring a trap *just in case* somebody stepped into it. It makes more sense that they knew we were coming and when."

Cutter nodded. "So they put out bait, and we took it."

Jo looked at Kay.

Kay's expression was not easy to read, even after the six years she'd been working for CFI, but Cutter thought she looked a little peeved. He said, "Kay?"

"Prey would of course lie to save itself, but the Rel believed it was telling the truth. Which means that Sims Captain is correct—we were specifically targeted." A beat, then: "Perhaps I should revisit the Rel and overcome my dietary distaste of them."

Cutter grinned. A Vastalimi joke.

He said, "How so? The targeting, I mean, not the diet."

"Not likely humans would think to question Rel in this matter. If Rel were given false information designed to draw hunters into a trap, it would be aimed at someone who *would* pursue this line of inquiry. Whoever did it knew that this was apt to be a Vastalimi. I would like to speak to this person."

Cutter nodded again. "Anybody want to jump in?"

Gramps said, "Well, it brings up the big question, doesn't it? Why?"

"Take out the people most likely to find the girl?" That from Wink.

Gunny said, "The old man has a point. That's a lot of trouble. Be a lot easier just to sit tight somewhere, com all shut down, bottled. Pack her up and move her every once in a while. It's a big planet. And they'd have to know that the Rajah can afford to hire more mercenaries. Why bother?"

Cutter said, "So they could have another reason. Any thoughts as to what?"

Nobody leaped on that one, and Cutter himself didn't have any ideas that made sense.

"What now?" Formentara asked.

"Back to what we were doing. We keep looking—"

Cutter's personal com chortled. The tone was the Rajah's ID. He held up a hand, tapped the com crowed to his belt, put it on loudspeaker: "Cutter."

"Colonel, the kidnappers have called with a ransom demand."

"I'm on my way."

He tapped the com off. Looked at Gramps.

The older man had his own com unit in hand, shaking his head as he looked at it.

"Nope, we didn't catch that call."

Cutter frowned. "Jo, with me. The rest of you stay loose."

He started for the door. "Oh, and think of ways we might make an extra million-and-some noodle, to pay for the suits you left in the forest."

He saw them grin at that. Well. Even though he would sacrifice a dozen suits to save any one of these people, he had a reputation to maintain, didn't he?

– – – – – –

In the Rajah's conference room, Ganesh looked as if he had been hit by a van, and neither Cutter nor Jo were surprised at his appearance, both of them having seen the vid showing the reason why. There was a vaguely medicinal smell about him.

*Fuck with the Vastalimi, get the claw.* He was lucky to be alive.

Jo noticed that Rama, the prospective son-in-law, was not there. She said so aloud.

The Rajah said, "I thought it better to speak to him of this privately later."

The big man pointed at the table, upon which was a sand-colored sheet of something like paper with writing on it. Looked as if it was Devanagari—Manak Hindi, a bit of which she could understand when spoken, but couldn't read. The sheet was inside a clear plastic cover, sealed all the way around.

Ganesh looked at the Rajah, who nodded once.

The security chief said, "This was found tacked to a lamppost at the end of Smuggler's Alley, two kilometers from the palace."

"Forensics?" Jo asked.

"Nothing apparent—no DNA, fingerprints. It is foolscap folio bamboo paper, made by Hakkas Manufacturing, in Depok, Balaji."

Ah. Rama had a hard-on for the ruler of Balaji. That the paper came from there might be enough for him to blow a valve.

Ganesh continued: "This paper is used for official archive hard copy from Pahal to Hem, including here in our country, and often in high-end POD editions of *The Vedas*. One of those rests on every other coffee table on the planet. The ink is standard India jet, available at any artist-supply market, applied, our technicians say, with a metal nib.

"It was affixed to the post by four brass thumbtacks, also clean."

"Cameras?"

"None directly covering the lamp. The four security cameras nearest to the location all malfunctioned precisely at midnight. Those farther away have been downloaded, and the recordings scanned. Thus far, nothing of use has been found there."

Jo and Cutter exchanged glances.

"What does it say?" Cutter asked.

Jo had already snapped an image, stored it in her optical aug. She would be able to call up the image whenever she wanted. Whatever Ganesh had to say, they could check it with their own translator later.

"It says, 'We have your daughter, and she lives but by our sufferance. Your mercenaries are no threat to us. The ransom will be the equivalent to ND ten million. Await further instructions.' "

Jo figured the Rajah could come up with ten million in pocket change, though that part was tricky. Any kidnapper with half a brain would know how easy it was to mark any kind of tangible ransom. Cash, even old, used bills, could be steganographed with something virtually undetectable, unless the scanner had the code. Somebody with the money could examine it under a microscope and not find anything, but the first note to pass under a scanner programmed with the find-it code would trip silent alarms. And in a case like this, every commercial and government scanner in the system would get that code. Buy a packet of soup mix at the local market way out in the country, in the middle of nowhere? They'd collect you before you got two klicks away.

Likewise, gems could be micronumbered invisibly, unless you were an expert and knew exactly where to look. A couple of those in a bag of one- or two-carat stones would be enough.

Platinum could be tagged with tracers that were inert until a coded scanner bathed them. Bank transfers could carry a find-me code.

The smartest way would be to have an e-transfer, then have that rerouted through additional transactions, which would strip out the original deposit code. Put it in Bank A, and by the time it got to Bank Z, which could be done quickly, following it would take a while. At some point along the way, the electronics could be changed into something more tangible: cash, gems, a shipful of guns or pharmaceuticals, and be half the galaxy away by the time the law caught up to the transfer.

That would take some organization, but the kidnappers had already proven they had plenty of that.

– – – – – –

Gunny saw Singh coming out of Doc's suite, and she drifted over to see how he was doing.

"Singh. How you holdin' up?"

"I am better."

Didn't sound like it to her, but she didn't press it.

"When we got back to the hopper, I saw you," he said. "You and the others, none of you were afraid, what we had done did not seem to bother you at all. It was"—he said something in a dialect she didn't recognize—"how to say it? A stroll in the field? for you."

She shrugged. "You get used to it. How old are you?"

"Twenty summers."

"When Ah joined the Army, you would have been two."

"Are you that old?"

She laughed. "Gramps would bust a gut laughin' at that one. Yeah, Ah'm that old. And trust me, Ah was way more rattled than you were first time we saw lethal action."

"I find this hard to believe."

"Oh, it's true. You like Doc's story? Let me tell you mine . . .

- - - - - -

"My first tour was with the Unified Terran Army, the Kiwi Police Action. Six of us on patrol came across a liquor still in the woods above the Lower Nihotupu Reservoir, Waitakere Ranges, maybe twenty-five klicks southwest of Auckland. We were hunting Maori insurgents, and we figured some of them were brewing it—the embargo was dogged down pretty tight by then.

"Ah was a doe-private grunt, just turned seventeen, my first field op. Our sergeant was a tight-ass from Beijing, the guy on point was from Fiji.

"Our com gear was for shit, off-line more than it worked, and we were using LOS jive-signs, maybe half of which I knew. First two of those you learn? 'Duck!' and 'Haul ass!'

"The Fijian was a third-tour guy who loved the forest, busted back to corporal from sergeant for punching out civilians in an off-base watering hole. The man could disappear behind a blade of grass. He found the still and doubled back to tell us. Him, we trusted.

"Sergeant Wang was a class-one asshole, chickenshit to the core, he would have called in a nuke-drone to take out an empty plastic barrel if our com had been working, but since he couldn't raise anybody, we went in for a look.

"Nobody home we could see. Our motion detectors didn't catch anything, our wide-look IR cams gave us nothing but the sig from the heat-pump induction heater under the barrel of mash they were cooking. No insurgent glows.

"Wang decided they musta heard us coming and trucked. He decided we'd toss a willy-peter into the camp and burn it down.

"The Fijian volunteered to do the grenade, and since Ah was the newbie, Ah got sent along to cover his ass. Walk in the park, blowin' shit up with nobody around.

"We got there, the others stayed back eighty meters in the woods. There was a two-hundred-liter aboveground camo tank half-full of hooch they'd already distilled. The Fijian emptied his water canteen and filled it from a spigot on the tank, tasted the stuff.

" 'Whoa! This shit has got some *kick*!'

"He offered me a sip, but Ah wasn't interested.

"He set a white phosphorus grenade next to the tank.

" 'Twenty seconds!' he hollered, and we were fixin' to truck, since it was gonna make a big, bright fireball when all that alcohol went up.

"Ah was already turned round, my back to the site, when the Maori came out the ground. Had a spiderhole dug next to the barrel, the heat from the inducer enough to hide his sig from our WLIR. Smart, and probably he'da stayed there 'cept he heard the Fijian yell out the grenade's timer and he figured he was gonna get barbecued in his hole, which he surely would have.

"That Maori had a drum-fed gunpowder shotgun, an antique, probably alternating buckshot and solid slugs, and he blew out the Fijian's face with his first shot.

"I dropped and spun as he fired, and his second and third shots just cleared my head.

"My weapon was an old BTY subgun, six-millimeter caseless-pistol plasma-capacitor. Piece of low-bid shit, as likely to jam or short-circuit after three or four rounds as not, even if you spent an hour every day cleaning and tuning the sucker, which Ah had done for all the fucking good it did me.

"I got off four and sure enough, that fuckin' Betty shorted—but three of those for sure hit the Maori solid.

"Big man, two meters, 130 kilos, easy, those tribal tattoos they like all over his face, body, and arms. No shirt, so I saw the puckers in tachypsychia-time when the pellets hit, the first two three centimeters apart dead-center sternum, the third one higher and to his left, all of them heart punches. I like to think the fourth went into one of the other three holes.

"Man was dead, but didn't know enough to fall down.

"Somebody in the squad started hollerin' and shootin'. My weapon was fucked. Ah ate dirt and the Maori laid onto the trigger and hosed the air over me on full auto, sounded like the rage of Yahweh. Ah figured Ah was history as soon as he realized all he needed to do was drop the muzzle a hair, but 'fore he could, the grenade lit and he got char-broiled into crispy terrorist. His ammo cooked off, that willy-peter burned the shit out of everything for twenty meters, but he was a fire shadow 'tween me and it, and Ah walked away without a blister.

"Eighteen years ago. Give me a stylus, I can draw you the pattern of tats on the man's face."

Gunny looked at the boy. "Nobody is a born killer. And nobody ever forgets the first time they get laid, nor the first time they spike somebody. Right now, it's fresh and warm, but it will cool, and you will get past it."

He looked doubtful, and he might be right. Some people never did get past it. They didn't continue on in the Army, unless they stayed REMFs. And what was the point in that?

Singh was rattled, but he didn't have the feel of somebody who would curl up and let it take him.

# SEVENTEEN

Kay went to see the Rel. If she could track down the source of information that led them into a trap, she might be able to find a connection that led deeper. It was a logical line of inquiry.

She returned to the public house where she had questioned the Rel. It was as dim and moist as it had been before, and there were Rel there; however, the one she wanted was not among them.

Again, the herbivores froze at her approach. She picked the one that looked the most terrified.

"I need to speak with Zeth of the Hallows," she told him. "Where is he to be found?"

"I-I-I d-don't kn-kn—"

"Then best you point me to somebody who *does* know, or you will regret it for the remainder of your short and miserable life." She was in no mood to be denied and wanted to be sure that came across.

Apparently, it did.

"B-B-Boot-Booterik is Zeth's sib."

"Which one is he?"

"H-He is n-n-not here." Off her look, he hurriedly added, "I have an address where he lives!"

"Provide it."

He rattled off a street and number.

She stood. "Do not attempt to contact either of these individuals, Rel. If you do, I will find out about it."

"I w-w-won't."

She turned and left.

Outside the pub, she activated her com, to call Sims Captain. She didn't think she would need help, but it was the unit's protocol.

"What's up, Kay?"

"I have a lead. The location is Footpad Alley, number sixteen. A Rel's domicile. I am on my way there and—" She stopped. What—?

Coming around the corner was a man with a sidearm pointed in her direction.

"Kay?"

She dodged to her left, jinked right and left again, and charged at the gunman.

He fired, but missed, a gas-propelled missile of some kind—

She sensed the second man behind her. She stutter-stepped and cut right, but—

—too late. She heard the second gun cough, felt the dart sting her high on the left side of her back—

She managed to reach the first gunman as he fired and missed again. She laid her right claws across his throat and ripped away flesh and cartilage down to the spine.

She spun . . .

Things went dark—

－ － － － － －

At the comshack, Jo said, "Kay?"

Behind her, Rags arrived. "What?"

"Kay's got a problem," she said. "Sounds like a dustup. Her com is on, but she's not responding."

"Got a location?"

"Yes."

"Let's go."

－ － － － － －

Formentara said, "The signal is not moving, it's right where we first located it."

As the hopper dropped low over the city, Nancy said, "Ninety seconds."

"You get that, Colonel?"

In the second hopper, coming in from the opposite direction, Cutter said, "Got it. We're fifteen seconds ahead of you." Gunny was with him, as was Wink. Along with Formentara, she had Gramps with her, and each hopper had six more troops. It was policy on a hostile world to split up command staff when it was reasonable to do so and to take enough firepower to get the job done.

By the time Nancy put them down and they boiled out, guns ready, Cutter was already on the ground and shaking his head. "Here's her com. She's not here."

"Probably still alive," Gramps said. "Otherwise, why take her?"

"Why take her at all?" Jo asked.

"Maybe Ganesh," Gunny said. "She made him look pretty bad"

"We'll have a word with him," Cutter said. "Formentara?"

"Let me trigger it," zhe said.

Jo looked at hir. "Trigger what?"

"Her implant."

"What? Vastalimi don't do implants, everybody knows that."

"Let's hope whoever has her thinks so, too," Cutter said.

Jo looked back at Formentara.

Formentara grinned, and waved a small flatscreen no bigger than hir palm. "She doesn't know about it, and no way she would. It's inert until somebody sends the coded trigger pulse. About a quarter the size of my little fingernail, a bit thicker."

"How in the hell did y'all get something like that into her?"

"Put it in her food. They don't grind all that much, got no real molars. Inside a piece of gristle. Acid-activated timer pops out burrs—tricky with Vastalimi, they got those short, meat-eater bowels—it digs in, usually in the small intestine, stays there, doesn't cause any problems. Hypo-allergenic, hooks of gold, coated in silicone, running viral moleculars, heat-diff biobatt. Good for ten years, easy. I check it every six months. Working fine a few weeks ago."

Jo shook her head. She, like the rest of them, had either an implant or a rider on an aug that sent out a locator signal, that was expected; you got killed, somebody would know where to come collect the corpse. But she'd never heard of a Vastalimi with one.

"She's gonna be pissed when she finds out," Gramps said.

"I can live with that," Cutter said. "Long as she's alive to get pissed."

– – – – – –

When Kay awoke, it was with a chemical hangover and a killing rage, the combination of which made her head hurt. She was on her side, in a vehicle, one rolling on a road, to judge by the vibrations, and a quick, surreptitious look showed her she was in a storage compartment, lying on a rubbery pad. A van of some kind, moving slowly, turning this way and that. It did not feel as if she had been uncon-scious long, her internal sense of time told her. Still in the city, then, and on their way . . . where? Who were they, and what did they want with her?

Perhaps the kidnappers? That would be good. Escaping

confinement might be difficult, but if these were the people for whom she was looking? So much the better.

She pretended to still be unconscious. If they had a camera watching her, they might have noticed her eyes open for a half second when she had looked around, but she hadn't offered any other signals that she was awake.

She would wait. An opportunity would arise.

— — — — —

In his hopper, Cutter said. "Once she gets to where they are taking her, we'll scout the location, determine the best way to go and fetch her."

It went without saying that they'd have to be careful. They'd only go in if they had a pretty good idea of what the situation was. The point was to get Kay back alive. But if it was the same people who'd kidnapped the Rajah's daughter? That would be a bonus.

His com chortled. "Cutter."

It was the Rajah. "I am afraid I have some disturbing news," he said.

"Go ahead."

"My prospective son-in-law has plans to field a large force of troops to invade Balaji. He seems convinced that the Thakore is responsible for my daughter's disappearance, and he does not wish to wait for you to find her."

*Great. Just what we need, a hothead with an army.*

"'Has *plans* to field'?"

"He is ready to go now, but I have convinced him to bide awhile before he launches any attack."

"How long?"

"Hard to say precisely. A few days. A week, perhaps."

"Thank you, sir. We're in the middle of an operation. Soon as we tend to it, we'll see if we might be able to talk some sense into Rama."

"I hope so, Colonel. If my daughter suffers as a result of his actions, I will be most unhappy with Rama."

Cutter disconnected. The Rajah had enough steel in him and enough money so that having him unhappy with you might present a real hazard to your continued existence.

Well. That was Rama's lookout. He had his own situation—

"Looks like they've stopped," Formentara said. Zhe waggled the flatscreen. "I'm not getting a signal, so they must be shielded, but I have a location where the sig cut out."

"Would it do that if she was dead?" That from Gunny.

"No."

Cutter said, "Gramps, get a snoop in the air on the PPS coordinates and get us some images. Careful, so they don't spot it."

Gramps mumbled something Cutter didn't catch.

"What's that?"

"I said, 'Teach your grandfather how to screw.' It's already on the way."

Cutter smiled. He did tend to get a little hands-on sometimes. "Sorry."

The snoop, a Dybercine M-3 Busybody, was a palm-sized drone with a low-rez forty-megapixel cam. It had whisper jets and a field-effect repeller, a cruising range of a hundred kilometers and an operating time of sixteen hours, as long as enough of that was sufficient daylight to recharge the cells. Not the absolute top-of-the-line gear, but good enough for their needs.

There were three ways to effectively use a snoop without the subject's spotting it. Either sheathe it in stealth gear; make it look like something natural, a bird, or, on some worlds, an insect; or fly it far enough away it couldn't be seen or detected. A palm-sized sky-colored drone three klicks up? Nobody using human eyes would see it; putting a scope on it would be almost impossible unless you knew exactly where to look; and sensors with gain set high enough to spot it would pick up all kinds of artifacts. The cam could collect a sharp streaming image in a single pass. Crisscross a few times, you could build a decent threedee hologram accurate to centimeters, more or less. The unit didn't have passwall viewtech, that cost a small fortune, but they could get that information later.

The snoop in the air, it would take a few minutes to arrive, and Cutter thought it best to tell the crew about the Rajah's intel.

He did.

"Isn't Rama's father the rajah of whatchamacallit?" Wink asked. "Why is he letting his son do this?"

Cutter shrugged. "Who knows what the agendas are out here."

"If it turns out we have to go into Balaji to collect Indira, its being a full-out war zone might cause problems," Gramps said.

"Or it could work to our advantage," Jo said. "If they are busy shooting at each other, maybe they won't notice us."

"And maybe if we do it right, we can find and collect her and be long gone before her boyfriend cranks up a shooting war." That from Formentara.

"That would be good," Cutter said. "We didn't come dressed for a war."

# EIGHTEEN

"Here we go," Gramps said. "She went in there and didn't come out."

The holographic projector over his board lit and the image of what looked like a row of warehouses appeared, three-dimensional and sharp. There was a pulsing purple dot above one of the buildings.

Jo looked at the structures. She had already tapped the coordinates into a flatscreen, found the address and a street map, and was running the search engine . . .

"Okay, this building is owned by something called the Hari Corporation. Hold on a second . . ."

Jo waggled her fingers at the sight-reader. More intel appeared.

"Looks like a shell. Officers listed are Krishna, Vishnu, and Durga. Might take a while to backwalk it."

"We can get that later," Cutter said. "Take us in closer."

Gramps waved his hand. The camera's VP did a slow zoom, so the one building filled the holograph. At ground level, the VP circled the structure, showing the windows and doors.

"All right, let's get the materials specs and start the tacticals," Cutter said.

— — — — — —

The door to the van's cargo compartment rolled up, and Kay caught the odors of three humans—one who had recently eaten meat, one who needed a bath, and one who stank of fear. She inhaled a bit deeper and caught the scent of a fourth, ten meters away. One or all of them could be armed, but surely the farthest one would be.

Only four—five, counting the one she had killed. She was insulted.

Of course, she was also captured, so the insult was overridden by shame.

How had she allowed it to happen? It was pathetic.

Best she prepare for what was coming.

Vastalimi learned as cubs how to enter an auto-trance state called *spokoj*, similar to hypnosis. This was usually done to enhance focus for detail work, or for rote memorization of a lot of data, but it could also alleviate pain. It wasn't enough to calm a serious physioemotional state, something like a *zrelost* seizure, but it was useful.

She whispered the trigger phrase under her breath and tripped into *spokoj*.

Good thing, too. Almost immediately, she heard:

"Is it still asleep?" one of the men said.

"Of course. The dart carried enough tranquilizer to put a giant out. It will be unconscious for another two hours, minimum," said a second man.

"Are you sure?"

"Watch."

She held her breath, sank deeper into *spokoj*, waiting . . .

There it came. A jab, into her side with something sharp.

It broke the skin, but was stopped by the rib. A short knife, probably. No real damage.

"You see? If it was awake, it would have jumped when I pricked it. Let's get it out and into the cage."

Four hands grabbed her, shoulders and behind the knees. A fifth hand reached between her legs to cup her *ruta* under her fur.

Ah. She might be a thing to them, but one of them was curious about her sexual organs. On this world, that would make him a deviant, but it was not a surprise.

Human males would mate with anything possible.

They lifted her.

"It is heavier than I expected," one of them said.

As calm as she was, Kay allowed her smile to play. They wouldn't know the expression even if they noticed it, not humans who called her "it."

"Hurry up," the fourth man said. That was the one in charge, she guessed. Best to keep that one alive.

Three of them were holding her, and the fourth's position was easy to mark. She had both scent and hearing; she didn't need to see.

She didn't need to see—but she opened her eyes—

- - - - -

Both hoppers were in the air, and the entry plan set. Jo and Gunny would kick in the southwest door while he and Wink blasted in via the northeast entrance. They could toss concussion and photon grenades to stun anybody close to the doors. Gramps and Nancy would keep one hopper aloft and the vehicle's guns ready to spike any enemy who came out or who arrived to come in after them. Simple, fast, direct, and in such chases, that was almost always the best way.

The warehouse did have sensor shields in place, which was not so good, so they couldn't tell where everybody was, but they'd deal with that as it unfolded. Speed and surprise made up for a lot of things.

"ETA, forty-five seconds," Nancy said.

"Pucker up," Cutter said. He wanted to tell them to be careful and not shoot Kay, but they all knew what the stakes were.

"And it would be nice if we could keep one alive to chat with."

"They hurt Kay, we'll have to draw straws to see who gets to end that conversation," Jo said.

－ － － － － －

*"Aaiie! It's awa—!"*

Kay twisted and slashed with her left paw, removing half that man's face. She stabbed him in the throat with her other claws as they dropped her—

—as she fell, she twisted and caught the second man with both hands behind his head and used her clawed feet to disembowel him—

—she shoved off his falling body, twisted, spun, and caught the third man, fleeing, from behind and swung him around as a shield—

—the fourth man fired a pistol at her, but the man she held absorbed the soft-target darts; he screamed as they punched into his flesh, *one-two-three-four-five*—

—the shooter was only four meters away, and she shoved the wounded man at the shooter, dived to the right, rolled, came up, and sprang to her left, jinked back and forth twice as she charged him—

—he backed off as he saw her coming, but his weapon was aimed away from her and she was moving fast—

He must have realized he wouldn't be able to get it lined up on her in time.

She showed him her fangs, gathered to spring—

—he had just enough time to shove the gun's barrel under his own chin—

"No!" she yelled, already in midleap—

He fired. The sound was muffled where the muzzle

pressed against his throat. He collapsed bonelessly, and she
sailed over his falling form.

*"Jebi mi!"* she said as she landed.

------

Jo had her augs cranked and she was through the door and
past any potential danger fast, before Gunny could get her
grenades in play. She skidded to a stop, senses on full alert,
questing for a target.

None in sight—

"Clear!" Jo yelled. No point in having the light show and
loud noises.

*"Jebi mi! Supak glupan glupak! Seljak mamlaz macola!
Mentol seronja kaka!"*

Jo grinned. Kay! And cursing like a pubful of sailors.
Fem could take the paint off a battlewagon with such language. She didn't sound hurt.

She sounded *mad* . . .

When Jo got to where Kay stood, looking down at four
dead men, she said, "You had to kill them all?"

"I did *not* kill them all. I killed *those* two. *That* one shot
*this* one, then shot his *jebanje* self. Holeass fornicator of his
mother!"

Gunny arrived and pulled up. Four seconds later, Rags
and Wink got there. They looked around.

Rags said, "Did you have to kill them all?"

Kay glared at him.

Jo laughed.

------

On the way back to HQ, Jo thought she might defuse some
of Kay's smoldering anger by getting her to talk.

"I've wondered: Why are the Vastalimi such fierce fighters? Yeah, you have the biological tools, the claws and teeth
and speed, but what is it in your makeup, can you tell us?"

Kay looked at her. She thought about it for a couple of seconds.

"There is on my world a small predator, called a *gmiza*. Something like a Terran lizard, but with longer and more powerful legs. The size of a house cat, perhaps five kilograms, a *gmiza* can leap vertically more than twice the height of a tall Vastalimi.

"Its primary prey is a small bird, the *ptica*, which feeds on grass seed.

"The *gmiza* mate for life and hunt in pairs. They will crouch in low grass in *ptica* habitat, and their skin will take on the coloration of the background. Nearly invisible, they will wait until a flock lands to feed, but they are fast and agile enough to take prey on the wing.

"They have learned how to use the *ptica*'s startle response, and often one will show itself, causing a *ptica* flock to take flight toward its hidden mate.

"It is quite impressive to see a flock of *ptica* three meters above the ground and rising beset by a springing *gmiza* as it snatches one from flight and drops back into the grass.

"They have few natural enemies. There are larger predators who will take *gmiza* when they can catch one, but mostly, they don't catch them. The ones large enough are generally too slow; the ones fast enough, not as fierce.

"*Gmiza* live in small, natural volcanic rock caves in the hills bordering grasslands, and anything big enough to threaten them usually cannot get through the entrance to their den.

"*Gmiza* have learned how to dry their food, using hot, flat rocks in the sunlight, and the plucked and desiccated bodies will keep for weeks. So even if a larger predator traps a pair of *gmiza* in their cave, they can feed and wait until it gets too hungry and leaves.

"There are Vastalimi who hunt *gmiza*. The creatures are not as fast as we are in a straight line, but are much more agile and able to turn quicker and more acutely. Catching one is a challenge, for they know how to use the terrain, and they can dodge and weave among the rocks enough to frustrate the most adept Vastalimi pursuer. You might go out a dozen times and not collect any.

"As a people, we are not known for our patience, and we aren't going to squat outside a cave and wait weeks for *gmiza* to run out of food. Of course, that is not the point—the challenge is to catch them afoot.

"It's much easier to catch the birds they eat than the *gmiza*. So one collects a dozen birds, fogs them with chem that makes them tractable, then uses them as bait. If one is lucky, one can fool the *gmiza* into thinking the birds are legitimate quarry.

"However, the *gmiza* are wary and easily spooked. They are sight-hunters, and their vision keen, so the smallest wrong detail will make them vanish. One moment, the pair is almost in range; the next, they are in the wind."

"Do you hunt them?"

"No."

"Why not?"

She said, "If you attack one, then you attack both; if you capture or kill one, its mate will go for you full out, and fight to the death.

"Picture it: They have no hope of winning, but they will sacrifice themselves to protect or, failing that, to avenge their mates. More than a few hunters have come home nursing wounds that festered, became infected, and caused serious illness, so it is not a completely trivial thing to hunt *gmiza*; still, the risk is minimal. A Vastalimi is bigger, stronger, and possessed of a sharper brain. All the *gmiza* has is an ability to dodge quickly, a defensive mode, and pure defense eventually loses to offense.

"But the creatures also have a willingness to die, and that makes them dangerous. They have a singular focus:

"A *gmiza* will attack a Vastalimi ten times, fifteen times

its size, certainly knowing it will not survive. How can one *not* admire the courage of such a steadfast being? And how could you take pleasure in defeating such? Only someone with a small ego would glory in besting an opponent with almost no potential chance of winning.

"If there is not much danger, how can there be much triumph?

"If you want to compliment a Vastalimi's ability? Say, 'She held. She fought like a *gmiza*.' "

Kay blinked, considered her words, said:

"There are better ways to improve your skills as a hunter and fighter. We have a saying: *'Borba neckta tjova veli'cina.'* It means, 'Attack one your own size.' "

They all nodded at that.

"A match against someone who might defeat you? *There* is a challenge."

She looked at Jo, who nodded. Their matches were play and usually in Kay's favor, but there was, Jo thought, a chance that she would prevail.

"There are among the Vastalimi fierce and adept warriors, males and females who can hold their own with half a dozen lesser-skilled opponents, those who live for the joy of close-quarters fighting, claw-to-claw. They are respected for their skills and ferocity, and they go places that provide opportunity for them to use both.

"The best of them tend to die young because they constantly test themselves against like fighters. A small error against an expert in a serious match often results in death for one or both.

"Those who survive sometimes become teachers of fighting methods, passing along what they have learned. I had such a teacher when I was a cub, an old male who had lost an arm in battle.

"When you must make one hand take the place of two, you either learn a new method, or you cannot compete.

"My teacher—*Stark*masc, call him Ess—developed a

sinuous kind of circularity in his upper body that allowed him to block and strike together. He could whip his single arm fast and hard, using his hips to generate speed and power, and the result was an unconventional system opponents either did not expect, nor could match if they did see it coming. And the stub of his other arm had uses opponents did not expect, as well.

"Ess never used his handicap as an excuse. He considered himself the equal of or better than any Vastalimi, and he won many fights against those who were bigger, stronger, and possessed of two good arms."

"What happened to him?"

"His final fight was against three attackers. He died from his wounds. So did two of the three, with the third left maimed.

"There are things that one walks away from," Kay said. "But when one chooses to stand? One seeks to fight like a *gmiza*, all out, no thoughts of defeat or death. Or like a one-armed Vastalimi who turned a handicap into an asset. That's how a Vastalimi fighter thinks. No hesitation, no qualms, move until you prevail or you cannot move anymore, whichever comes first."

Jo nodded. Good to know.

# NINETEEN

Formentara was in hir augmentation trance when Jo arrived, hands waving back and forth in a sensor-hula over hir console.

Jo had seen this often enough to know it was better to let it run its course, so she sat and began to mentally review the operations so far. One needed to revisit tactics, to see if there were things that could have been done better, and there almost always were ways to improve. Even a small move left instead of right might make the difference between life and death; one needed to examine the process and consider. Better to learn from someone else's fatal mistake . . .

"I'm done," Formentara said. "Gone off into your own trance, I see."

Jo looked up to see hir grinning. "XO's work is never done," Jo said.

"But you love it, so it's not really work, is it?"

Jo returned hir grin. "You got me. So what's up? Am I due for a balance?"

"Nope, your augs are in perfect sync, as of course they would be."

"So . . . ?"

"I have a new thing."

Jo's interest blossomed. Formentara was unrivaled when it came to biological augmentation. "You found it *here*? I thought you said this planet was the equivalent of the Stone Age."

"I didn't find it, I *created* it."

"Really? Can I have it? Please?"

Zhe grinned. "This is why you are my favorite patient. Because you ask that before you even ask what it is."

"You created it, I don't need to ask."

"Absolutely true, but still, I'm touched by your confidence. Okay, here's the deal . . ."

Jo listened, and by the time Formentara was done telling her, her mouth was open in wonder. "Holy shit. When can I get it?"

"When are you free for an hour?"

"Now. How about now, is now good?"

Formentara laughed. "On the table."

— — — — —

Deep into the augmatrix, Formentara shunted, adjusted, revised, retuned, and did hir dance among the hormones and viral molec, a maestro conducting a complex symphony, every note important, the smallest gestures critical. This was hir realm, hir universe, hir reason to get up every day. A hair this way lay failure; a hair that way, genius, and it was a delicate juggling routine that could crash down in a heartbeat. Any decent augmentor could take a piece of off-the-shelf wetware and spin it up, make it work exactly as designed. There were a million keyboard players who could play Mozart's music—but only *one* Mozart . . .

There, the shuttle of enzymes for hypothalamic registration; here, the adrenals rebalanced. There, the new battery ignited; here, the redistribution of power on the afferent/efferent exchange. Eliminate those senescent dregs; reroute the output of those neurons.

Dance, dance, and dance again.

There was no sense of time in the augmentation flux, the flow could be a minute, an hour, an eon. It was as in-the-moment as zhe could be, and it never got old.

Formentara blinked and looked at hir system's time sig. Fifty-six minutes.

That was excellent. Better than zhe expected.

Once again, zhe had gone into the Void and become, at least on a small scale, God. Time to wake Sims up and see if it worked. Zhe raised the oxy level and gave her a squirt of stimulant.

"Jo."

"I'm getting dressed, Mum, I'll be down in a minute!"

"Jo."

Sims blinked up at her. Focused. "Ah. How did it go?"

"Perfectly."

"Can I try it?"

"That would be good."

Jo sat up.

– – – – – –

Once she had calmed her rage, Kay was left with a question. She went to Cutter Colonel's office.

"A few moments of your time?" she said.

"Come on in."

She sat on the hard chair in front of his desk and considered her approach. She was not an expert in human communications though she was more adept than most of her kind. How best to begin so as not to sound as if she were challenging her leader?

"You are wondering how we located you after you were taken," he said, cutting to the heart of the matter.

That surprised her. "Indeed. I was not followed from the

base. My com was left at the scene of the attack, and thus of no use. It is possible that cameras recorded the vehicle and that was somehow tracked, but that seems unlikely."

"You have an internal tracker," he said. "Surreptitiously administered and inert until remotely triggered."

Her immediate reaction was a flash of anger that threatened to erupt into an attack. She held herself in check. He was her leader. "The Vastalimi do not hold with such devices."

"I know."

"And yet you had it done in spite of that."

"Yes."

"Why?"

"The end in this case justifies the means."

"I had the encounter under control."

"So you did. We did not know that. You are a valuable employee. We would prefer to keep you alive."

"Was this not my choice?"

"Yes and no."

"Explain."

"You signed a waiver when you contracted with CFI."

"I do not recall that the contract specified I was to be given such a thing."

"It was worded very carefully and unlikely you would have noticed. A reference to another lettered and numbered reference: 'Pursuant to Subsection Alpha-Theta Seven, the corporation reserves the right to employ such technology as specified in Codex Delta for the health maintenance and welfare of its employees.'"

"I thought that referred to medical treatment in case of illness or injury."

"That's what you were supposed to think. It's buried in the fine print list of devices, and IDed only by a model number."

"So you legally had the right to do this."

"Yes."

"But it was a deliberate, devious ploy to subvert Vastalimi objections."

"It was." He paused. "You are one of us, Kay. A solider, a warrior, as much a member of the unit as anybody. We don't let our people die if we can help it, nor go missing without some recourse. We would have spent as much time and energy as necessary to find you, and that would have subverted our primary mission to some degree. Better that we knew where to look."

"I see. I understand your position if I do not agree with it."

"I thought you would."

"When the contract expires, if we renegotiate it, that clause will be removed, or I will not endorse it. Our association will end."

"Okay."

"And I will have the tracker removed. If our medic will not do it, I will find one who will. Along with any other devices I may have hidden within me."

"All right. I understand."

She stood. "You do not. You think this is some superstitious alien taboo, that there is no valid reason for the Vastalimi to routinely refuse much of what humans consider benign medical technology."

He didn't say anything, which she took as verification of her statement.

"It is impossible to explain to one who is not of us, but it is as much a part of our psychology and spirituality as your innate curiosity. It speaks to who we as a people *are*, and how we feel about ourselves and our place in the cosmos. You do not have to understand it, but it will be respected."

He nodded.

She left.

– – – – – –

After she was gone, Gramps came in. "How'd she take it?"

"I'm still alive. There was a moment when I wondered if I might not continue to be."

Gramps chuckled.

– – – – – –

Jo stood on her right foot, her left tucked against her supporting leg just above the knee, her eyes shut.

"Five minutes," Formentara said. "That's enough. Try the hop."

Jo nodded. She bent her supporting knee slightly, pushed off and lifted a few centimeters above the floor. In the air, she switched feet, put her left down, landed in balance, brought her right foot to rest on the left leg.

All with her eyes still closed.

Not even a wobble.

"Wow!" she said.

"You think?" Formentara laughed. Zhe was pleased, Jo could tell, and why wouldn't zhe be? This was a big deal, this new aug.

SPK, Formentara called it.

*Somatic Proprioceptive Kinetics.*

Anybody with even moderate physicality could stand on one foot for a few minutes. But close their eyes? A fit, trained person of twenty-five might manage forty or fifty seconds. The older you got, the less you could do. At her age, thirty seconds would be unusually good. A woman of sixty? The average was seven seconds; at seventy? Four seconds.

Jo had done *five minutes*, and not a tremble. That was amazing. As was the in-air switch. Her balance was perfect, and she felt it.

Not that there was a lot of call for standing on one foot in the dark, but that was only the tip of the iceberg.

Jo was aware of her entire body, what was where, how

gravity worked on it, and what she could do. She could freeze in midstep, knew exactly how much space was between her and the walls, the ceiling, Formentara, and every stick of furniture in the room, even with her vision off-line.

It was a real sixth sense. In a hand-to-hand situation, having that much of a center would be a real advantage.

"Open your eyes."

Jo obeyed. "I could get a job walking a high wire in a traveling circus," she said.

"Walking? You should be able to run on a wire at full speed and do a tumbling run, with the aug lit. Shut it off for a second."

Jo did. "Whoa! I feel as if I'm going to fall over."

"That will pass."

In a couple of seconds, the sensation ebbed. "I still feel like a cow trying to balance on stilts. Like the first time I came out of the O/O and felt as if I were going blind and deaf."

"That's the price."

Jo nodded. She knew. That was part of the reason that augmented folk tended to have shorter lives. The enhanced senses, the superhuman abilities, they were addictive, a seductive, nearly irresistible drug. Once they were lit, you didn't want to extinguish them. If you didn't have the discipline to flip the off switch, you'd burn yourself out, even if the balance in your system was as well regulated as Formentara could make it.

"This is terrific," Jo said. "Thank you."

"Yeah, well, keep it to yourself. When we get back to civilization, I'll probably put it on the market, but I might want to tinker with it a little more before the commercial version."

"Not a word," Jo said.

"And you must use these powers wisely, my child."

They both grinned.

— — — — —

"Rags, you have a caller waiting."

"Uh-huh. And . . . ?"

"He's on the limited-access opchan, and he's not some-body who is supposed to have the access code."

Cutter looked at Gramps. "Really?"

"His ID is a cutout. He won't say who he is, wants your ears only."

"Well, let's have a chat with him, shall we?

"Cutter here."

"Greetings, Colonel."

The voice, on speaker, sounded masculine, but that didn't mean much, given the state-of-the-art voxware you could pick up in any large market. A twenty-year-old Rel fem could be made to sound like an eighty-year-old human male, with a different accent and a lisp, and there were versions slick enough to alter speech patterns to match, less than a millisecond's delay, so that even colloquial phrases wouldn't give the game away.

Cutter waited for five seconds, then said, "You called me."

"Indeed I did. You seek Ramal's daughter, Indira."

"Yes. Do you have her?"

"No. And I do not yet know who does."

"And why are we having this conversation?"

"Because I know who does *not* have her."

"I'm still listening."

"The Thakore of Balaji is no more than a convenient scapegoat."

"And you know this how?"

"I have . . . a close association with Thakore Luzor."

"And you are telling me that he had nothing to do with Indira's kidnapping."

"This is so."

"I have to ask: Could it be you are offering this because

the Rajah of Pahal's son is about to lead an invasion into Balaji? Do you think I can call him off, based on this?"

There was a pause, and maybe a quiet sigh. Then: "Rama Jadak is an idiot, full of wind and fury, which he expels constantly from both ends. He abuses the help, he is a kicker of innocent dogs. I doubt he would listen if both Vishnu and Shiva materialized, put their hands on your shoulders, and vouched for you. His motives are impure."

"How so?"

"He has been looking for an excuse to attack Balaji. Wars are expensive, they cost taxes and lives, the populace is not quick to embrace them. But what man would begrudge a royal son trying to save his bride from dishonor or death? Such things stir a nation's blood. We remember the *Ramayana*, which features the mythological Rama, and speaks to this very thing.

"The heir to the Rajah's throne in Pahal could not manage it alone, but his father-in-law-to-be will have to honor his end of the mutual aid pact between the two countries. And how could he not? It is his daughter. The result will be bloody and costly, and in the end, will not achieve the stated goal of returning Indira."

Cutter thought about that for a second. "Suppose for a second that I believe you. What would you have me do?"

"No more than you are already doing. Continue your search. Just bear in mind that attention to the Thakore will be a waste of your time and resources. If the Thakore finds her before you do—and be assured we are looking—he will send her to her father in the royal yacht."

"Really?"

"I guarantee it."

After the caller discommed, Cutter looked at Gramps. "What do you think?"

Gramps shrugged. "Intrigue on these backlane planets is thicker than bird turd on a park statue. Can't tell who's lying without a program, and even then, you'd want your best guy running the stress analyzer to double-check. Could be just like the caller said. Could be he just wants to throw us off the track. I don't see how anything changes."

Cutter nodded. True enough. But it did bring up an interesting line of inquiry.

# TWENTY

Because she had been taken unawares before, Kay was determined it would not happen again; more, this time when she went looking for the Rel who could tell her where to find yet another Rel, she was not alone. Jo Captain and Gunny, along with a squad of CFI's best had her back, and woe to any who stood in their way.

It was the smart thing to do. Not that she liked doing it.

Investigation into the men who had captured her proved less than useful. They had names and background available, but the men were, as far as they could tell, low-level thugs. Since they were all dead, that would not provide much in the way of intel. Presumably, they had kin, and those relatives could be determined, then questioned, but that was, Kay felt, a low-percentage option.

The neighborhood in which the Rel supposedly resided was more upscale than Kay had expected. Rel tended to herd together, sometimes a dozen to a plex, and all they needed was a cool and humid place. They mostly slept when they weren't working or socializing, and they didn't need much in the way of bedding since they tended to clump together, back to front, or side to side. They didn't spend much money on living quarters, but this place was new and, from its look, not cheap.

Herd mentality, that social structure. Repugnant, too.

Kay approached the entrance to the plex. Jo, Gunny, and the troops stayed back, ready to move, but they'd only come in on her signal. Better she talk to the Rel alone. Arriving with a group of armed soldiers would not strengthen her in the eyes of prey.

"Who calls?"

Kay gave her proper name. "I seek Zeth of the Hallows."

"He is not here."

"Then I would speak with his sibling Booterik."

"A moment."

The door slid open, and a single Rel stood there. A male, and his decorations muted, mostly dull blues with hints of purple.

"You are Booterik."

"I am. You may enter."

Kay smiled. "May I? How kind of you."

She walked into the place, following the Rel as he waddled ahead of her. It was clean, neat, not much in the way of furniture. Dim, damp, cool—a relief from the tropical heat outside.

Something was wrong with the smell, and it took her a second to realize what it was: There wasn't any scent of fear from the Rel. None.

And he was alone.

How interesting.

"Why do you wish to speak to Zeth?"

"My business and his."

"And mine. I am his elder sibling."

She regarded the Rel. This Booterik was insolent, at the very least impertinent. Something was wrong with him, that he would dare speak to a Vastalimi thus.

Carefully, she inhaled, searching for something in his scent. Drugs, perhaps. Chemical bravery? She couldn't detect any such.

Madness?

Kay resisted the urge to open his belly with her claws. She was here for information. If this being could provide it, he could go on with his life, such a sad thing that it was.

"Zeth gave me information regarding the whereabouts of the Rajah's daughter, who has been kidnapped."

"And . . . ?"

"His information was inaccurate."

"Allow me to apologize in his stead. I am sure this was not done deliberately to deceive."

"Are you?"

Booterik moved to a cushioned chair and sat upon it. He gestured at a similar seat across from him. "Sit if you wish."

Kay glanced around but sensed no threat. They were, as far as she could tell, alone, just the two of them. But she remained standing. Not wise to sit in the presence of prey behaving thusly.

"Zeth is not the smartest among us, but he is not given to deliberate falsehood. Especially to . . ." He trailed off, waving a hand in her direction.

She understood that well enough. *Especially not to a predator who would as soon kill you and eat you as look at you.*

"I look forward to his explanation," she said.

"Unfortunately, you will not be able to hear it from him directly. He has . . . left this world. He departed yesterday."

"Where would his destination be?"

"Far, far away." Booterik smiled. "Where you won't ever be able to find him."

*If it isn't drugs? Then he* must *be mentally deranged.*

"I find your tone disturbing."

"Do you?" Again the smile.

Kay relaxed her stance slightly, bent her knees a little,

sank a hair lower. Enough to be able to move a little faster. Because if it wasn't drugs, and if he wasn't mentally off the beam, then Booterik here had a weapon of some kind close to hand and the belief that he could get it and use it before she got to him. Which was hardly sane by their standards, but still.

Hidden in the chair?

Interesting. She had heard about Rel who had overcome the prey response and offered a challenge to a Vastalimi. She'd never run into one herself, and that was because they were few and far between, and those who had tried it only did so the once since they were surely no longer among the living, having gone down that path. If not killed instantly, then soon afterward.

She let it percolate, to see what would happen. "Do you know how Zeth came by this misinformation?"

"As it happens, I do. But I don't think I shall tell you."

Kay took a step toward him—

The Rel came out of the chair, impossibly fast, faster than she had ever seen one move, faster than it should be possible. As he did, a knife appeared in his hand, snatched from a hiding place in his chair. He came straight at her, the knife leading, and he shoved it toward her belly, intending to skewer her—

He was faster than any Rel she had ever seen, but that didn't mean he was faster than she was. Nor was he trained. He was depending on his speed, his lines were all open, save for the knife, and his attack was out of balance—

—when the blade's point was two centimeters from her belly and the Rel's attack fully committed, Kay pivoted. The blade tickled her hair below the navel. The Rel might have tried to slash inwardly, but she dropped low and slammed her elbow into his arm as she pivoted, felt the bone break just above his wrist, then she threw her body into his, knocking him sideways and sprawling.

He hit the wall, bounced off, somehow kept to his feet.

*Don't kill him—!*

The Rel recovered, the knife fallen from his limp hand, and he came at her again, arms extended, face contorted, his sad, dull, grinding teeth bared in a poor imitation of a snarl.

She kept her claws sheathed, snapped her right hand out in a straight punch, and hit him on the nose. The force of his charge and the hit straightened him out, stopped him, and knocked him unconscious. She danced to her left, and he fell and slid past her on his back.

She triggered her com. "We are going to need to transport an unconscious Rel out of here and back to the base for a medical examination," she said.

"Why?" Jo asked.

"He attacked me, and I had to put him down."

"A *Rel* attacked you? What, is he stoned or crazy?"

"I cannot say for certain. But perhaps we should determine his reason."

– – – – – –

Wink knew Rel physiology well enough to offer standard medical treatment, of course. Every alien species had its own quirks, and he was far from an extee specialist, but he could do lumps and bumps and sniffles and wheezes. He'd trained at enough hospitals to have run into most of the alien species who interacted with humans.

It didn't take more than a minute into his exam before he realized what he was dealing with, and it was beyond his ability to get into it.

"Wow," he said.

"What?" That from Jo, who was the only other person in the room.

"We need to get Formentara in here."

Jo looked at him. "Why would—? Really?"

"Yeah. Our friend Booterik here is wired."

"A Rel on augs? I never heard of such a thing."

"That makes two of us."

"I'll get hir."

"Formentara is gonna be as happy as a Malay monkey on mushrooms."

— — — — — —

Jo stepped out as Formentara came in. Outside the exam room, Kay stood, waiting.

"Your Rel is augmented."

Kay nodded. "Yes."

"You knew?"

"It seems a reasonable assumption. I did not detect hormone or somatic drug odors from him, so the augmentation is unusual. His demeanor was most un-Rel-like. His speed beyond that of a normal Rel. Augmentation would allow for that. From our short conversation, I got the impression his brother was no longer among the living. This one will have answers we need."

"Formentara will figure out what's what, then we can ask your Rel about it. It would seem to be connected to Indira's kidnapping."

"So it would seem—"

"Shit! *Shit*—!" Formentara yelled.

Jo and Kay blew through the door, Jo's pistol out and Kay's claws ready.

The Rel on the table jittered like a spider on a hot griddle. Wink frantically waved control-jive at his computer diagnostics, and Formentara did likewise to hir gear.

As they watched, the jitters stopped, and the Rel lay suddenly still.

"He's arrested," Wink said. "I'm going to pump adrenaline directly into his—"

"Don't bother," Formentara said. "His EEG is flat. He's not coming back. Shit! I *missed* it!"

Jo said, "Missed what?"

"The second burner, dammit!"

Jo and Kay exchanged glances.

Formentara said, "He's running a myotonic speed rig, custom augware, adjusted to Rel physiology—got a suppressor, too, so that's why Kay couldn't smell him.

"He has a brainburner implant, a high-voltage capacitor, set for query-discharge. If somebody opens his aug for inspection and doesn't shut the CNS implant down, it zaps his limbics.

"First thing I did was close it. But there's a *second* burner, wrapped around his cortex. A neural net. It fried him before I realized it was there. Stupid!"

Wink said, "Nobody would have caught that, it doesn't show, it's completely biological, there's nothing to detect—"

"*I* should have caught it! Some asshead slipped it past me! And I tell you what, whoever did it is not from around here. This was done by somebody who knew what the fuck they were doing, and it is recent. Days old, no more."

Jo had never seen hir so angry. She said, "Well, well. This is another whole ugly jar of worms, isn't it? A Rel on aug, and with enough suicide in him to be doubly sure nobody could poke around in his head. Why?"

## TWENTY-ONE

Cutter looked at his team. He was getting tired of having these meetings. "It seems that we keep getting more questions than answers."

Nobody spoke to that.

"And it also seems apparent that there is more going on here than a simple kidnapping for money."

"Figure out what, that probably gives us the 'who,' " Gramps said.

"Go back to your contacts," Cutter said. "Look for connections. Get some useful intel that doesn't lead us into a dead end or a trap. Do it quickly."

They all nodded at that.

- - - - - -

Gunny took less care with her clothes than she had the first time she'd gone into Lakshmi's Lair. Stavo Parjanya had already seen what was under them, so she didn't need to get his attention that way.

"Hey. My favorite corporate warrior."

"And my favorite bouncer. Well. On this world."

"You wound me, fem."

They grinned at each other.

"Here to, ah, pump me for more information?" he asked.

"Think you can produce any more?"

"Oh, yeah, or die trying. I'm off in fifteen minutes."

"I know."

Again, the smiles.

- - - - - -

The woman had a lovely comvox: "So, smashball soldier, what can I do for you this time?"

Gramps stood outside, in the hard shade of the main building, watching a distant thunderstorm flash heat lightning. Too far away to hear the thunder. He said, "I thought I might buy you dinner and ask a few more questions."

"When?"

"At your convenience, Lareece."

"Tonight is good for me. Say . . . 1500 or so?"

"That would be good. How about Krishna's Song?"

"Here only a few days, and you already know the best restaurant in town. But it will be impossible to get reservations on such short notice."

"Already have them."

"Ah. A confident man. I like that. But what would you have done if I'd had other plans?"

"Eaten there alone," he said. "Who could replace you?"

She laughed. "And a flatterer as well. Fifteen it is."

- - - - - -

"Dr. Tomas Wink," came Vanyu's voice over the com.

"It is I. How's the one-and-a-half coming?"

"It's getting there. I'm doing a session tomorrow, maybe. Forecast says there's a chance of weather."

"What kind of feeblet lets a little rain stop her from diving? Easier to see the water's surface that way."

She laughed. "A little rain doesn't bother me. It's the lightning and gale-force wind I worry about."

He knew. There were players who would risk electrical storms, divers rarely got cooked, but more than a few had been blown over land in wind-heavy storms, which made for a really hard entry. Part of the risk.

"You going to be there?"

"I was thinking I might."

"Weather probably won't start until afternoon. We could get in a few dives if we get there early."

"What's early?"

"How about 0600?"

"I suppose I can cut my beauty sleep a little short. See you then."

She laughed again.

– – – – – –

Formentara met the augmentor she had dealt with before. The place was a small autocafe, run entirely by dins, invisible rails guiding them back and forth among the table. She sipped at maté as he arrived and sat.

He was more than eager to talk to hir. He practically ran into the place.

"I need more information."

"Anything."

"I believe there is a high-level augmentor working on this world."

"Yeah, and I'm looking at hir."

"Other than myself. This person would be keeping a low profile, and perhaps doing some experimental work."

"Experimental how?"

"Possibly working on Rel."

"Rel? Rel don't do augs, everybody knows that."

"Assume for a moment that everybody is wrong. Who would have that ability?"

"Nobody local, I can assure you of that."

"Are there serious players who might not be local?"

"None I know about."

"Can you find out?"

"I can try. What's in it for me?"

"Have you heard about Rampant Systems newest Erector Set?"

"Of course. Supposed to be the best dickware ever made, infinitely adjustable, costs a fortune, raise wood on a dead man. But it's embargoed here. We can't get it."

"If you knew the augmentor who created it you could."

He stared at hir. "Really? No shit? That's *yours*?"

Zhe smiled.

— — — — — —

"More tea?" the Rajah asked.

"Sure," Cutter said.

The Rajah didn't have to lift an eyebrow, a server was there and pouring two seconds later.

This was a different room than he'd visited before, the walls of some dark, spalled wood with a thick coat of wax covering them. The ceiling was draped with cream-colored silk sheets and had some kind of indirect lighting that made the sheets glow warmly. The couch upon which he sat was a full-form biomechanical, the surface clone-suede, that adjusted itself perfectly to his contours. There was a faint tang of cedar to the air, from burning incense stuck in a large rectangular container of fine white sand near the door. The sand's surface was raked into parallel lines, like a zen stone garden. The effect was most serene.

Cutter wasn't much of a tea-drinker, but it was a popular beverage in some circles, and he'd learned to appreciate the taste. The local brew, whatever it was, had an astringent, slightly bitter tang, with flowery overtones and something like ginger under those. A little kick, too. He sipped at it. "It's very good."

"Thank you. Our cha-master is most adept."

Cutter nodded.

"How may I help you, Colonel?"

"If your son-in-law-to-be invades your next-door neighbor and cranks up a shooting war with the Thakore, what will you do?"

The Rajah sipped at his tea, paused to enjoy the flavor a moment. "I would have little choice, I am afraid. New Mumbai and Pahal are allies, we have a long-standing mutual defense pact. My enemies are theirs; their enemies, mine. And he is to be my son-in-law. I could do nothing else but support him."

"So if one of you decides to go to war, the other has no say in the matter?"

"Not precisely. This is one of the reasons that Rama has not yet stormed into Balaji. I can hold him off for a time on the pretext of preparing my forces, but since his stated purpose is to recover my daughter, it would be unwise of me to refuse to honor our pact—on many levels."

Cutter was careful how he phrased his next question: "What of Rama's father?"

There was another pause as Ramal sipped his tea. "Rajah Jadak, who is a distant cousin, is a likable man. He smiles a lot, he is beloved, but his mind is not the sharpest, nor most nimble, and his ambition long banked and essentially cold. He is not a strong ruler. Rama does as he will, and Jadak does not stand in his way."

Cutter thought about following that up, but waited a moment, since it seemed the Rajah was not finished. He was right:

"Rama is well aware that I could not allow my daughter to wed, nor remain married to, a patricide, so Jadak's life is safe enough. Should he die prematurely, I would see to it that the cause should be found, and if not natural, such would greatly stress Rama's and our own relations. So I expect that Jadak will live out his normal span, waving at his subjects, attending dress functions, blessing babies, and so on. Rama is already the power in Pahal, he does not need the title to make it so. He is ambitious but pragmatic.

"At least he has been so far."

"Noted. I have another question, the nature of which you might find offensive."

"I engaged you to recover my kidnapped daughter. Any question that will aid in that is acceptable."

"All right. Who will benefit most from a war with Balaji?"

"Other than munitions makers and funeral-pyre builders?"

Cutter offered a small, wry smile, to acknowledge what they both knew about combat.

"It would depend on how the war went. Pahal and New Mumbai's armies combined outnumber Balaji's by more than three to one. The Thakore has the home advantage, but we are equally well equipped and trained. It would be a matter of time before our victory. Afterward, there are always reparations. War is expensive, but more so for the loser. Eventually, both Pahal and my country would make a profit."

Cutter knew that the loser paid the majority of a war's cost, assuming there was anything left of him to generate revenue.

The Rajah zeroed in on Cutter's drift: "Have you valid reason to suspect Rama's motives are anything less than honorable?"

"No, sir, I can't say that. But the question has been raised as to whether or not the Thakore of Balaji is in fact responsible for your daughter's absence. And going to war on that suspicion alone without evidence seems, well—"

"Foolish?"

Cutter shrugged. "At the very least, it seems precipitous. If the Thakore has her, and if he doesn't kill her the second the first Pahali soldier steps across his border, thousands, maybe tens of thousands of troops from all three countries are apt to be wounded or killed, based on Rama's *belief* that she's there. If she dies as a result of Rama's action, or if she isn't even there . . . ?"

"Either would be a tragedy," the Rajah said. "More so if we were wrong."

"Yes, sir."

The Rajah waved away a server come to refresh his tea. "What you are really asking here about who benefits from this potential war is whether my son-in-law-to-be would benefit from it, isn't it?"

It was, but his protestations about his daughter aside, Cutter was leery of saying so out loud. He'd never been that much of a diplomat, but he had learned enough along the way to know if you didn't watch your ass, there were ways of losing it other than having it shot off.

He let that one lie.

The Rajah did, too. Finally, he said, "What would you have me do, Colonel?"

"Tell Rama that before you can commit your troops to an invasion, you need proof that your daughter is being held by the Balaji."

The Rajah nodded. "I had already considered such a condition. Yes. I will do that. And if the proof is provided?"

"It will give us more information we can use. Maybe in time to prevent a war."

# TWENTY-TWO

At the afternoon intel meeting, the group presented their new information.

The weather had turned stormy. The lightning arresters were getting a workout, and the rain came down amidst loud thunderclaps and hard winds. They were snug enough inside, but if you had to leave shelter, you'd be soaked before you got ten meters.

Tropical worlds tended to provide some fierce downpours.

Not much had changed, insofar as the substance of their knowledge.

Gunny allowed that Rama was not known for his patience, nor his kind nature, but outside of rumors, there was little to indicate he was particularly despotic. No dungeons full of political or personal enemies, though there were some of both who had apparently disappeared mysteriously.

Wink allowed that local doctors did not seem to have any indications that other Rel were being augmented.

Formentara's search along those lines had thus far been fruitless.

Gramps had found that money was being shifted in the city. The rumors of impending war had caused military-armament stocks to rise, along with emergency supplies. Fuel costs had also begun centimetering up. Local gun stores were having runs on ammunition.

Kay was out in the rain somewhere, seeking something.

Cutter told them about the Rajah, they batted that around for a couple minutes, then he officially closed the meeting. Nobody was in a hurry to leave. There was little they could do outside that they couldn't do under a roof, and they all had slogged through enough mud and bad weather so they didn't need more practice.

Gramps had the thousand-meter stare, and Gunny roused him from it: "Hey, fossil-man, your brain short out?"

He looked at her. "Not yet, Chocolatte. Just thinking about another rainy day, long ago and far away, when I was young."

"They had *rain* when you were young?"

Deadpan, he said, "My uncle invented it. I was also remembering that story you told the kid after we got back, about your first kill."

She looked at him. "How could know about that? You weren't around when Singh and me were talkin'."

"The walls have eyes and ears, remember?"

She shook her head. "That's right, Ah forgot, you ain't got nothing better to do with what little time you have left than run the surveillance gear to spy on folks."

"Rust never sleeps."

"Your uncle invent rust, too?"

"Nah, my aunt did that."

The sound of the rain sheeting against the roof was loud.

"So what about Gunny's story?" Wink asked. "Why were you remembering it?"

Gramps shrugged. "Reminded me that I have that story, too."

Gunny said, "Rainin' pretty good out there. I don't have anyplace I need to be for a while. Ah don't mind listenin' to an old man ramble."

Gramps nodded.

— — — — — —

"Before the Army figured out I was a better desk-commando-photon-pusher than a field soldier, I did my first tour as a cricket-crusher. I was stationed at Fort Kharanji, whose crappy climate was a lot like New Mumbai's—hot, except when it was wet.

"One evening, there came a torrential rainstorm, fifteen centimeters in a couple hours, and the transmitter-generator that fed the fence juice somehow overloaded a circuit and shorted the wire out, so I was on fence patrol. Cheaper to send a pair of boots out into the storm than to install sufficient backup.

"It was still raining, getting dark, and the ops helmet I wore was old and crappy, the motion sensors, spook-eyes, and Doppler were all going in and out every time the lightning crackled, the com mostly static, so it was slog through the puddles and shine a flashlight, looking for trouble.

"Not that we expected trouble. The base was in the middle of a forest in the middle of nowhere, and we'd never had any problems from the locals, so I wasn't looking to catch anything but more rain.

"Half an hour before my relief was due, I was in the northwest corner of the base. The trees had been trimmed back a few meters short of the wire, but the post-mounted lights were out, and it was dark, the downpour keeping the camp glow pretty dim.

"My com crackled, and I thought I heard somebody, but I couldn't make out the words, and when I toggled a repeat-request, I got nothing—it didn't seem to be working from my end at all.

"Then I saw a darker blob in the darkness right at the fence, and it was moving.

"I did just like I'd been taught in basic: brought my weapon from sling-ready to off-hand, and hollered out, 'Who goes there? Identify yourself!'

"For which trouble I got three sidearm rounds fired in my direction.

"My weapon was an RK-32 carbine, and I indexed the pistol flashes and unloaded a magazine at the shooter."

Gunny said, "RK-32? What, is that a flintlock?"

"Yeah. A thirty-round magazine flintlock," Gramps said. He smiled. "And I used every one of those cartridges, full auto."

Gunny shook her head. "Wasting the Army's ammo."

"SOP—never use one when thirty will do. Hey, I was eighteen. Shooting and all the while yelling into my dead com for help.

"When nobody shot back anymore, I changed magazines and lit a lantern.

"Once I got more light, I saw there were two men on the ground, one inside the fence, the other just outside, and both hit multiple times.

"The outside guy died before the medics got there, the other survived, and lived to be court-martialed.

"The dead guy was a local, he was the one who shot at me. The one who survived was an assistant quartermaster, an old lifer sergeant about to retire. They decided that a big rainstorm with the fence's power down would be the perfect time to do a little redistribution of the Army's wealth.

"The sergeant loaded up some stuff—mostly electronics, viral-molecular chips, visual-purple control switches, some timers, and like that, probably eighty, ninety grand worth on the local black market. He met the guy at the fence, they cut a hole, and were making the switch when I happened upon them.

"I wasn't supposed to be there. The sarge had arranged

for the broadcast power to the fence to be interrupted, and he'd somehow managed to get a fake report-to-quarters call out to the sentries, only my com wasn't working, and I didn't hear it."

"Their bad luck," Gunny said.

"Yep. And my cherry."

"War is hell," Wink said. He looked around. "What about you, Jo? You got a story?"

"Not one that is particularly interesting," she said.

"Aw, c'mon," Gunny said, "it's not like you have an appointment you need to keep, is it?"

Jo shrugged. "Okay . . ."

– – – – – –

"My first military action was at the Zamadani Riot that led to the Second Holy War.

"What happened, it was a summer day, a hot and arid wind off the desert, a crowd milling around a local shrine, chanting prayers. Maybe five hundred of the Zamadani faithful. Rain was a once-every-other-year event, and when it happened, you couldn't walk for the mud that caked your boots, or so they told me. Didn't rain while I was there.

"Our platoon had been dispatched as backup for the local police, but nobody was expecting any real trouble. They were pilgrims come to see the shrine, make offerings, whatever.

"Nobody ever figured out exactly what set it off. One second, nothing; the next, the loons went loose on us, and we had to dodge and cook.

"They didn't have guns, though every adult in the faith carried a short, heavy, convex-curved-inside-edged sword. It had a shape something like a Gurkha *kukri*, and the length of the blade was supposed to be from the tip of the owner's middle finger to the crook of the elbow.

"*Rikotilo de Dió*, they call them—God's Sickle. Two kilos of razor-edged nastiness.

"In the first few seconds, one of our guys was beheaded,

and a couple others lost hands, or were badly butchered. They knew how to use the things. Three of my squad didn't make it.

"Once we commenced firing, we chopped them up by the scores.

"I probably shot a dozen fanatics waving those fucking swords in the five minutes before somebody cranked a Hot Screamer Pulse through the crowd and shut it down.

"Afterward, there were a hundred bodies and way more who were seriously wounded, and some of them were surely mine, but I couldn't tell you which one was the first.

"They all wore those white robes with cowls and scarves across their faces, so telling one from another once we started blasting? No way to be sure."

The others nodded.

Gramps said, "I was in an MCC during that one, once it got cranked up good. Saw a lot of those sea-of-white attacks on the feeds. They did all look alike."

"There you go," Jo said. "My story. And I do have some training I need to go do. See you all later."

She headed out of the conference room, padded down the hall. Actually, she wanted to try out the new aug in the rain, see how it worked with things being slippery and slidey. She'd strip down to tights and slippers and run through the mud a little, do a systems check. Never hurt to work on different surfaces, in bad environmental conditions. It wouldn't always be a bright, sunny day on clean plastcrete when the line went hot, and practice might not save your ass in every situation, but it would give you as much advantage as you could give yourself, and that was worth something.

Everything she'd just said to the others about her first military action was true—but it wasn't the whole truth . . .

At sixteen, she had been on a field trip with her science class. They'd gone to Adelaide, to the new Extee Museum. Afterward, a few of them went to a local bar that apparently looked the other way when underage customers came in.

Jo had been sitting with a couple of her friends when a guy came over and offered to buy them a drink. He was tall, good-looking, a few years older, maybe twenty, twenty-two, and he had a slick line.

They were impressed, and while she was careful not to drink more than two of anything alcoholic, it wouldn't have mattered if she'd been drinking water.

Because he doped her drink.

Things got hazy, and the next thing she knew, she was naked in a cheap room somewhere on a bed on her back with the guy on top of her pumping away. She was aware of it, but she was unable to move.

He turned her this way and that, used her until he was too spent to continue, then got dressed. He walked away laughing.

"Welcome to the big city, Outback. Hope you enjoyed the ride. Come back anytime."

Hours later, when the drug wore off, she put her clothes on and found her way to the place where the class was staying. She didn't tell anybody. They assumed she'd gone off on her own and had a good time, and she didn't say any different, only smiled.

She hated it. Hated how she felt. How helpless she had been.

She vowed that nothing like it was ever going to happen to her again.

She saved some of his DNA. If you had money, there were semilegal ways to ID the person it came from.

Once she was sure she wasn't pregnant and hadn't been infected with some disease, Jo took some of the money she'd saved from working in the opal mines the last couple of summers and found an augmentation medic in Port Augusta, a couple of hours' drive away from her home in Woomera. She wasn't old enough to have the implant, but she did the research and found out the medic was a drinker and willing to do work to keep himself in booze.

She took the pubtrans bus to town, got herself a room, and went to see the medic.

He was a drunk, but skilled, and the outpatient implant a basic one, what was called CAS, which stood, she learned, for *Citius, Altius, Fortius*—the old Olympic motto: Faster, Higher, Stronger . . .

She was already pretty fit from digging in the mines, but the implant, which included hormones, genes with spliced viruses, and connective-tissue strengtheners, worked just like advertised. A few weeks later, she was half again as strong as she had been, measured by how much weight she could lift; her speed was only 20 percent more on hand stuff, a little less on things like running; and she could only jump about a quarter meter higher than before, but those were enough to bring her up to par with a lot of male unaugies.

She was careful not to let anybody know what she had done. Her parents didn't suspect; neither did her sister.

A follow-up visit to the medic in Port Augusta showed that everything was working fine and as good as it was likely to get without a lot more training.

The medic was even willing to check the database for a few dollars more and ID the DNA sample she gave him. He had given her a funny look, and at the time, she thought he might have had some idea of what she was up to, but if he did, he didn't care enough to say anything.

Roxby Norse was the name of the man who had raped her. Twenty-three years old, a resident of Adelaide, SoAus, occupation salesclerk, at the Outdoor Produce Market on Currie Street, near New Light Square. Married, no children, no criminal record. A predator, and not one you'd likely spot looking at his stats.

She spent the next month working on her plan.

She had learned from research that the less complicated something like this was, the better. There were few links that anybody knew about between her and M. Norse, and it was unlikely anybody who knew her would remember him.

She lived in a town five hundred kilometers away from where Norse lived.

She did the research. Ran the maps. Found his place of work, where he lived. She was careful to do it from a computer that didn't leave ways to backlink it to her, just in case somebody thought to look.

She memorized the maps, sat images, transportation lines, and schedules. It was like studying for an important test, and she'd always been good at that.

She found a place in Port Augusta where she could buy a full-head skinmask retail, no ID necessary. She bought one.

She waited for fall break, when there would be a lot of students out and about.

She mailed a package to herself at a mail drop in Adelaide.

She took a flight to Victor Harbor, well south of Adelaide, and caught a feeder maglev to the big city, buying her ticket with cash and flashing a fake ID she had made herself. It wouldn't pass a careful check, the ID, but nobody was apt to do that.

In the crush of travelers, nobody gave her ID a second look.

She got to Adelaide, rented a covered trike at the train station.

She rode to the mail drop and picked up her package, using a different phony ID. She stuck the package into a cheap backpack.

She rode and parked the trike two klicks away from where Norse lived. She had determined that the best time and place was when Norse left his cube for work. He was on a night shift, and it would be dark.

In the night, at a ratty public fresher whose camera watching the door had been smashed and not yet replaced, she went into a stall and opened the package. She removed from it the skinmask and put it on. Once it was smoothed into place, she put on an outback cap, an old shirt and sweater, and baggy pants. She donned thinskin gloves and pulled the last item from the package, an old ball-peen hammer that had belonged to her late grandfather. It had been in a box of tools in the attic of her parents' house for years. Nobody would miss it, even if they had known it was there.

She tucked the hammer under her sweater, loaded her street clothes into the backpack.

She walked the two klicks to the plex where Norse lived, timing it to arrive half an hour before he was due at work. It was only a ten-minute trip by bus from his place to the market.

It was dark, though the streets were well lit, and she felt conspicuous in her disguise, but nobody paid her any mind that she could tell.

She saw Norse leave his cube and head for the bus stop.

She fell in behind him, far enough back so as not to draw his attention.

There were a few people on the walks, shift-changers going or coming.

She had thought about it long and hard and decided that any kind of righteous announcement, about who she was and why he was about to die, was a bad idea. The walls had ears and eyes, and it didn't matter that he knew because he wasn't going to remember it anyway.

She was ten meters back, and the bus kiosk was half a block ahead.

She pulled the hammer from under her sweater, took a deep breath, and sprinted.

The aug kicked her natural adrenaline surge even higher.

At the last moment, he sensed or heard her coming and started to turn, but too late. She smashed his skull with the hammer just over his left ear, felt the bone give and the hammer sink in.

He collapsed, jittering, and she stopped, dropped, and hit him again, five times, all to the head.

Each strike punched through the bone.

By this time, some of the pedestrians and cyclists had seen the attack and somebody would be calling the police.

She came up, put the hammer into her pocket, and took off, her new speed giving her feet wings.

Nobody moved to stop her.

She ran, found the alley she knew was there, turned into it. Ran, cleared the end, made another turn. Ran faster.

There was a small park with a dead zone, no camera, and under a thick bush, she changed clothes, removed the skin mask, and tucked the hammer away in the backpack.

She got back to the trike and climbed onto it, headed for the Grange Street Ferry Terminal.

She caught the next hydrofoil ferry heading for Wool Bay. It was ninety kilometers, an hour-and-a-half trip.

Halfway across and running at speed on the foils, she leaned out over the lower deck rail, used the hammer to weight the skinmask and gloves, and dropped them into St. Vincent Bay.

When the ferry landed, she dumped the rest of her disguise into a recycle bin.

She caught the morning maglev to Victor Harbor, then took the maglev from there to Port Augusta, and finally, the pubtrans bus home.

The StatNet news the next day listed the killing of Roxby Norse in Adelaide. The police had no motive, nor any suspects. Eyewitnesses could add little. One of them indicated that the man who had done it seemed to move really fast, but nobody got a good look at him. There was a partial recording from the bus kiosk, but it was blurry and useless.

And Jo didn't feel helpless after that . . .

She went to her quarters, stripped, stretched, and put on her tights and slippers. Time to go run in the rain . . .

# TWENTY-THREE

Kay enjoyed the storm. It blocked the sun, cooled the air, yet was warm enough so it was not unpleasant, a giant shower. Running and climbing helped her to work off her frustration at not finding the Rel.

Prey that did not behave as such was disturbing on a visceral level.

Back at the perimeter of the base, the skies still dumping steadily, with strong wind gusts, she became aware of another running in the rain.

The rain washed away scents, and the heavy clouds dimmed the light, but there was no mistaking the other: Jo.

The woman was aware of Kay. She angled in her direction, slowed her run.

"Great day," Jo said.

Kay nodded. "Good weather for play."

"Want to dance?" Jo said.

"Yes."

"I have to warn you—Formentara has given me a new toy. Proprioceptivity enhancement."

Kay whickered. "Perhaps that will help make it more of a challenge for me."

Jo grinned.

They were five meters apart, on muddy ground. The footing would be inconstant. If Jo had a way to better augment her balance, that would offer her an advantage; then again, Kay's feet were clawed, which gave her a better grip.

Jo turned slightly and edged to her right.

Kay mirrored the pose and motion.

When the two fems played, each had strengths that could give her the match:

Jo had more formal training as a fighter.

Kay was slightly quicker.

Jo's reach was greater.

Kay was more agile.

Both could see deeper into the red and violet than most humans, and both had better hearing and olfactory functions. though the rain would dampen their senses about equally. Of course, at contact range, eyes, ears, and noses were less important than positional sensitivity.

Jo stole a half step toward her.

Kay settled into a lower stance.

In their early matches, Kay had won; the first eight times, she had prevailed. As Jo had gotten more experienced in dealing with Vastalimi tactics, she had taken a few matches. Then, it was every fourth time. Then, one in three. Recently, her skills had improved to the point where Jo could prevail 40 percent of the time.

Four of ten was better than any human had a right to expect in a one-on-one with someone of Kay's species. Jo was the most adept human opponent Kay had ever played with, and likely as adept as any human who had faced a Vastalimi anywhere. Which was impressive, but still less than her goal.

Any mistake by either was usually the match-ender; both had learned to capitalize on errors, forced or accidental.

In the beginning, Jo could be drawn into traps. Now, she was more wary and apt to offer traps of her own.

Of course, it was but play—claws sheathed, and Jo did not use bioweapons, nor knives or zapwands.

Kay still had the edge, but it was not that much sharper.

Jo slid another half meter closer, switched her feet into an angled left lead.

Kay unfocused her gaze, alert for any giveaway motion. She dropped her stance a bit more. Lower was better in a clinch. Legs bent to spring gave the potential of a farther and higher leap.

Vastalimi usually caught their prey from the side or behind, by bounding for it and launching themselves into a grab. A million years of that was hard to overcome. Of course, they fought each other, the Vastalimi, and thus knew how to deal with an attack rather than fleeing prey, but leaping was part of that, too.

Jo had learned this and devised ways to counter it.

Jo switched her leads again, stealing another half step. It was simple but effective against one who had not seen it: Lean forward, then as you lean back, slide your foot ahead. Your body appeared to stay in the same space, but you were closer.

Kay had seen the trick and was not fooled. She waited.

At four meters, the woman was well within Kay's standing-jump range, and just a hair outside her own. But a leap, once committed to, took a relatively long time to arrive. Velocity was limited to ground speed at launch. An alert opponent had plenty of time to get out of the way or set up a counter. The first time Jo had stepped in and thrown a long sidekick when Kay had flown at her from a distance had been a surprise. Vastalimi were agile, but unlike creatures with long and heavy tails, they could not change direction in midair. She had managed to tuck and twist, so that the kick caught a raised thigh instead of her belly, but it had been enough to off-balance her landing and allow Jo to follow up effectively.

She hadn't made that mistake again.

No, the way to victory now lay in gaining position and being able to get an attack off faster than it could be defended, or to set up a second or third move to follow it equally fast. This was why pure defense was the path to a loss. You could block ninety-nine of a hundred attacks but if you failed on the hundredth, you lost—

Jo cross-stepped to her left, offering what seemed to be a weak position.

Kay whickered. "Really? Have I gone blind?"

Jo grinned.

Kay switched leads, allowing her hands to drift back into defensive position a little slower, leaving her highline open.

"Yeah, I'm not buying that one," Jo said.

Lightning sizzled, and the instant blast of thunder made it *right there*—

Jo attacked, churned through the mud, her augmented speed turning her into a wet blur as she used the light and sound for a distraction. She fired a right punch high—

—Kay dodged to her left, shot her right hand out in a stop-block punch—

—Jo snapped her right knee up wide, aiming for Kay's thigh. She slid over the muddy ground on her left foot as if she were skiing, no loss of balance—

—Kay barely avoided the knee strike by a spin away, and she slipped while doing it, took a heartbeat to regain her own balance—

—Jo dropped her raised knee and pivoted on both feet, but her momentum kept her skidding past a hair—

—Kay crouched low, the squat almost touching her buttocks to the ground, and leaped, hands leading for a low tackle—

—Jo sprang up and forward, tucked into a ball, and threw a forward somersault *over* Kay—

—Kay turned her dive into a shoulder roll. Splashed mud and water, bounced up in a 180, sank to her ankles in a boggier patch—

—Jo landed the flip, right leg leading, and stepped out of it, pivoted on the balls of her feet, turned to face Kay, five meters between them—

"Halt!" somebody yelled. "Identify yourself!"

Kay came out of her crouch, saw Jo do the same.

An unsuited sentry.

"Captain Sims and *Kluth*fem," Jo called. "At ease."

"I need a password, Captain."

The sentry, a hard-faced human with his weapon pointing between the two of them, was ten meters away, backlit by the lights of the main structure in the compound. Likely that Jo or Kay could get to him and take him down before he could do anything useful, and if he knew who they were, he knew that, but he was one of theirs, and this was his job.

"The password is 'Boogie-woogie.'"

The sentry lowered his weapon. "Sorry, ma'am," he said.

"Not at all," Jo said. "We forgot where we were, our fault. Good job."

The sentry nodded.

Jo looked at Kay. "A draw?"

"Draw. Tell Formentara the new augmentation is most impressive. I thought you would fall when you threw that knee."

"Me, too," Jo said. "Amazed me I stayed up."

"It will be interesting to see how it works on firmer footing."

"I'm looking forward to that. What say we get dry, and I buy you a drink?"

"I am open to that."

– – – – – –

Gramps said, "We've intercepted another com, Rags."

Cutter looked up at the man in the doorway.

"Should be up on your screen. Oral, no visual, but you need to listen to it."

Cutter saw the pulsing com-dot on his computer's holo-proj. He said, "Play on-screen com recording."

"*—can't talk long, they are coming back, but I am alive, Father, and—*"

The voice stopped.

"That's it," Gramps said.

"How did we come by it?"

"Rama sent it to the Rajah about five minutes ago, according to the Rajah's security, along with a barely polite frothing-at-the-mouth demand for the Rajah to get his ass in gear and get his armies on the march."

Cutter leaned back in his form-chair. "Is it her?"

"Formentara says it is, but with reservations. Zhe's on hir way over."

"Reservations?"

"Voxmatch uses twenty-six points for a perfect mesh. Realistically speaking, anything above nineteen points is good enough for a positive ID and you almost never get a perfect mesh. The message is a twenty-three."

"So we believe it is her."

"Yes, but—"

Formentara arrived at that moment and moved past Gramps into Cutter's office. Zhe said, "It is her *voice*, but she didn't send that message."

"Explain."

"We have access to more than a hundred hours of recordings featuring Indira. So a baseline is easy to establish. The kidnappers would know that. This snippet of monologue is her saying those words, no question, but they weren't spoken in that order."

He raised an eyebrow.

"It's a mash," Formentara said.

Cutter looked at hir expectantly.

"A construct. Listen to this." Zhe tapped a command into the small handheld.

Cutter's computer's speakers cut in:

"—*can't talk long, they are coming back, but I am alive, Father, and—*"

"Sounds about the same to me," Cutter said.

"Not *about* the same, it is *exactly* the same," zhe said. "Voxmatch puts it as a twenty-six when compared to the first message. That never happens.

"The second one is a mash I put together using a computer-cull to give me the set of words that matched my query. I linked them together in order, ran it through a smoother to fix the cadences so they'd be more like they would be in that sentence's order. A word at the end of a normal sentence usually gets a different emphasis than it would at the beginning or middle, and if you move it, it sounds wrong."

Cutter nodded. "Okay."

"My mash is a perfect match. Couldn't happen that way coincidentally. Somebody did the same thing I did."

"So it is a faked message."

"Absolutely."

Cutter considered it. "The question then is, who? Somebody trying to fool Rama? Or Rama trying to fool the Rajah?"

"There's something else," Formentara said. "There's a carrier sig under the message, part of which is a com unit's hardware hash. I ran the number, and it's IDed as one of the units Indira had, which is reportedly missing."

Cutter thought about that for a moment. "So whoever is responsible for the message has the com unit Indira probably had with her when she was taken."

"Or access to the hash number and enough sense to append it, to convince us she sent the message," Gramps put in.

"Gets even more interesting," zhe said. "The backwalk on the sig shows its origin in the southern reach of the Asana Forest."

"That seems sloppy," Gramps said. "The other messages

were bounced all to hell and gone, no way to trace them. Why wouldn't this one be?"

Cutter said, "Refresh my memory: The Asana Forest is where . . . ?"

"Southern Balaji."

*Of fucking course it is.*

"Looks like Rama is going to get his war," Gramps said.

"Why fake the message if they have her?" Cutter wondered aloud. "Why not just have her parrot whatever they tell her to say?"

"Maybe she isn't in any condition to talk," Formentara said.

Cutter sighed. Always a possibility—that the victim was dead before they ever arrived. It had happened before, not much you could do with that, save maybe recover the body. A small and cold victory.

Cutter's com announced an incoming call.

"The Rajah?" Gramps said.

"Yes. I'll go talk to him. And then maybe we need to have another word with Rama. Call the team in. We are probably going to have to hurry."

# TWENTY-FOUR

Kay got the call as she finished grooming her fur, combing out undercoat shed and tangles. She wasn't particularly vain about her appearance, but there were basic minimum standards a Vastalimi would adhere to when it was possible to do so. You might not have time to groom in combat for days, but there was no excuse for not doing it sitting idle, waiting for something—for anything—to happen . . .

She opened the com, said: "I am here."

"Is this the Vastalimi?" came the voice.

A female Rel, she didn't doubt. "It is. Speak."

"I am told you wish to talk to me."

"And you are?"

"My name does not matter."

"Then you should have no problem giving it to me. And better that we should talk face-to-face."

"I won't give you my name, nor will we meet can I help it. Two of my kind to whom you recently spoke face-to-face are dead. I have no desire to join them."

"I killed neither of them."

"All the same, they are dead, and certainly due to that contact. Death rides on Vastalimi shoulders."

So, Booterik's thinly veiled reference to his sibling Zeth's being dead could be so if this Rel was telling the truth.

"So Zeth *is* dead. How did he die?"

There was a long pause. "I understand it was suicide."

Kay nodded to herself. Yes. That made sense. Under stress, Rel were quicker to do that than many species. Or it could have been murder, to keep him quiet.

"It was you who told Zeth the location of the kidnapped human fem."

"No. I told someone else, who told someone, who probably told Zeth. I did not know Zeth."

Yes, she could see such a possibility. What one Rel knew was apt to be shared with others, which was likely how Zeth learned of it. They were herd creatures; among themselves, they were quick to talk about anything and everything. Which was why she went looking there in the first place.

"How did you come to learn this information?"

"By way of a human native."

"The human's name?"

"I—I need assurances."

"What assurances?"

"That if I help you, you will not hunt me."

Kay considered the comment. Augmented Rel. Those who didn't roll over and show their bellies immediately? How very strange. "You bargain with me? Have you forgotten who I am?"

"I know what you are. And I know, too, what the word of a Vastalimi means. Give it, or I discom and run."

"And you believe I won't find you?"

"Eventually. It might take years."

"Or days."

"Yes. But that is my offer."

The Rel did not matter, only what she knew. "All right, done. If you give me information—and if it turns out to be true and useful—I won't hunt you."

"The human's name is Brahmaputra Siddhartha. He is the manager of the TotalMart in Dep-by-the-Sea."

"How did he come to reveal this information?"

"By accident."

"Explain."

"I worked for TotalMart as a contract accountant, and Bram Sid was my employer there. While balancing ledgers, I came across a file that was out of place. When I read it, I found the information about the Rajah's daughter. It was thinly disguised—'R.'s daughter, being held at the lodge, under guard.' Like that. I mentioned it to my lover."

And her lover could not keep it to himself, Rel being what they were. It spread from there.

"Is that all you know of it?"

"It is."

"Then we are done," Kay said. "Graze free."

The Rel broke the connection.

They could find out her name, of course. If she worked for TotalMart, there would be records, and Cutter Colonel had deep connections with TotalMart. But why would she bother? The CFI team could verify it if they wished. The Rel was but a tool, history of no import. And Kay had given her word, which *was* important.

This was most clever, the planting of false information. It was done by somebody who knew that Rel were quick to mouth, who knew that it would be too good not to share. And by someone who knew that it was likely a Vastalimi hunting for information would eventually speak to one of the Rel who had it. Most clever.

Perhaps they had made this information available elsewhere, as well.

It seemed an elaborate and complicated effort to set up

a trap. Of course, it had worked, if not as well as they doubtless wished.

Certainly it was not done by some half-witted kidnapper looking to make money; no, this opponent was smart and, so far, had been ahead of them. That was good. One wanted a decent match. There was no real joy in a fight against a markedly inferior opponent.

She needed to speak to the colonel.

– – – – – –

Once more, the core group sat in the conference room. Jo glanced at Cutter, who nodded. She began:

"Kay has information that the false lead we followed to the hunting lodge was a plant, and that the source was one Brahmaputra Siddhartha, who manages a TotalMart in Dep-by-the-Sea. At six million inhabitants, Dep is the second-largest city in New Mumbai. It is north of here, located between Lake Dep and the Kali Sea. Bram Sid is a local by birth."

"Any confirmation?" Gramps asked.

"We can confirm the identity of the source and a possible connection to the Rel who steered us wrong."

"TotalMart?" That from Gunny. "The same TotalMart who we do a whole shitload of our business for?"

Cutter said, "Yep. Check your flatscreens, you will find everything the corporation knows about Bram Sid."

"Why would he be involved in this?" Wink asked.

Jo said, "We'll be taking a little run up the coast to speak to M. Sid later this afternoon to find out."

Jo said, "Formentara also has some news for us." She looked at hir.

"My reports are that Booterik had his augmentation surgery done four days before he died, at a facility also in Dep-by-the-Sea, by an *ajnabi*—an offworlder—arrived here but two weeks earlier. This programmer is human, ostensibly from Filay the Moon, in the Filay System. Goes by the name 'Gee.' Local augmentors says this is the only person who has the capabilities outside myself."

"Kind of a coincidence, isn't it?" That from Gramps.

It was a rhetorical question.

"What's the drill?" Wink asked.

Jo said, "We pay M. Sid a visit. You bring some of your happy juice and administer it so he wants to play nice and come along to answer our questions truthfully. If he did it, we squeeze him until Indira pops loose. If somebody put him up to it, we find them and do the same."

Jo looked at Cutter, who raised one hand in a continue-on gesture.

"The TM is one of the midsized plenipotentiary stores, a Zanzibar-Design, with many small, specialty-shop fronts linked together. Two kilometers by two kilometers under-roof, nineteen thousand full-time employees, most of whom live in cheap housing on the premises.

"They are a main stop on the maglev line, have their own airport and spaceport, complete with customs. In addition to employee housing, there are hotels, hospitals, banks, fire department, wooded parks, entertainment, restaurants. Got a two-hundred-person security force, power stations, dedicated water supply—it's essentially a town owned by the corporation, and it draws shoppers from New Mumbai, Pahal, and the Kali Islands. On an average day, there will be more than a hundred thousand customers cycling through this place."

"And this guy is the manager of all that?" Gunny said. "What kind of money does a job like that pay?"

"With commissions, I'd guess 2.5, maybe 3 million noodle a year," Gramps said.

"Doesn't seem like somebody who'd want to get into kidnapping for the money," Wink said.

"No, it doesn't," Jo said. "And we'll have to be careful. It's not a good idea to let their security know we are coming—

we don't want word to get to M. Sid and have him decide it's a great time to take a vacation. If we get in trouble, the colonel can pull some strings, but better we avoid that.

"Formentara and Kay will go see the augmentor. Gunny, Gramps, Wink, and I will find the manager."

"Two-hundred-person security?" Gramps said.

"They won't all be on duty; besides, we'll give them something else to think about."

Cutter said, "Something not too expensive, please. We don't want to piss off the golden goose here."

"I have just the thing," Jo said.

# TWENTY-FIVE

"Never fails to amaze me, looking at one of these monsters from the air," Wink said.

It was a huge building, segmented-eplast construction with channels and drains, so if part of it collapsed, not all of it would, and with all the infrastructure you'd expect, just like Jo had said: roads, a monorail station, air- and hopperports, a spaceport over there.

Big money in big stores, and TotalMart was the largest shark in the galactic-shopping food chain by far, everybody else running a far distant second. Other sentient species would sometimes look at such a place and shake their heads: Can you *believe* what those humans do?

Jo said, "Security requires that customers leave their hardware at the door when they enter. We won't, we have the proper licenses, courtesy of the Rajah, but that means they will be keeping a closer eye on us. At least for a while."

Wink nodded to himself. Of course. Mercenaries who could carry, you bet you'd keep a careful watch on them. In the land of the unarmed, the man with a rock was king.

"We have Formentara's toy," Jo continued, "so that should give security something else to keep 'em occupied."

"If it works," Gramps said.

Formentara smiled sweetly at him but didn't say anything.

Gramps smiled in return. Hard to ruffle hir feathers. Everything Formentara came up with *always* worked.

"We are in the landing slave's grip," Nancy said. "Fifteen minutes until they park us."

Gunny said, "I knew a guy, ex-Army, worked security for the system-megastore grand opening on Zand, place was twice the size of this one. They had a doorbuster sale on agro-dins, and 90 percent of what they do on Zand is farming, so they were lined up for days, camping.

"Twenty-six people were killed, nine of them security, dozens seriously injured when they let shoppers enter. Guy I knew said it was the scariest engagement he'd ever been in. Security was limited to the use of LTL hardware only— zappers, puke spray, hand sonics, like that. Said once the crowd surged, it rolled over them like a tsunami, nothing slowed 'em down."

"Sad way to go," Gramps said, "in a store, stomped by some farmer shoving to get a cheap hay baler."

"No Screamers installed?" That from Formentara. "No stupesonics? No seizure flashers?"

Gunny said, "My guy said they had Screamers, but elected not to use them. Bad PR to lay fifty thousand customers out in pools of their own urine."

"And twenty-six people dead is *good* PR?" Wink said.

"All about the money," Jo said. "Cheaper to pay off the survivors and families of that many than to alienate a few hundred thousand possible repeat customers. Cost of doing business."

Kay said something Wink didn't catch.

"Say what?" he said.

"I said 'Humans.' " You could have etched diamond with her tone.

*Yeah, that about summed it up.*

"How would you have handled it on your world?" Wink asked.

"On Vast, we do not have these places. If we allowed them, there would be no such riot. Such things are not permitted."

"You'd have used the Screamers?" That from Gunny.

"No. We would have used lethal weapons and continued doing so until the illegal activity ceased. The customers would have known that."

"You'd have killed maybe thousands of Vastalimi, just like that?"

"If that is what it took. They would have been responsible for their own fates."

Gunny shook her head. "Hard-asses on your world."

"We value life differently than humans do."

"No shit," Wink said.

Jo looked at Kay. "You've heard some of our stories about our first killings. Would you care to share yours? We have a few minutes."

- - - - - -

Kay looked at Jo Captain.

"The first *person* I killed, or the first *human*?"

Kay saw the teeth revealed in smiles, indicating amusement.

Even after years, she still had to overcome her instinctive reaction to that—it didn't mean the same thing as it did on her homeworld. Vastalimi smiles didn't reveal the teeth.

Many things among the humans were that way. Such an odd mix of predator and prey, they were.

"Person will do," Jo said.

Kay allowed the memory to surface:

"I was *dijete*. This does not translate exactly into Basic, it is a phase of late cubhood. A period older than babies, younger than fully grown, during which we were still called by our den-noms.

"We were twelve standard years, and on *Seoba*. This is a ritual trek of two months, undergone during *dijete*. You are taken to a reach and left with nothing save what you brought into the world at your birth.

"Our pack, comprised of three different family litters, roamed the South Reach of *Travnjaka*, the Great Grassland. Mostly, we hunted *vepar*, large, tusked rodents half again our size.

"By that day, there were still fifteen in my pack, down from twenty."

"Down from twenty? Five dropped out?" Formentara asked.

Kay looked at the speaker.

"Five were dead on the trek. Two from wounds incurred hunting *vepar*, one from an attack by a *div macka*, something like a Terran liger. One stepped into a serpent burrow, broke her leg, and chose *izvaditi utrobu*—suicide."

"Suicide? How?" Jo asked.

"Disembowelment by her own claws."

"Nice. And the fifth?" From Wink.

"The fifth disappeared, and we did not know what happened to her. There are several large predator species who live in the grass. Probably killed and eaten by one."

"Tough playground." That from Gramps.

"It was a cold and gray evening, we smelled snow coming, and we were closing in on a pair of young *vepar* when Blue Eyes had a *zrelost* seizure."

She saw that none of them knew this term, either.

She explained: "Blue Eyes was male, and the seizure was due to the sudden and unexpected onset of sexual maturity.

"Normally, the Vastalimi do not Blossom until their fourteenth season. The first rising in males is overwhelmingly powerful, and in society, he would have been restrained and given to a mature female trained in the ways of safe release. Because he was early, and we were far into the grass, this was not possible.

"Gripped by conjunction-lust, Blue Eyes attacked fem Tawny.

"None of the fems were mature enough to accept Blue Eyes that way. Males who have lost control drive to their climax without thought for their partner. *Zrelost*-driven intercourse can result in injury for even an incautious, mature female. In cubs, it can be fatal. The claws and teeth dig deep, the member thrusts to the hilt.

"Blue Eyes knew this intellectually, of course, but the Blossom is impossible to resist. He was crazed with hormones and not in his right mind.

"I was the first to reach him as he clawed and attempted to mount Tawny. I killed him."

"*Killed* him? You didn't try, I don't know, restraints? Knocking him cold?" That from Wink.

Kay offered a slight turn of her head. "We were on *Seoba*. We were five hundred kilometers from the nearest settlement. We had no means of communication, no tools other than our own claws and fangs, no way to hold him. Blue Eyes' *zrelost* Blossom might have lasted thirty hours. Trying to restrain a maddened male would have likely resulted in serious injury or death to some of the pack. We might have knocked him out, but an attempt that failed might result in a fatal injury to one of us. It was the safest way."

No one said anything for a few seconds. Then Jo said, "And what happened to Tawny? Was she hurt by the attack?"

"Minor injuries, a few bruises, some scratches."

"Something, at least."

Kay looked at her. "It was the proper response."

"And how did you feel about this?"

"Blue Eyes was my littermate. We had grown up together, with our three sibs."

They all looked at her.

"He was your *brother*?" That from Formentara.

"It was unfortunate; but it was the proper response in the circumstances."

None of them spoke to that.

There was another thing she might have said, but Kay withheld it. Humans indeed had a different life-view than Vastalimi, and she knew from her experiences with them that hearing that Tawny—her sister—had died the next day when they took down the two *vepar* they'd been hunting would bother them. As if killing Blue Eyes was somehow made less valid because Tawny died so soon afterward. They wouldn't understand that such a thing did not matter. Death came, and when it left, it seldom did so with clean claws. That was the way of it.

Humans simply did not view this as did Vastalimi.

As she considered this, Jo looked at her. "I'm curious; how many of you made it to the end of your trek out there in the grasslands?"

Kay nodded. "Eleven of us."

"Tawny?"

"She was not among the survivors."

Nancy said, "Better strap in, folks, we are approaching the ground. These slave programs don't always get it exactly right—I've been let go a meter up, and I don't want anybody biting their tongue off if that happens."

# TWENTY-SIX

There were cameras on the transport, as well as bird cams and bug cams overhead, and probably many more such devices hidden in vehicles and other objects on the ground. The tram picked them up at the end of a line of parked hoppers, probably two klicks away from the store's nearest entrance. They could have walked, but that would have marked them immediately. None of them were in clothes that screamed "military!" and all weapons they had were concealed.

Formentara and Kay caught a different tram to the maglev station for their visit to see the offworld programmer in Dep. Things going well, Jo and the rest of them would pick up Formentara and Kay after they were done here.

Things going well . . .

Knowing you were being watched and recorded was part of living in civilization. You learned not to do things that would come back to haunt you if they were shown in a criminal court as evidence against you. Even though the standard contract the Rajah had signed gave them immunity equal to that of an offworld ambassador, and they would not be charged for what they were about to do, CFI did do a fair amount of work for TotalMart, and even if they suspected, better that the store's security couldn't *prove* they had anything to do with it. It was a fine line to walk.

Thus they all wore skinmasks—high-end, but simple. And they watched every move they would make.

The device was rigged with a timer and a hellfire tab. Fifteen minutes after it was triggered by an encoded radiopulse, it would be no more than hot smoke in the sunny day.

When the tram arrived at the store and people began alighting, Jo "accidentally" dropped a handbag she carried. When she squatted to retrieve it, she stuck Formentara's toy under the tram, her actions hidden from view by the strategic stances of her team.

She stood less than two seconds later.

The kwik-stik adhesive made a permanent bond with the underside of the tram. Well, it would be permanent under normal circumstances. Once the encoded radiopulse stroked it, the adhesive would release. The device, about half the size of her palm, would fall onto the roadway. A repeller would pop it into the sky, albeit only a few hundred meters up. On the way down, the gadget would be consumed by the hellfire tab, leaving a smoke trail and little else.

Security would tag it, of course, but determining the source, and what it had been? Certainly not beyond a reasonable doubt.

It was possible that store security might eventually puzzle it out, but backwalking it to Jo and the CFI team would be difficult. Should be enough to keep them off TotalMart's corporate shit list.

It would have been much easier if she could have just carried the sucker in her pocket into the store and dumped it into a recycle bin once she'd used it, but TotalMart was big on radio controls inside its stores. Any coms in use inside went through their own repeaters, incoming and outgoing, and signals they didn't recognize were automatically jammed. Even Formentara couldn't figure out a way past a five-hundred-thousand-watt damper with something you could hide in your hand, so the complicated gadget was necessary.

The days when you could start a fire or set off an explosion *here* while you hustled over *there* to do something and have it go without a warble were gone.

Civilization didn't like surprises . . .

– – – – – –

They ducked into the last loo in the line. Nobody else there. They changed the simple skinmasks they'd been wearing for a second set, just enough to screw up a facial-recog program. Local law didn't allow cams in the loo, but Gramps had a bollixer running just in case there were voyeurs in security. Wouldn't be the first time somebody got off watching people pee.

Gunny leaned against the door to make sure nobody else came in as they masked up.

Gramps said, "Sid's schedule puts him in his office from 0800 to 1130 hours, then he heads for lunch. He travels with two security guards and sometimes takes other executives to lunch. They favor the restaurant Makri, which features a large, edible spider as its premier dish. The place is within easy walking distance of Sid's office, but he always rides in an electric cart that picks him up on the ground level outside his office."

"Ah think Ah had one of those spiders once," Gunny said. "Pretty tasty. 'Cept if you cook it wrong, it's poison."

They had gone over all this several times, but Jo ran through it again:

"Once more: Gunny takes the driver's place. We'll be at the hallway leading to the public loo, three stores down. She makes the turn, we take down the guards—we are all checked as loading trank darts, right? We don't want anybody works for TM dying."

They all nodded.

"We go out through the exit past the loo. Doc, you have your gadget ready?"

Wink opened his right hand and held it so they could see the injector stuck to his palm. "IV punch," he said. "Gas-jet into the vein, no hypodermic necessary, nine seconds to take effect. He'll be awake but so stoned he will do whatever we tell him and smile as he does it."

"Okay, let's get into position. I won't trigger the switch until he is in the hallway. Once it is lit, we will have fifteen minutes before the sat's foot steps off the mall. Nancy will have the hopper ready to lift when we get there. Let's do it, people."

– – – – – –

Gunny waited until the cart passed into a cam-shadow under a conduit-covering drop ceiling, then slid into the front seat next to the startled driver. "Hey! Who the fuck are—-!"

Gunny shot him in the forehead. They said it didn't matter where you put the trank dart, long as you got a solid hit piercing the skin, but she figured the closer to the brain, the better. Besides, she had a reputation to maintain. Head-shot Gunny . . .

He toppled, and she eased him off the cart and dragged him to the storage compartment in the front. She pulled his ID tag free, shoved him inside, and closed the lid. He'd be out for forty-five minutes. She stuck the tag onto her shirt pocket so the edge showed, the holograph and stats hidden. If she passed by a scanner, it would indicate that Doy Bergive, the driver, was at the wheel. As long as there wasn't a cam that showed her face and found that it didn't match the driver's, she'd be good. It didn't have to hold up for more than another five minutes.

She drove in the cart lane, hit the warning horn to beep at pedestrians who had strayed into the cart's path. "Hey, stay on the walkway!" Like she'd been doing this job for years.

Gunny pulled up in front of the office exit a minute before the door opened.

One of the bodyguards, a tall and wide man in a faux-sharkskin suit cut to hide his shoulder holster, stepped out. Frowned at her.

"Where is the other guy?"

"If the usual guy is Doy? Fuck if I know. Dispatch told me to take his cart and get over here. I drive where I'm told."

The guard hesitated a moment.

It went to Plan B, he came out with hardware, she'd shoot him and haul ass. If he went for his piece, she'd be faster coming from her right hip carry, he'd never make it . . .

He looked up and down the hall. "Clear," he said.

The door opened again, and Sid came out, the second guard behind him. The second guard was a short, thin, woman.

－－－－－－

When Jo saw the target, she triggered her radiopathic pulse.

In the parking lot somewhere, the hidden transmitter sent its radio sig to a satellite in low orbit. The sat was a surplus Navy Warbird that now belonged to the Rajah, and the radio wave that spoke to it switched on a preprogrammed sequence.

The Warbird generated a beam. It zipped across the twenty thousand kilometers in a hard, focused, electromagnetic pulse that splashed onto the TotalMart building and scrambled com frequencies seven ways from Saturn. Anything within a certain bandwidth, which included communicators, wireless cameras, and repeaters, went wonky. And they'd stay that way for most of fifteen minutes.

Probably going to be a lot of silent alarms going off because they had lost their carrier links.

Security was going to be hopping. And electronically blind and deaf. If they had any sense, they wouldn't go into lockdown because it might cause a panic if people who wanted to get out couldn't, and there was no indication of a physical attack from without.

Jo grinned.

- - - - - -

The lights flickered as the store's mainframe adjusted power flows, trying to sort itself out.

"Where is Doy?" Sid asked Gunny.

"I don't know, sir, Dispatch sent me."

Tall-and-Wide said, "My earbud just went dead."

"Mine, too," Short-and-Thin said.

Sid looked at the guards. "Great. Another fucking computer/communications glitch. Nothing I can do about it from here. They'll send a runner if it's any kind of real problem." He looked at Gunny. "Let's go. I have people meeting me in four minutes."

"Yessir."

The three of them climbed into the back of the open cart and sat.

Gunny engaged the motor, and the vehicle hummed away.

When they neared the loo corridor, Gunny said, "Sorry, sir, but I have to stop at the toilet!"

"What?"

"I have a touch of intestinal flu."

By then, Gunny had made the turn.

"Crap on your own time!" Sid said. "Turn around!"

Gunny heard the small *whumps!* of darters going off.

Both bodyguards spasmed and collapsed.

"What the fuck is going on—!"

Gunny stopped the cart and turned to grin at Sid, just as Wink arrived.

"Happy daze!" Wink said. He slapped Sid on the neck, under his left ear.

"What a nice afternoon for a walk in the park," Wink said. "What say we go outside and enjoy the hot sunshine."

Sid grinned at him. "Sure!"

- - - - -

The building was plain, some kind of prefab panel, no markings on the door to identify it. It was a one-story light-industrial unit in a row of others just like it, save for small signs and a couple of personal touches, different-color doors, like that.

A few people came and went.

Formentara looked at Kay. "This is the place. Shall we?"

"Stay behind me," Kay said.

"Glad to."

Kay stepped into the motion detector's range. The door slid open. Kay hurried through. Her dart pistol appeared in her hand as if by magic.

Formentara strolled in much slower, hir own weapon still tucked under hir tunic. Kay was eminently more capable of dealing with resistance, was there any, and if it was formidable enough to defeat an armed Vastalimi, chances that Formentara would offer much of an additional challenge were slim and snowball.

The anteroom was empty. The door leading to the next room was open and Kay was already through it. "Hold," Kay said.

Formentara arrived and saw a tall, redheaded human male in a zentai skinsuit, covered neck to toes—face open—in a thin, green material. Guy had muscles on his muscles, and the smoke-thin material revealed that he was hung like a pornoproj star, too.

He seemed full of nervous energy, bordering twitchy.

He was next to a console, stopped now, but obviously working on the lit board. No patient, so he was doing b.g.

There were no signs of weapons, and no place he could hide an external one under that outfit.

"My God, it *is* you. Formentara! I'm honored." He gave her a military bow.

"Do I know you?"

"I wouldn't think so. We've never met, and my work is still in the budding stage. But of course any augmentor worth his own piss knows who *you* are." He waved at the console. "I'm Gee."

He pronounced it with the soft-gee sound, like the karate suit.

"Well, M. Gee, I would like to discuss your work in the realm of alien augmentation, if you have a few moments."

"You saw my Rel?"

"And the traps you left in him."

Gee smiled. "I didn't believe them when they said you were here, but just in case, I added the second. Any local augmentor on this dirt ball would have been flummoxed by the first, but if you were looking at the Rel? I knew you'd blow past that like it was nothing."

"And you also knew I wouldn't expect anybody here to be good enough to hide the second."

He gave hir another slow nod of acknowledgment. "Indeed. Did it work?"

Zhe was tempted to tell him it hadn't, but one rewarded skill with honesty. "It did."

He grinned widely. "Ah. My greatest accomplishment. Thank you."

"His augmentation was not detectable by a Vastalimi at close range. I would consider that a greater accomplishment."

"I am honored."

Formentara shook hir head. "You have promise. I have some questions about the Rel. I need to know how one came to such a place that he would seek out an augmentation. And how you just happened to be here when he needed it."

"Coincidence?" he said.

Zhe smiled. "Oh, no, I don't think an augmentor of your caliber, the only one on the planet capable of rigging an undetectable-scent cross-species meld, just *happened* to be here. Somebody hired you. I need to know who and why and what else you have been up to. And why the Rel needed to die."

It hardly seemed possible, but his smile increased yet again. "I would like nothing better than to sit and talk about it with you, believe me. But I am bound by ND confidentiality agreements."

Kay said, "*He* reeks of hormones, some real, some artificial."

Formentara nodded. She couldn't smell them, but she knew the signs, it was in his every gesture.

"He's wired, big-time. Surely has a biozapper," zhe said. "Stay back."

Gee laughed. "Of course, you would see me for what I am."

"How many?"

"Twenty-four."

Zhe nodded. Gee was an aug-hog, an addict, running too many systems, barely in balance, and burning himself up. Addicts thought they could manage that, especially programmers, and of course, they couldn't. Gee could put himself under and run his own robotics, but it was a fool's game. Robots could be finely tuned, but even the best AIs didn't have intuition. They could be masters of the craft but not artists. Without that, it was not a matter of "if," but "when" the crash would happen. Might be months, years even, but he'd never live to see fifty.

"I can tune you," zhe said.

Zhe saw him consider it. He knew what his eventual fate would be. And if he was half as knowledgeable as he pretended, he knew what that offer meant. Even a onetime tune could self-replicate enough so it would probably add six or eight years to his longevity, as long as he didn't add more systems.

"You would do that?"

"We can help each other."

Ten seconds passed. "Once I'm under, you could change your mind."

"You'd have my word going in."

He nodded, almost to himself. "And to be under the probes of the great Formentara? Another signal honor. But—no. I can't."

"Listen—" zhe began.

He charged Kay, moving much faster than a normal man could possibly move—

— — — — — —

Kay saw the human in green coming at her, raising one hand to point his finger at her, and she knew he was too fast for her to step out of his way—

She collapsed, let her muscles go limp, and dropped to the floor as the bioelectric bolt crackled from the man's finger at her, singeing the fur on her left shoulder as she fell—

He was moving too fast to stop as he leaped for her, hands open to grab—

Formentara yelled, "Contact shocker!" but it was too late, Kay was already on her back and she thrust her right foot up hard in a kick at his crotch even as he flew over her—

The jolt of electricity surged through her bare foot from the contact even as she felt his testicles mash under her heel—

Kay blew out a hard breath and entered *spokoj*. She might be injured from the electric jolt, but she'd have to deal with that later. Now she needed the ability to *move* and *spokoj*-mind wiped away the pain that would hinder her—

She came up as Gee landed and turned to make another run—

She was ahead of him. She leaped, claws extended—

He tried to twist *and* step out of the way, and trying both at once was too slow—

She caught him across the chest with her right hand; the claws sliced through the green fabric and his pectoral muscles, opening four gashes from his left shoulder to his right side—

She caught his frown as he triggered his own pain dampers—

She was on him, but his bioelectric charge was depleted—

She felt a tingle, no more as she shoved him and swept his lead foot—

He fell onto his back and she dropped—

Formentara, yelling: "Don't kill him! Don't kill him—!"

At the last instant, she retracted her claws and hit him with a palm to the forehead, banged the back of his head against the floor, hard—

She saw the whites of his eyes roll up as he lost consciousness . . .

— — — — — —

Kay said, "I might break one of those restraints. Three should be sufficient to hold him."

Formentara said, "Maybe. Or he could overload his Golgi stretch-reflex and snap half the bones in his body with the force of his contractions. Get loose, or kill himself, neither of which we want."

Kay had glued the claw wounds on his chest shut and helped Formentara strap him to the augmentation table. He was coming around, blinking, disoriented.

"Can you get him to tell us what we want?"

"Oh, yeah. I'll be able to shunt stuff back and forth enough so he'll talk."

"I wouldn't bet on that," Gee said. He managed a weak smile.

"You could have a dozen traps in you," zhe said. "Now that I know what I'm dealing with, I'll be able to find and disarm them all."

"I don't doubt it. But you won't get that far. See you on the other side, hey?"

Zhe reached for a control, but it was too late. His eyes

bulged, and the whites went red with hemorrhages. He exhaled, a death rattle, and was gone.

"Shit! Shit, shit, shit, *shit!*"

Kay looked at hir.

"He had a demand-explosive charge in his skull! A bio-bomb powerful enough to cook his fucking brain! Shit!"

Kay stared at the body.

Well. This could not be counted a major victory.

## TWENTY-SEVEN

When the hopper landed, and they picked up Formentara and Kay, Jo caught the grim expression of Formentara's face. "That bad?"

"Don't fucking ask."

Kay said, "We captured him. He suicided before we could question him extensively."

"Before we got a fucking thing," Formentara said.

"Not precisely so," Kay said.

Zhe looked at her. "What are you talking about?"

"Consider what we did learn. Gee worked for somebody well-off. He was hired offworld and transported here, at what was probably no small cost, and he was willing to kill us and risk death, and when that failed, kill himself before he would give us the information we sought."

Gunny said, "Yeah, so?"

Jo said, "So even if he was making a shitload of money for the work, what would possess a man to kill himself rather than just roll over on whoever hired him? What's worse than dying?"

They considered that for a moment.

"And why an augmented Rel?" Gunny said.

Nobody had an answer for that one.

"We'll see how much we can backwalk the late M. Gee," Formentara said. "I have contacts who will know."

"Might not need to know," Gramps said. "We have the store manager."

In the backseat, Sid sat staring at the ceiling, grinning stupidly.

Formentara said, "I'll want to scan him. Make sure *he*'s not carrying a death pill, because they have been dropping like fucking autumn leaves around me."

Jo nodded. After Booterik, she had considered that, which was why they decided to make sure Sid was stoned enough he couldn't trigger a suicide if he was so inclined.

Wink said, "I'll make sure he stays under deep enough so he won't do anything foolish even if he is rigged."

"The disruption at TotalMart is done, and they are screaming loud and repeatedly to every authority on the planet," Gramps said.

Jo picked it up: "If Sid is innocent, he'll be turned loose, and the Rajah will fix whatever needs to be fixed. TotalMart isn't going to shut down a store making that much for the corporate coffers, and if they want to do more business here, the Rajah can stop it.

"If he is guilty, TotalMart will cut him loose in a nanosecond to keep the Rajah's goodwill."

"Nice to know how money works, isn't it?" Gramps said. "All about the bottom line."

- - - - - -

Formentara scanned M. Sid and determined that he was free of aug and mechanical traps. Zhe stomped off to make some calls about the late M. Gee.

Wink ran his diagnostics and confirmed there weren't any poisons set to release inside the store manager. He fiddled with the inflow of neurochem and put Sid into a more blissful state that made him receptive to questions.

Jo took the lead, with Wink standing by; Gramps, Gunny, Kay, and Cutter were in the next room watching through a one-way glass.

"How are you feeling, Sid?" Wink asked.

"I feel fucking great!"

"Good, good. My friend Jo here wants to ask you some questions, how would that be?"

"That would be fucking great! She is fucking gorgeous. I'd like to see her naked!"

Wink smiled. "All yours."

Jo shook her head. "Let's talk about the Rajah's daughter, Indira."

"Sure!"

"Do you know where she is?"

"Nope."

"Do you know who kidnapped her?"

"Un-uh."

"Do you know how a file that speaks to this got into your accounting records?"

"Yeah, sure!"

"And how did that happen?"

"I put it there."

"Why?"

"Because Larro told me I should."

"And who is Larro?"

"Larro is my best old friend from forever! We go waaaaaaay back."

"And does Larro have another name?"

"Yes!"

Jo glanced up at Wink, who shrugged. "The chem tends to make them literal."

"What is Larro's other name?"

"Vattack. Would you take your clothes off so I can see you naked?"

"Not right now. Where might we find Larro?"

"Can't find him." He shook his head. His demeanor changed from giddy to sad.

"Why not?"

"He's dead. And cremated."

Jo and Wink exchanged glances.

"How did he die?"

"Hopper accident. It crashed. Poor Larro." He started to cry.

Wink said, "Don't cry, Sid. Think of seeing Jo here naked."

Sid stopped crying. He smiled.

Wink's earbud popped: "Got it," came Gramps voice. "Larro Vattack, age fifty-one, killed in a one-hopper crash three days ago off the southern shore of Lake Dep.

"Police reports indicate that the main repeller blew, and the safety couldn't keep the craft from landing in the water. Emergency floats deployed, but the hopper leaked, filled with water, and Vattack drowned before help could get there. Attempts to revive him were unsuccessful. I'm digging into his background now."

Wink shook his head. Vattack was dead and it looked as if that would kill their lead, too. Fuck!

Jo said, "Did Larro tell you why he wanted you to put that file about Indira into your accounting record?"

"Yes!"

"What did he say was the reason?"

"He said that it would be good for business."

"Did he say how?"

"Yes!"

"And what did he say about that?"

"That there were people who would be more disposed to loosen regulations up if the Rajah was gone."

Jo frowned.

"And how was this supposed to help the Rajah to, ah, go?"

"Larro didn't say." He paused, his face going sad again. "Larro's dead now."

"Don't cry," Wink said. "Jo is thinking about taking her clothes off."

Sid went back to his happy face.

"Jo is also thinking about slapping that shit-eating grin right off Dr. Wink's face," she said.

"That would be fun to watch!" Sid allowed. "Especially if she is naked!"

Wink chuckled.

"How is Indira's kidnapping connected to the Rajah's leaving?"

"I don't know."

Jo asked several more questions, circling around the subject, but it was apparent that Sid didn't have anything else of substance to offer. He'd done a favor for a friend that he thought would benefit them both.

Wink shook his head. Well. So much for this road. Zeth the Rel was dead. His brother Booterik was dead. The guy who had augmented Booterik was dead. The guy Sid could give them, Larro, was also dead.

It seemed an awfully convenient set of coincidences.

– – – – – –

"So, what do we do with Sid in there?" Gunny said. "We gonna turn him over to the Rajah's security?"

"He's guilty of something," Cutter said, "but I'd rather keep him to ourselves for now. No point in risking any more intel leaks than we already have out there."

Gramps said, "So we are now looking at a conspiracy to kill the Rajah as part of the kidnapping?"

Cutter shrugged. "Maybe. We seem to be looking at something pretty convoluted, being run by somebody who isn't taking any chances it will come to public light, and who is rich and ruthless enough to eliminate anybody who might try to do that."

Gramps said, "Incoming call from XTJC for the colonel."

Cutter smiled. "Put it on speaker, no visual.

"Cutter here."

"Hatachi here."

"Good evening, Colonel Hatachi."

"You think so? I'm looking at a report regarding a major disturbance at the TotalMart upcountry in Dep-by-the-Sea. Something about a missing manager and an EMP bath that scrambled the entire store's comnet."

"I think I heard something about that."

"Imagine my surprise."

"Why would this concern J-Corps? Wouldn't it be a local police matter?"

"Unless it was an attempt to screw with interplanetary commerce, which would put it into my jurisdiction. Big store goes down, it can cause a ripple effect."

"That's true."

"Somebody footprinted the store with a warbird's tuned EMP and bollixed the com and cam circuits. By the time security got it all sorted out, the store's manager was gone and a cart driver and a couple of bodyguards woke up with trank-dart hangovers. Somebody with pretty good strategy and tactical skills shut the sucker down and waltzed the manager out."

"Interesting," Cutter said.

"Just before they went down, the store and parking-lot cams got good images of some particular customers coming and going, and they sure did look like military."

"In uniform? You have IDs on them?"

"No, of course not. Facial recogware doesn't match them to anybody we know, and I'd guess skinmasks made that so. Which is good; otherwise, I might have to make some arrests."

Cutter waited.

"Look, we both know you did it. We also know it had the Rajah's blessing, or you wouldn't have gotten access to that satellite. And TotalMart doesn't want to piss off the Rajah, so while local security is screaming, TM Corporate is not making waves. Nobody will back me up on this, but I don't like it, Cutter, not a deminoodle's worth. You are perilously close to stepping over the line, and if you do, I am going to hammer you into the ground like a piton."

"Always good to know that the XTJC is on the job," Cutter said. "Maybe once our contract here is over, you and I can get together and have a drink. I have a bottle of Hiram Connery's White Label that's about ready to open."

There was a pause, then a chuckle. "White Label? You can afford that? If you aren't in the stockade when you get done, I'd be pleased to raise a glass with you."

Cutter smiled.

After the disconnect, Gramps said, "Scotch? You're a bourbon man."

"Yep. But Hatachi drinks scotch, and a bottle of White Label would cost him three months' pay," he said. "Probably be a good idea to buy some—TotalMart will have it in the locked liquor room. Be sure to get our discount."

"'Know your enemy,'" Jo said. "*The Art of War.*"

Cutter nodded. "Yep."

— — — — —

Outside, with a rainstorm threatening to cool off the still-hot twilight, Jo approached Kay. "How was it with Gee?"

Kay knew she was asking about the fight. "He was armed, fast, and strong, but relatively unskilled. The end was never in doubt."

Jo nodded.

Kay knew what she really wanted to know. "You would have defeated him."

"You think?"

"It might have taken you a little longer than it took me."

Both fems grinned at that.

— — — — —

In the com room, Gramps tuned the screen so Gunny could see it. He said, "I have chapter and verse on one Vattack, Larro

Herome, and none of it tells us why he would have planted false information about the kidnapping. He was a businessman, he owned a string of warehouses up and down the coast in three countries, from Westwood, in Pahal, to Long Port in Depal, most of 'em in Dep or the capital, and used mostly for agricultural storage. Guy was worth eight or nine million."

"Another rich guy who ought not be involved with kidnapping for money," Gunny said. "Anything else in common?"

"Nothing that seems to matter," Gramps said. He sniffed. "Is that perfume you are wearing?"

"No. Body wash. Quartermaster said they were out of unscented."

"Uh-huh. Wouldn't have anything to do with that hot young bouncer you've been working, hey?"

"No more than your new haircut has to do with the businesswoman you've been talking to."

"My, my. Spying on me?"

"You got room to talk."

Gramps smiled.

– – – – – –

Formentara leaned back from the subspace com and pondered what zhe had learned. Gee had gone to TAU. He had been a rising star on the biggest Venusian wheelworld, Vesta, he'd had fast hands and new ideas, according to hir sources, and was making good money in the Solar System as a backup augmentor. He'd space in, do something tricky, and move on. If you were good and willing to travel, you could always find work.

He was too fond of sampling his own product, and that was going to kill him eventually, but on a scale of one to ten, with most of the augmentors here being a one and Formentara hirself being a ten, Gee would have rated a four, maybe a five. He could have make a good living staying in-system and ghost-programming for others.

So the money to come halfway across the known galaxy to fiddle with Rel must have been pretty attractive.

Zhe put in a call to a professor zhe knew at TAU on Earth, and waited for the SSC to make the FTL links.

SSC was an expensive way to do research. The units cost a small fortune, they didn't always make the connections right, and they dropped coms frequently. Charges for bandwidth were spendy, even if piggybacked on a larger carrier. Cutter didn't like them to use the things much; even with scrambled and encrypted stuff, the pipes were easy to break into, and while you surely didn't want anybody knowing *what* you were talking about, sometimes you didn't want them to know you were talking at *all*.

Zhe needed, however, to find out about this kid.

And somebody on the team needed to find out something that gave them more to go on PDQ. The longer a kidnapping ran, the more likely it was the victim wouldn't come back alive.

Zhe waited for the SSC. *Come on, you piece of GU shit, connect the call!*

# TWENTY-EIGHT

Cutter called the meeting for 1300, and when they all got there, he laid out his take first. "Okay, we have been cycling our drives too long on this, too much time having meetings. Intel keeps getting more complex but less useful. This sucker is obviously a big enough conspiracy that we should be able to locate a thread to unravel. Find it and pull it, and if you have to get proactive, remember we have immunity. The digits are flashing, time is running out.

"All right, what new do we have?"

Formentara said, "A professor at TAU confirmed basics on Gee, and I've got a tracer on the money put into his account when he was on Vesta. We are talking half a million noodle, way more than it's worth to fiddle with a few augs, even on Rel. It came from here, but all I've got is a transfer number."

"The Rajah's carte blanche will get us into the banking system here—Gramps?"

"I'm on it. But I wouldn't bet on their leaving a pointer."

"Let's look at the rest of it. Theories?"

Jo said, "I go back to stuff we knew before. It doesn't look like Indira's kidnapping was for the money. Whoever is behind this seems to have plenty of that. Plus enough influence to drag millionaires into it, who also don't need the noodle. Something else going on."

Cutter said, "So it could be personal or political. Somebody wants to put the screws to the Rajah? Somebody he pissed off, maybe."

"Perhaps they seek to achieve serious strategical or tactical advantages for something," Kay added.

"The Thakore next door?" Gunny said.

"I don't see his gain," Cutter said. "Rama stomping into his house and kicking the shit out of him, and his treasury looted? I'm guessing that was him telling us as much on that com, and he didn't sound like somebody quick to shoot himself in the foot. Got to look at the classics: money, love, hate, power. If money is out, that leaves us the others."

Gramps said, "Given the players we know about, I'm starting to like Rama for it."

"Your reasoning?"

"He's already de facto running his own country. If he's got an excuse to invade Balaji and more or less screw it over, that's more power. He's making a lot of irate noise, but that could be a diversion. He's got the wherewithal to pull it off—money, men, connections."

Cutter looked around the room. That thought had crossed his mind, too.

"So you figure he starts a war, gets reparations from Balaji when he either wins or agrees to call it off, then miraculously finds Indira and rescues her?"

"Which cements his relationship with his prospective father-in-law all to hell and gone," Gunny said. "Win-win-win. Money, power, the bride, the hero of the day. Even if she doesn't make it, he can lay the blame on somebody, he's got two out of three."

Gramps nodded.

Kay whickered.

"What?" Jo said.

"One who searches for the definition 'devious' can find it listed under 'human.' "

"Can't really argue with that," Gunny said.

"So what now?" Wink said.

"Go back to the bushes and beat them harder. See what runs out. I'm going to the range to vent some steam."

"Ooh, ooh, can Ah go, too?"

Cutter grinned. "If you are feeling masochistic."

- - - - -

The range was up and running.

"You ready?"

Gunny smiled. "You need to ask?"

When they played, it was augs off, no help from chemistry or nanos.

If Cutter and Gunny were side by side, and each had a single target already there, she beat him every time: Nobody was as fast out of the holster as Gunny, nor were they as accurate, certainly not in CFI.

But with unexpected attackers?

Cutter's advantage, every time.

It had to do with his ability to read a scenario and instantly apply tactics—choosing which targets to shoot and in which order, when beset with choices.

It wasn't a skill he could claim to have learned but something innate. He had always been able to do it reflexively, without thinking: If six soldiers came round the corner and started blasting, Cutter's choices of how to move and the sequence of which one to plink first, second, third, and so on, gave him an edge. It wasn't as if he was unbeatable, but once action commenced, he could sometimes shoot where he knew an opponent was going to be *before* they went there. Like leading a bird on the wing, only in these cases, sometimes he would shoot to the sides or even behind a target, and that target would somehow step *into* the round.

That was freakish. He didn't know anybody else personally who could do it, though he had heard about some who were able.

He didn't even know how *he* did it.

He'd done research, and unless there was some kind of psionic precog power at work, the only thing that made sense was neurological lead time; he was somehow bypassing that half-second delay in human brains between intent and action; he was skipping some part of the Readiness Potential or the Conscious Wish, and arriving directly at the Act a little ahead of schedule. It was as if his gun hand knew before his brain did.

He couldn't do it elsewhere, but in combat scenarios, he could.

It was most useful. A half second ahead was a big deal when death zipped through the air on bullets or darts.

He didn't think it was something that could be easily learned, if at all, which was good—if Gunny could develop that, she'd be unbeatable.

She tried, but so far, hadn't managed it.

So when it was a simple dueling tree, he expected Gunny to plug it first. His goal there was to improve his own time when it came to pure speed. He was on the downhill slope, though, and, unless he tweaked his augs, was going to keep getting slower.

Sometimes he could get within a quarter second, and in a shoot-out, that would probably result in *ai-uchi*, mutual slaying. But if Gunny moved first, he couldn't catch up. She liked to practice against a simulacrum with a gun already pointed at her. With a normal reaction time programmed, she could sometimes beat them. Even when the opponent's laser painted her first, she could take him with her much of the time. She liked to say she might be goin' to hell, but whoever shot her was gonna be holding the gate for her when she got there . . .

"The range is hot," Gunny said.

Cutter blew out a quick breath . . .

The computer popped up a single attacker for each of them, armed with a knife and charging.

Cutter drew, but he heard the *thwip!* of Gunny's dart gun before he squeezed the trigger of his own darter.

Point to Gunny.

The next scenario was a falling ball the size of a man's head, dropping from six meters high at one gee.

Gunny hit it four meters up.

Cutter hit it two meters above the ground.

The third scenario was two shooters each, left and right.

Gunny tapped the first and swung to tap the second.

Cutter was a half second behind her.

"Ah do believe that is three for three. Maybe you need to take a rest?"

"Not over yet. And I am immune to your trash talk."

She laughed.

The next scenario was four soldiers in basic armor, which left gaps and unprotected spots where a dart would work.

Gunny was fast, and she was dead-on. She potted all of them, *one-two-three-four!* but—

She was aiming at the places where the armor didn't cover them, and it took a bit longer to line up. He was on autopilot, shooting at where he somehow knew those spots would be before the soldiers got there.

She was right behind him, not more than three-tenths of a second, but he was done first.

"Damn! Ah still don't see how the fuck you can do that."

"Me, neither."

As long as there were more than three targets, he beat her. When the generator gave them fewer, it was Gunny's point.

After twenty minutes and thirty scenarios, they were tied, and down to the final match, the Chinese Army Drill.

In this, a plethora of opponents sprang up, charging and screaming and shooting, and it was a no-win scenario. You couldn't defeat the oncoming horde, so the contest was to see how many you could take down before they wounded you to a point where shooting back would be impossible. The computer knew, and while players bitched that they were tougher than the machine thought, by the time it shut things down, the theoretical wounds would invariably have proven fatal. And the computer's scanner knew if you got hit in the head or spine, and that was an instant game-over.

The pistols held thirty darts, so that was the upper limit—a reload would take way too long.

Cutter's personal best was eighteen, and that was the record anywhere, as far as he knew. There were a couple of old army buddies who claimed they knew somebody who had done twenty, but no verified records of it to be found. Pure speed wouldn't let you get more than that because you'd get hosed first unless you dodged enough to get missed. Not enough just to shoot, you had to avoid getting shot too hard, and the incoming tags were impossible to avoid for long.

"Ready?"

"Ah am."

"Go—!"

The army materialized, forty, sixty, eighty, filling the scenario into the distance—

Cutter fired, ducked, fired, leaned left, fired, fired, again, again—

He lost track of how many darts he sent downrange.

He heard Gunny's game-over beep and was aware that her scenario had dimmed and frozen, but he kept shooting—

His own gallery went dim, and his game-over beep sounded.

"Ah will be gawddamned. It just ain't fair!"

Cutter grinned. The blinking scores told the tale. Gunny,

who was the best pure shooter he had ever been around, had tagged fifteen attackers before they took her out.

He got nineteen.

"My lucky day," he said.

"Luck, hell. Once, twice, three times, yeah. Setting a new record every other time you come to the fucking range? That ain't luck. That's magic!"

Maybe it was. He'd take it . . .

"You can use your augs next time," he said.

"Piss on you! Ah don't need your pity!"

He laughed. "I'm going back to work now. Our boy Singh is dropping by."

– – – – – –

Singh, looking none the worse for his earlier adventure with CFI, stood at attention in front of the colonel's desk.

Cutter looked up at him from his chair. "You sure about this?"

"Sah, yes, sah."

"Why?"

"I may speak freely, sah?"

Cutter grinned. "Say on."

"My Rajah's Army's training is as good as any on our world; a man who is steeped in it is the equal of any solider trained elsewhere on the planet and better than most."

"But . . . ?"

"It is no offer of disrespect to my Rajah to say that your unit is better and more experienced than any to be found locally, and I include the XTJC in that assessment."

"Got that last part right. Continue."

"My father taught me that a smart man learns everything he can about his chosen trade and by so doing, and with good luck, may thus live to become a wise and, perhaps someday, old man. It is better to have knowledge and not need it than to need it and not have it."

Cutter nodded.

"A smart man would learn from the best teachers. On this world, in the ways of war, that would be you, sah."

"The Rajah might not be inclined to let us have you again."

"I am certain that he will if you ask, sah."

Cutter shook his head. "You got balls, kid. I'll see what I can do."

Singh grinned.

— — — — — —

Singh was eager, though Wink thought he probably didn't have a clue what he was getting into.

"Do you like your knife?"

Singh looked at Wink as if he had grown a second head. "*Like* it? My *chhuri*? It is part of me. May as well ask me if I like my *hand*."

Wink grinned. The people here were members of a knife culture—at least in the military and police; they all carried those forearm-length slightly curved knives Singh had just named *chhuri*. The rank and file had plain-looking ones in Kydex or leather sheaths mounted on their belts; the high-ranked sported bejeweled versions.

Wink said, "Are there prohibitions regarding your knife? May I examine it?"

"No prohibitions, it is a working tool. Of course you may."

Singh pulled the knife from its scabbard with a whisper of steel on the formed plastic. Singh did a little twirl using two fingers and positioned the handle toward him.

Wink took the knife.

It was about thirty-five centimeters long, nearly two-thirds of that blade, with the cutting edge on a slightly convex curve, just under two fingers wide, tapering to a sharp point, like a scimitar. The handle was a rich, chocolate, chatoyant wood, half-round, bonded and riveted to a full tang, butt slightly knobbed. The handle was polished but bore slight nicks and dents; the blade was a polished steel without maker marks. It felt like an old weapon.

"This *chhuri* was made by my great-uncle for my grandfather. It was blooded by my grandfather when he served in the Army, at the Siege of Kapil. My father carried it when he was in the Rajah's Rangers, though he never needed to use it in war. I am given to understand that he once fought a man who insulted my mother and opened him from neck to crotch though he survived. My father gave it to me on my seventeenth birthday, as is customary in our family. If I have sons or daughters, it will pass to the eldest when they are of age."

"A fine weapon," Wink said. He did a spin, reversed his grip, and offered it back to Singh, who raised an eyebrow at the manipulation. "You have skill with a knife even though you are a medic?"

Wink grinned. "I'm a *surgeon*. Before they let us play with the lasers and plasmas, we learned how to handle steel and obsidian and sapphire scalpels. You know the worst person to get into a knife fight with? A surgeon."

"Or a butcher," Gunny put in.

"There's a difference?" Gramps said.

"Fuck you both very much." He turned back to Singh. "Though I have to admit, they have a point. Knowing where to cut is almost as important as having the wherewithal to make the cut. And the tool is vital, as well. Surgeons and butchers both have that."

Casually, Wink reached behind his right hip and came out with his belt knife.

Singh took a reflexive step backward.

The knife, from a Terran master bladesmith named Pippin, was a spear-point design he and the maker had collaborated upon. The blade was short, wide, and thick—only ten centimeters long, but nearly three centimeters wide, and a full six millimeters thick. It was single-edged, made from random damascus, composed of four different kinds of tool steel: three layers of this, four of that, three each of these, then folded and hammered five times, until there were 416 layers. The metal had been acid-etched to showcase the folded pattern, making the steel a dark gray, almost black.

This kind of forging made for a strong and pliable metal, and the temper gave it a hardness that would take and hold a razor-sharp edge. The handle was fat and round in cross section, longer than the blade, a deep, rich red of stabilized maple-wood burl that was both functional and attractive. The guard was a sculpted oval, the same steel as the blade. The knife felt good in his hand, it was easy to manipulate, perfectly balanced, and exactly the knife he wanted for close encounters of the deadly kind.

"You're probably wondering why it's so stubby," Wink said. "And why I wouldn't use something shaped more like a scalpel."

If that was what he was wondering, Singh didn't say anything.

"Scalpels are designed to cut and leave as little tissue damage as possible. This thing can reach all the major arteries on humans and most other intelligent species, and the thick blade leaves a big channel for bleeding out. Shorter is easier to carry, less likely to break, and, like medicine, you want to use the minimum amount necessary to do the job. The best knife is the one you have, not the one at home in a drawer."

Singh touched the handle of his resheathed blade and smiled.

"Sure, if you are in uniform, but what if you have to go to somewhere that won't allow a visibly strapped knife? Hard to hide something as long as your foot under a thin tunic. This, I can stick into a back pocket or under a shirttail, though I usually wear it in a leather sheath. Rare-earth magnets hold the knife securely, and there's a safety strap if I feel like tumbling.

"Of course, if you are in a duel with another knife fighter, bigger is better, unless you are nose to nose, but if you can stab him in the back, that's a lot smarter and safer.

"This knife fits my hand exactly as I want it to. It lets me put the point, edge, or the butt where I need it to go."

"The butt?"

"Sometimes you want somebody down and out but not dead. Saves wear and tear on your hands."

Singh nodded. "Ah."

"I'm not telling you to get rid of your knife," Wink said. "I'm saying you would be better served with the ability to use more than one size or shape. Sometimes shorter is better. We'll work with that."

"I bet you tell that to all the women you are with," Gunny said.

"Well, which is better, Gunny—to touch the bottom of the well or the sides?"

"Both," she said.

Wink laughed. To Singh, he said, "Suppose that you lose your knife. Or that it breaks. Then what do you do?"

"We have been trained in bare hand-to-hand fighting."

Wink nodded. "Which among us do you think you might best defeat that way?"

Singh looked around. "I do not wish to offer any insult," he finally said.

Wink said, "Oh, we're hard to insult, don't worry about it. Who?"

"Captain Demonde."

Gunny's laugh was the loudest, but not the only one, and there were a few choice comments from the others, too.

"You wound me, son," Gramps said. He put his right hand over his heart.

More laughter.

When it died down, Wink said, "Why'd you pick him?"

"He is the oldest and least fit-looking. I would expect him to be slower, to have less stamina."

"Reasonable criteria. Jo and Kay would eat you alive, no

contest. Gunny is harder than a bag of rocks and death on two legs, armed or bare; and I'm something of an exercise fanatic myself, plus I know all the best spots to hit you.

"Okay, show us something. Spar with Gramps a little, demo us what your system can do. No blood or broken bones or anything, just a few friendly taps or throws."

Singh nodded. He stepped out onto the practice floor and started to unstrap his knife belt.

Gramps pulled a dart pistol, tapped a control with his thumb, and shot Singh in the thigh.

"Ow—!"

Gramps pointed the pistol's barrel at the ceiling and blew imaginary smoke from the muzzle. "Just a stinger, no juice in it," he said. "But if it had been venom, you'd be deader'n last year's news."

"You cheated!"

"Hell yes, I did. I learned a long time ago, better you learn to fight smarter, not harder."

"If you had not had the pistol—"

"Then I'd have used some other tool. Knife, stick, a chair, whatever. Fighting fair gets you killed unless the other guy also fights fair and you are better than him *and* lucky. First rule: Don't do it.

"But just to keep the demo going . . ."

Gramps tossed his pistol to Gunny, who snatched it one-handed from the air without looking at it.

He stepped up closer to Singh, stopping a couple meters away. "Okay, let's see what you got."

Singh said, "Wait. Why would you be loading only stingers in your pistol?"

Gramps looked at the others, then back at Singh. He smiled. "Because I knew you'd pick me for the demo."

"How?"

"Because *I* would have picked me, too. So would everybody else here."

Singh shifted his feet into a front stance and raised his arms, fists loosely doubled.

"Twenty years ago, I'd have already decked you while you settled into that dueling stance. But I'm a little slower than I used to be."

"A *little* slower?" Gunny said.

He turned his head away from Singh to look at her. "That's a good thing, Chocolatte. Don't want anything going off prematurely, do I?"

Singh, probably thinking Gramps was distracted, charged—

He leaped, fired a fast one-two punch at Gramps's face—

Only Gramps sidestepped, stuck his foot out, and caught Singh's ankle, turning the charge into a fall—

Singh turned the fall into a half-assed roll, but by the time he'd come back to his feet, Gramps was right there, and he kicked the back of Singh's left knee. The kid collapsed on that side, and Gramps threw his arm around Singh's neck into a carotid hold. He squeezed—

*One . . .*

Singh struggled, pulled on Gramps's forearm with both hands, a mistake. He tried to poke Gramps in the eye with his fingers extended, but Gramps had his head turned away.

*Two . . .*

Singh squirmed, twisted, tried to get out of the hold—

*Three . . .*

Singh's body started to sag. He gave a last effort to turn his head to the side—

*Four . . .*

Singh's eyes rolled up—

*Five . . .*

Gramps let him down easy onto the floor and stepped back a couple of meters.

The blood made its way back into Singh's brain. He opened his eyes. Frowned. Sat up.

Gramps said, "You were right. I'm the least among us

when it comes to fighting, slower and older. But why I am still here is that I know that, and compensate for it.

"Old and treacherous beats young and strong every time."

"I will remember."

"Good. Let me show you how you could have gotten out of that carotid hold . . ."

# TWENTY-NINE

There was beating the bushes, then there was beating the bush . . .

It had been a good day. He'd shown the kid Singh that he wasn't so old he couldn't keep up.

And he'd shown a good-looking woman the same thing. In a different way . . .

Gramps watched Lareece pad across the thick rug, admiring her bare and firm ass. Particularly attractive in the natural moonlight shining through the cleared ceiling panels.

If the optics were good enough, maybe somebody monitoring a spysat overflying twenty thousand klicks up was enjoying the view, too . . .

*A thing of beauty is a joy forever,* he thought. *And what is more beautiful than a statuesque naked woman with whom you have just made mad, passionate love?*

She opened the bar's chiller. "You want any more of this champagne?"

"I'm good."

"For an old soldier who plays political smashball, yeah, you are pretty good."

He chuckled.

She topped her flute off with sparkling gold. The bubbles were tiny, and that was supposed to mean it was good stuff. Given it had cost him 120 noodle a bottle, he didn't need to measure the size of the bubbles to know that. He could charge the two bottles to the expense account, but probably he wouldn't. Nobody needed to know what he was drinking and how much it cost, and it was definitely worth it.

She returned the bottle to the chiller and headed back to the bed.

If the view was great from behind, it was every bit as good from the front. She was forty, fit, and in this light, could easily pass for twenty-five. Carpet matched the drapes, too.

She set her flute on the bedside table and slid across the red silk sheet to sit cross-legged next to him. "Well, that was fun. Want to go again?"

"Sure. You lean back, let me unlimber my magic tongue—"

"Oh, no, I don't think I could manage another one of those right now. I had something a little harder in mind."

"My age, you have to learn how to do it smarter, not harder."

She laughed. "Well. I do have something else for you, though."

"Do tell."

"It's more in the realm of business."

"What a shame."

She shook her head. "You know, you have this patter down pretty well. Lots of practice, I expect."

"Well, actually, I'm more of a natural. Would you believe I was a virgin when I met you?" He kept a straight face as he said it.

That cracked her up.

When she was done laughing, she said, "That was wonderful. I haven't had so much fun in years. Um. Okay, here's what I found out. There is a fabric company in a small village, Dera, at the north end of the Rajaja Forest, near the border with Pahal. They make Surakarta Batik, a high-end material, used mostly in ceremonial dress clothing—robes, sarongs, capes. The owner of the weavery is a high-caste rich woman named Udiva.

"On the day the Rajah's daughter was kidnapped and the news got out, the Ramali stock market dropped 350 points. Lot of people lost a lot of money, but Udiva sold short and made more than ten million on the overnight turnaround on half a dozen different stocks."

Gramps nodded. "And this was unusual?"

"Very. Udiva's portfolio is conservative, mostly bonds, and she leaves it to her broker; however, on that day, she personally handled the transactions, buying and selling things she had never dabbled in before."

"Insider trading?"

"Had to be. The stocks that went down? She shorted them no more than a few hours before the drop. As nearly as I can tell, nobody in the country made as much on the market that day as she did. Somehow, I missed it before, but it checks out."

"Well, well. Somebody told her the market was going to take a nosedive—and that had to be somebody who knew *why* it was going to drop."

"That's what I would bet. Listen, I wouldn't presume to tell you how to go about your business—save how it concerns our activities right here in this bed—but you might want to have a word with Fem Udiva."

"Gotta love smart women," he said.

"Talk is cheap, old man."

"Yeah it is. Lie back and be amazed, young woman."

# THIRTY

"This is what the manor looks like," Formentara said.

The image on the projection had a scale across the bottom of the image.

"Crap, it's a monster."

"Yes. Fifteen thousand square meters in the main house," Formentara said. "Thirty-six sleeping chambers, each with its own toilet and shower. Living, dining, recreation, kitchens, you could house a small army there. Four hoppers, twenty small ground vehicles. Staff of forty domestics housed in the servants' quarters, plus eighteen live-in guards, all the bells and whistles a rich woman's castle needs. Spends a million-plus a year on upkeep.

"Udiva lives and loves large," Formentara continued. "She has parties that sometimes turn into weeklong orgies, and she's the largest consumer of dopesmoke and exotic liquor in that part of the country."

"How do we get to talk to her?" Gunny asked. "Ah'm guessing we don't just kick in the door?"

"Nope," Cutter said. "Her guards are first-class pros, and the place is wired tight enough to detect a mosquito fart. Plus she's got the local police and military ready to hop when she says 'Jump.' We maybe could set it up that way, but it would take a while.

"However, as it happens, Fem Udiva is having one of her bashes in a few days. The Rajah has a standing invitation. If he were to show up with some new attendants . . ."

Jo said, "Why spend time and energy trying to crack a locked door if somebody will stand there and hold it open for you?"

"Exactly," Cutter said. "We get in, have a chat, find out what we need to know, go on about our business, everybody is happy."

"You think this rich woman will just tell us who gave her the tip?" That from Kay.

"If we ask properly, she will," Wink said. He held up a small medical case. "Dr. Feelgood can always find a way."

– – – – – –

Unlike the foray into TotalMart, this would be a stealth operation. Done right, nobody would even realize what they had done—Wink had enough chem to find out what he wanted, then to make the subject forget he'd asked.

There were only two of them going in—Wink, because he had the medical skills, and Jo, because she was the best equipped to stand guard while he asked questions.

"Scanners will pick up anything we try to take in," Wink said. "And if they have half a brain among them, they'll know that Jo is augmented to the toenails. I see that as a problem."

"Except that they won't look," Cutter said. "It would be considered insulting to the Rajah to ask him or his entourage to pass through a scan field. And even if they do a surreptitious peek? Wink is listed as the Rajah's personal medic, thus his having medical supplies is expected, and Jo is going as a 'security consultant.' Even though they don't much hold with augmentation, nobody is going to begrudge the Rajah an augmented bodyguard, especially after the recent assassination attempt."

"So this is going to be as easy as that? Waltz right in, corner the woman, find out what she knows, and leave?"

"Sure. Even if you get caught, the Rajah has but to snap his fingers, and all will be forgiven. *What? My people wandered into a place off-limits to visitors? My apologies.*

"No matter what they might think, they will grin and bear it; he's the Rajah."

— — — — —

Jo stood by the bedchamber's door, listening for company. Wink had shined his not-inconsiderable charm at Udiva, who was an attractive, Rubenesque woman of sixty or so. Her outfit of fine green-and-orange static-held silks had probably cost as much as Jo made in six months.

The room smelled of roses, almost overpoweringly so, even with her olfactories damped way down.

Wink had taken Udiva down a path different than she'd expected. She'd thought Wink was interested in quick and dirty sex—right up until he slapped a derm on her neck and put her into a chemical fog.

With her augmented hearing, Jo could follow the conversation as she listened for anybody who might wander down the hall.

"Who told you the market was going to fall just before the reports of the Rajah's daughter's kidnapping broke?"

"Rama Jadak," she said.

*Just like that. Son of a bitch. Gramps was right,* Jo thought.

"You sure? Directly?"

"No, via com. The message was encrypted, but I have

had dealings with Rama over the years. He is the power behind the Rajah Jadak; to do serious business in Pahal, you deal with Rama, everyone knows that."

"Could it have been somebody using his voice?"

"The com had his ID number."

Wink glanced over at Jo. "That enough?"

"Get the ID sig."

Wink turned back to Udiva. Asked her for the number, which she gave him.

Jo said, "Let's go."

"Hold on."

Wink peeled the pink derm spot from Udiva's neck and replaced it with a second, blue one. After a moment, she began snoring. He looked at his timer. "Fifteen seconds."

He waited that long, then peeled the second derm off. "She'll sleep for an hour, won't remember what happened."

He reached down and worked her silk pantaloons down and off.

"What are you *doing*?"

"Setting the stage." He tossed the pantaloons onto the floor, spread her knees a bit, and untabbed her tunic, to expose her torso. She had large breasts, and they'd been augmented. Her mons was depilated, smooth as could be.

He stood. "Whoa, look at that."

"You're a doctor, you've seen plenty of those, haven't you?"

"Wave the light panel off."

Jo looked at him.

"Go on, you'll like this."

She did.

The room dimmed to a faint glow.

And it wasn't the only thing glowing. The snoring woman's pubes and nipples pulsed, each a bright, phosphorescent orange, dimming and brightening in synch with her heartbeat.

Jo waved the light back up. Shook her head.

"I guess some of her lovers must get lost in the dark," Wink said. "So she lit some landing beacons, just in case."

"Let's go find the Rajah and get out of here."

"We gonna tell him it's Rama?"

"Not us, that's for Rags to decide. But now that we know, we can finally get off our asses and *do* something."

# THIRTY-ONE

"So, it *is* Rama," Cutter said.

"Told you," Gramps said.

"And given your lack of short-term memory, you'll probably tell us ten more times before the day is done," Gunny said.

"And I'll enjoy doing just as much each and every time."

Gunny shook her head.

Kay said, "Our course of action would be to capture Rama and get him to tell us where he has the Rajah's daughter." Not a question.

"Pretty much," Jo said. "Since we are relatively sure he is responsible, that knowledge will make it easier to proceed."

"And where is he?" Cutter asked.

Formentara said, "As of now, in northwestern Balaji."

"What is he doing there?" Wink asked.

"Starting a war, it appears," Formentara said.

"Fuck! I was hoping to get to him before he did that. I wonder why the Rajah didn't give us a heads-up?"

Formentara lit a projection, a view from orbit, with a map that included four layers of overlay. "It seems that Pahali forces crossed the border into Balaji, just south of the Inland Sea in the Kadam Forest within the last few minutes. They have been just firing the odd potshot at each other, lighting up the night with a flare now and then, but our sat feed shows that ground troops began their advance at oh-dark-thirty."

"Has the Balajian army engaged?"

"Not so much. The border guards retreated in a hurry. Lot of commercial timber in the forest there, which straddles both sides of the border. Been a hot summer, the wood is dry. Nobody wants to burn it down, so the Thakore's main army is waiting on the plain to the southeast. There's a mountain pass that bottlenecks south of the forest, so they'll have to throw some big rocks to soften it up."

"Shit, shit, shit. What about the Rajah?"

"Ramal's army is still in New Mumbai, on the eastern border, but it is packing up its tents. I had to guess, I'd say he'll be heading northeast to get behind the Thakore's forces while Rama's troops hit them from the front. The capital city is all the way across the country on the east coast, but Balaji's navy is pretty strong, more gunboats than Pahal's, and New Mumbai won't be able to get their ships there without sailing all the way over the Roof, so it'll take them a while to make any difference at sea.

"Pahali and Mumbaiian air and missiles will hit Balajian ground forces, but Balaji actually has as many fighters and bombers as they do, so that won't be a rout. I don't think we are talking nukes here, but there will be some noise."

Cutter nodded. Yes.

"It won't be a surprise," Formentara continued, "but it won't matter. The Balajians are outnumbered. Knowing it's coming isn't the same as being able to stop it."

Gramps said, "We got to go pretty quickly."

Cutter nodded. "Yeah. Either way—if Rama has Indira, and he's planning on 'rescuing' her, or dumping her body deep in Balajian territory, then she'll be there already, or he'll have her with him. Find him, we find her."

"If she knows he did it, she's a dead woman."

"Yes. But what we have so far, I see Rama as greedy. If he can get it all, I think he'll try for it. Somewhere in the upcoming battles, Indira will show up, dead or alive."

"Okay, people, you know the drill. Saddle up."

They filed out, save for Gramps, who lagged behind.

"What?"

Gramps said, "We got an incoming com. It's from the guy who called us about the Thakore," Gramps said.

"Put it on speaker."

"Colonel. We spoke before."

"Yes, sir, what can I do for you?"

"My country has been invaded by Rama's army and is about to become a bloody fucking battlefield."

"I know. Sorry. I'd stop it if I could."

"I take it you haven't found Indira."

"No. But we have what we think is a strong lead. If we can collect her before it goes too much further, it might help."

"What can we do to assist you?"

"Nothing, sir. Better that nobody knows where we are or what we are up to. The air has ears."

"It does. You have this com number. Please let me know if you have news."

"I will."

The connection went silent.

"You think it's him? The Thakore hisself?"

"I'd offer good odds, yes. He's hoping that we can find Indira and get the war called off. But that's a really narrow window. Man is looking at an invasion he can't stop, he'll check everything that might help."

Another incoming com cheeped.

"You are getting popular, Rags. Another on the private pipe. Hurry up. We have to go."

Cutter gave him a fuck-you look: "Cutter here."

"Hitachi on this end."

"Good evening, Colonel."

"Dark, yes, nothing good about it."

"We didn't start the war," Cutter said.

"I know. And since it's a local dustup, J-Corps won't get too involved unless it trips one of our beams."

Cutter knew what "too involved" meant. XTJC would have speckunits roaming in the field, monitoring. They'd be broadcasting GU ID sigs high, wide, and repeatedly, and woe be to anybody who fired on them. J-Corps had a certain rep on backrocket worlds, and deservedly so: Shoot at us, we will nuke you all and let God sort out your radioactive dust. When you had only a relatively few troops to cover an entire world, you went to the big hammer fast. J-Corps wouldn't think anything at all about deploying tactical nukes to take out a small force. Mama Terra was paying for the boomware: What was a two-klick crater to her if the Army decided it was necessary? More where those came from . . .

"Just in case any of CFI's people somehow find themselves roaming around in a war zone, I am hereby advising you to be careful where you do any plinking."

"Understood."

"And unofficially, Colonel, if you can come up with a way so they stand down, I'd be happy to buy some of that bourbon you like if we get around to that drink. I know you don't really care for scotch. Lot of forms I have to fill out when the locals decide to go to war."

Cutter grinned. "I'll drink the bourbon, you can have the scotch."

"Done. Discom."

Well, well. Best get this show in the air . . .

## THIRTY-TWO

Formentara said, "Colonel, we got a J-Corps force on spysat, debarking from a carrier near the border where Rama's army crossed over."

"Figures. They'll be monitoring the action. How many?"

"Short company, a hundred or so."

Cutter nodded. "We'll have to make sure we don't shoot any of them by accident. Hatachi has let it be known that a bottle of good scotch won't buy us out of that."

Zhe didn't speak to that.

"Everybody ready?"

Zhe said, "All green on the log-ins."

"Okay, you're in charge. Don't break anything while we're gone."

Formentara grinned.

— — — — — —

"You ready to fly, Nancy?" Jo asked.

"Honey, I'm always ready to fly."

"Might get shot at."

"I been shot at. Not a problem if they don't hit me. I am allowed to dodge, right?"

Jo looked around. The team was all on board: Rags, Gunny, Gramps, Wink, Kay, and herself.

And Singh. The colonel had him come along, and Jo figured it was more because he wanted to be sure that Singh wasn't bending the Rajah's ear. When you hire the locals, you always keep a sharp eye on them, JIC.

"Okay. Let's go places and rescue people," Jo said.

The hopper's engines revved, and they lifted.

— — — — — —

The colonel said: "Okay, once more, here's what we will be dealing with. Rama won't try to run his armor through the woods, so it'll be infantry. And it's gonna take a while because there is a huge forest, hundreds of kilometers wide at the border and that far extending into Balaji.

"The forces at the front will be his best and toughest, and Singh here has indicated that they aren't too shabby.

"Rama's Navy will sail round the Eastern Horn of Pahal, and there will be armored vehicles hauled that way. Tanks and juggernauts will be airlifted via VTOL lifting bodies and plunked down where he thinks nobody will be expecting 'em, somewhere east of the Inland Sea.

"Air will overfly where it can—the Thakore has a decent-sized air force of his own, so that won't be overwhelming.

"Nobody uses nukes, if they keep to the treaty. No satellite-deployed ceepee. No biologicals, and not even poison gas, outside of civilian crowd-control stuff.

"Both armies will be plugged and sonic-damped, so they won't be spraying puke 'n' crap, nor cranking up the amps to blow out eardrums and addle brains, except for civilians who get in the way. We will don our nares filters and pass-through wolf-ear plugs, just in case. Might get messy otherwise."

Gunny chuckled.

They'd all done training that involved exposing themselves to various noxious chem, and "messy" was an accurate term.

"We're leaving the suits home. Both sides will be throwing stuff hard enough to hole them, and we won't be doing any stand-up fighting if we can help it. Getting in and out fast and staying off the pradar is a better way to go. We'll have Formentara's magic transponders, and those should help."

"Nancy is going to sneak us in ahead of Rama's advance, and it will be cutting it close, but that's the best option. Once they engage, the armies will be shooting at anything that moves, and transponders or not, we run the risk of getting friendly fire from both sides.

"We collect Indira, Schrödinger's—either way, we get the hell out ASAP.

"Questions?"

Nobody had any. They had covered all this before, it was just to make sure that he went over it again.

"Nancy puts us down in that clearing, we go through the woods, get to where we want to do, and take care of business. You need to pee, visit the head now."

- - - - - -

The edge of the forest was just ahead, and since that's where Rama's camp was, the going would be faster once they cleared it, but that would mean air attacks would be a risk. Lot of dumbot drones on both sides flying around, looking for something to shoot. Plus J-Corps wandering around on the QT.

Not that they couldn't be detected in the thick of the woods with DLIR or pradar, but with all those heavy-boled trees to absorb the shock, the explosives didn't work as well. Nobody was supposed to be throwing nukes, and having a meter-thick tree between you and a shower of bomb fragments was way better than having to absorb them yourself.

Plus nobody wanted to burn down the valuable trees, so more likely they'd send in infantry to deal with them.

Nobody was particularly likely to notice a handful of un-IDed troops during all the goings-on.

But: Speed was of the essence now; they had to get in and out or risk getting crushed between the two armies. The fog of war made everything that moved a target for everybody with a weapon. Lot of friendly-fire killing went on.

Cutter looked at his team. He was getting too old to be doing this shit though he had to admit to himself that there was an element of, well, *joy* in it.

Never felt so alive as you did after you came out of a battle in one piece. And if you were dead? You wouldn't feel that . . .

Jo said, "Two klicks, southeast, Colonel. Kay and I have the point."

"Go for it," Cutter said.

The tricky part would be getting next to Rama. In theory, Formentara had adjusted their transponders so they would be autotoggled by any military pradar ping. If Rama's army looked at them, their ID sigs would match his; if the Thakore's army did the same thing, the sig would show up as belonging to him. There were always rangers and speckunit boots on the ground in a battle, and as long as the sig matched yours, you tended not to worry as much. Plus a handful of troops weren't any real threat anyhow.

At least that was the theory.

If they got painted with pradar from both sides at the same time?

Formentara had shrugged. "Transponders will schiz out, offer one, then the other. You'll be in deep shit, both sides shooting at you. Better to not let that happen."

Cutter adjusted his low-ready grip on his carbine and watched Jo and Kay take off.

"Move out," he said.

– – – – – –

Jo was up for a party, but she kept her augs running at minimum. They needed to move quickly, but it might be a long engagement, and better not to burn up her energy too soon. No suits for them this time, only helmets and pliable-ceramic armor, and that minimal cover. Fast and sneaky were the keys here, not round-resistance. No way for six of them to offer a stand-up fight against two armies.

She and Kay were LOS lasercom only, so if they couldn't see each other, they couldn't hear each other. Not that they needed to talk that much, they'd use jive to signal each other, and both of them had enough night vision to track each other even here in the trees—it was dark, but not completely so.

If they came across resistance this early, they'd need to avoid it or take care of it quietly if they could.

Kay stopped, raised her hand, closed it into a fist.

Jo froze.

Kay pointed, and Kay followed the line in the dark forest . . .

There, a picket, not looking in their direction, but rifle held at his waist. Not quite low ready. Expecting the possibility of company, Jo figured, but from another quadrant, and no target in view.

Kay pointed at herself, then the soldier.

Jo nodded.

It was always fascinating to watch the change as Kay went into her stalk. She seemed to shrink, become something less conspicuous, and she moved with a stealth Jo could only envy. She crouched lower, stepped slowly and with great care to avoid making any noise.

She stole to within five meters of the soldier.

He wore spookeye goggles hinged to the front of his helmet, so if he glanced in her direction, he'd see her, but so far, his concentration seem to be to the north. Jo didn't ping his transponder, didn't want to risk alerting him, so she wasn't sure whether he was Pahali or Balajian, but it didn't really matter—either was as much a worry as the other.

Kay crouched, silent, still as a rock. Waited.

Something must have subconsciously spooked him. The soldier turned toward Kay.

Jo raised her carbine and put the floating green dot on the man's throat, above his pec-plate. She was forty meters away, and the scope compensated for parallax automatically to ten times that distance. The carbine was suppressed, but it would make some noise—

Before the picket could bring his weapon to bear, Kay sprinted in, incredibly fast, and lashed out with one claw—

The false image her aug gave the blood that spewed from his neck made it a maroon color in the spookeye field. He dropped his weapon and reached for his ruined throat, no more than a fading gurgle accompanying his fall as he dropped onto his side.

Kay dropped next to the dying man and hastened his end with another claw.

She did like that throat strike, and with good reason: Land it, it always worked. And so far as Jo could tell, Kay always landed it. If you planned on hand-to-hand with a Vastalimi? You wanted to wear a nice, thick titanium collar . . .

Moving on now, people . . .

– – – – – –

There were supposed to be two sentries outside Rama's temporary shelter, but it turned out there was a third. Kay and Jo were set to deal with the expected ones.

"I got him," Wink said.

The third man was behind the building, a dome-shaped thing with surface e-camo lit to hide it from an overfly.

Wink worked his way into position.

He gripped his knife, the fat cylindrical handle familiar

and comfortable in his hand, and edged his way forward, moving as smoothly as he could. When the sentry moved, Wink stopped. Motion, especially jerky motion, caught a human's attention in a hurry. You might hear a funny noise in the night and puzzle over it, but if you saw somebody creeping up on you with a knife, you wouldn't wonder over it very long. The trick to overcoming that was to be close enough to use the natural reaction a man had to deadly danger to finish the attack.

People would freeze, run, or fight, and usually in that order.

Wink had been on death's doorstep often enough so that the hormonal rush didn't kick in the same way for him that it did for most. The chemical cascade that flooded a man's mind and body, driven by the reptile brain that wanted to survive at all costs, came to him, but seldom as the tsunami. These days, it was more like a small wave that lapped at his thighs, rocking him, but not threatening an uncontrolled tumble.

He missed that.

Here he was, stalking a man armed with a carbine who wouldn't hesitate to shoot him if he spotted him. His transponder was off, he wasn't in uniform, he was a wild card, and fair game to either army. And yet he was only mildly edgy.

Once they were inside and hidden, noise was less of a factor, those guards would be easier, but here and now, with this unexpected extra one on patrol, quiet was the main factor. They were in the middle of a military encampment; there were a lot of nervous, heavily armed soldiers geared up for battle. Such situations were volatile. Throw a rock through a window in this kind of situation, and when the smoke cleared from the startled gunfire, there might be dozens of corpses from friendly fire, the shooters convinced they had seen the enemy.

Wink took another step. Two. Three. Stopped.

Perception was a strange thing. One of his uncles had

been a hunter, had liked tromping around in the woods with a small-caliber rifle, shooting tiny tree-dwelling animals called squirrels. It was all highly regulated; one had to take safety classes, obtain a license, wear special clothing, and use an approved and registered weapon. The season for such hunts was short, and the managed parks in which they took place were crawling with forest rangers sent to enforce the game limits and safety rules.

After a hunt, his uncle Val used to have an ale or four, snort, and offer that there were more wardens in the woods than hunters. That back when he'd been young, things had been much more relaxed and fun. It was all so fucking civilized now.

Val was a large man, pushing two meters and a hundred kilos. His hunting costume was a brilliant, phosphorescent pink: a vest, cap, and gloves that the quarry's vision supposedly couldn't differentiate from any other solid color. That wouldn't spook the prey, but it would allow hunters to easily see and identify each other.

That was part of the safety-first attitude for which Val had little use. Sissy stuff. What kind of hunter couldn't tell the difference between a squirrel and a man?

The sentry turned a little, giving Wink a profile, and for a moment, he felt a tiny thrill course through him. Then the sentry turned his back again.

The thrill ebbed.

Maybe he could make a deliberate noise? Spike the fear factor?

No. It wasn't about him, it was about the mission.

Wink took another step. Two . . .

The last time Uncle Val went hunting was on a clear, cold morning, the sun shining brightly. The season had just begun, there were a lot of hunters and wardens out.

Thirty minutes after he stepped into the groomed forest, somebody shot Val in the back of the head. The bullet passed *through* his bright orange cap and hit him in the hindbrain, shutting down his autonomic system. By the time medical help arrived, it had been too late for a long time. Val was effectively dead before he hit the ground.

So much for safety first.

How *was* it possible for somebody to mistake a two-meter-tall, hundred-kilo human in a bright, glowing pink costume for a tree-dwelling creature the size of his hand? To shoot him *through* the glowing hat?

But: On every planet where hunters went forth to take game using projectile weapons, be they guns, bows, or atalatl-hurled spears, they sometimes took out each other instead of the prey.

If you had a knife, you'd have to be blind to accidentally stab a human instead of a squirrel, but distance and excitation and a way to reach out from afar?

Some small number of such instances were deliberate. Somebody who wanted to see what it felt like to kill a fellow human, and a hunting "accident" was punished much less severely than intentional homicide, sometimes not at all, under the "assumed-risk" principle. But most were true accidents, people whose adrenaline fogged their vision and caused them to see what they wanted to see instead of what was there.

A rat-sized creature with a bushy tail? Or a man's glow-in-the-daylight hat?

Hell. Shoot it—and find out.

Almost. Almost. Five meters. Three . . .

*Now!*

Wink sprinted, raised his knife, and drove it into the man's spine at the base of his skull, slipping it between C2 and C3, the spear point severing the cord entirely.

The sentry never knew he was coming, nor what hit him.

It was a paralyzing stab. The man collapsed, unable to move, speak, even breathe. With help, he could recover, the cord could be repaired, a few months and he'd be as good as new.

"Sorry," Wink said quietly. He squatted and nicked the right carotid artery. The sentry would bleed out quickly, no pain, he'd go to sleep and not wake up. Wink didn't enjoy this part particularly, but it was necessary. The man was a soldier. He had to know there was risk involved here—

"Wink?"

He activated his com. "I'm done. You aren't waiting on me."

"Stet that."

Wink wiped his knife on the dying man's sleeve and resheathed it.

## THIRTY-THREE

The dome was spacious, a prefab iglu, filled with luxurious furniture, like silk couches and ornate, hand-carved tables, chairs, and a desk. The interior was broken up into rooms by shimmering curtains of brightly colored silk hung from the high ceiling. It smelled of spicy cooking.

When Cutter stepped into the main room, Rama was on a cushy couch, wearing silver silk nightclothes, and not the least bit pleased to see him.

"Cutter! What are *you* doing here? How did you bypass my guards?"

"We have reason to believe that we can find Indira in your camp."

"*Here?* Are you mad?"

"Maybe just a little bit pissed off, but not entirely mad, no."

"What are you saying? You think *I* had something to do with my fiancée's disappearance?"

Cutter nodded. "It certainly looks that way. We have run down a bunch of leads, and they all point in your direction."

"Leads? Any such things are false! Planted by Luzor to throw you off his track!"

Cutter shook his head. "See, that's one of the things. There's no way that the Thakore benefits from kidnapping Indira. What he gets for that is you kicking in his door and slaughtering his people wholesale, blowing things up, plus a big bill for it all afterward. Why would he do that?"

"Because he is insane, a fool, a man so devious they will have to guard his corpse after he dies, or he will steal it himself!"

"On the other hand, what do you get out of it?"

"Excuse me?"

"If you recover Indira, you are an international hero. You are acclaimed across two countries, and you cement your connection with the Ramal family forever. The Thakore has to cough up a shitload of money, trade agreements, whatever, because he'll likely lose the war."

"Not 'likely.' He *will*!"

Cutter continued: "If you find that Indira has been slain, then you punish her slayer, and either way, you come out of it smelling like a rose."

"You must be as insane as he is."

"There are days when I wonder. But: We do have all those reasons."

"You cannot have any that are legitimate!"

Cutter rattled off a set of names. "You do know these people?"

"Of course I know them! They are wealthy men, in Pahal and Mumbai. One cannot help but know men of great means on our world."

"You know a woman named 'Udiva'?"

"The cloth merchant in northern Mumbai, yes, yes, I know her! What of it?"

"You admit to having dealings with them."

"Did you not *hear* me? Yes, certainly, I deal with them

and others like them all the time! They are pillars of society, businessfolk, they are the upper castes. How would I *not* deal with them?"

"Listen, I'm not a judge to decide who knows what about what. What say we just collect Indira and lay it all before the Rajah? He can sort it all out."

"There is no one to collect and nothing to sort out! I am in the middle of a campaign! I have no time for your crazed stories, Colonel! I have battles to fight, ground to capture. Once that is done, then we can discuss your silly notions, and the Rajah can laugh at them with me."

"If Indira is not here, you can go on about your business. I'm assuming if you had anything to do with this, you weren't foolish enough to let her know because that will mean you'd have to kill her."

"Enough! I command an army! I will hear no more of this. Guards!"

"They, uh, won't be coming."

"What? What have you done?"

"Nothing fatal to the ones inside. Just made sure they wouldn't interrupt us until we finished our conversation."

"It is finished! I will speak no more! Leave, or—"

"Or what? It seems we have the advantage here."

"You are wrong in this, too!"

He swept his hand under a silk cushion and came out with a small pistol.

Cutter was faster. He cleared his holster and indexed Rama, fired one dart from his own weapon. It hit Rama square on the chest, and that should have been that, only—

Rama grinned and thrust his pistol in Cutter's direction—

*Fuck!* Cutter dived out of the chair and to his right. He hit the floor, rolled on the thick carpet, and came up, jinking left as he did, in case Rama tracked his trajectory—

Which Rama did—he fired at where Cutter would have been had he kept going forward—

Too far away to jump at him, and he was either immune to the darts, or that thin fucking nightshirt was some kind of special armor—

Cutter pointed his pistol at Rama's head and triggered off four quick shots—

Rama screamed and clapped his hands to his face—

Maybe he wore beddybye armor or was antichemmed, but a dart in the eye? Always a good attention getter—

Rama screamed loudly, rage and anger mixed, and pointed his pistol, but before he could line up on Cutter with his good eye, the nearest curtain flapped open and there came the quiet *fhump!* of a suppressed weapon.

Rama's head blew apart as the explosive round hit it.

"Shit!" Cutter said. He came all the way to his feet.

Behind him, Jo stood there, carbine extended for another shot if necessary.

Certainly wasn't going to *be* necessary for Rama to get to whatever afterlife might be waiting for him. No medic in the galaxy could fix that.

It made things more complex.

Wink came in behind Jo and bent to look at the corpse.

"I'm just guessing without a full autopsy, but I'd say that Rama here is considerably dead, and the cause probably an explosive carbine round to the head."

Jo held up Rama's pistol: "His magazine's loaded with full-on toxics. He'd have killed you if he'd hit you, Rags. No help for it."

"Well. We'll just have to explain it to the Rajah as best we can. Better that we find his daughter and bring her back—that'll go a ways to keeping us on his good side."

"I'd guess we just got on the Thakore's good side, too."

"There's that. Okay, we go to Plan B: We need to arrange for Rama to take that secret trip."

"I have the recording."

"Let's get moving."

Jo stood there for a moment.

"Something?"

She nodded in the dead man's direction. "Yeah."

"Go ahead."

Jo told him.

He shook his head. "Motherfucker! You sure?"

"Pretty much."

Cutter chewed on it for a moment. "Well, it doesn't matter to the immediate situation. Let's go."

It didn't take long to load Rama's body, along with the unconscious guards and the three dead sentries from outside, into Rama's private transport, conveniently docked at the south side of the dome. The ship could be entered from inside the place, didn't even have to get wet, it was pouring rain.

Once that was done, Cutter said, "I'll ditch the hopper somewhere and meet you at the rendezvous."

"Could be a long way."

"I saw a scooter in the back. Sig is going to show it as Rama's, so his guys won't be shooting at me if they see me."

"Copy," Jo said.

Once he was clear of the dome, Cutter lifted and triggered the recording.

"This is Rama," came the dead man's voice. "I am flying west for a meeting with Rajah Ramal's envoy. Do nothing until I return."

The incoming com lit with several queries, but Cutter ignored them. He expected that's what Rama would have done had he been alive and actually going somewhere.

Not likely anybody here was stupid enough to shoot down their commander's private yacht; though from the way he had been, it might have been tempting. One less asshole on a planet, who'd miss him?

# THIRTY-FOUR

"Right there?" Wink said.

Jo nodded. "Actually, it's pretty clever. It's what the late Rama and his command staff all use. What's one more iglu among scores just like it? The ranking officers will have guards posted, so that's not a tell. I doubt there's a functionary whose job it is to count temporary structures every day, and if there is, he could easily be in on it."

"Hiding in plain sight," Gramps said. "Got to give him credit for that one."

"Rama didn't strike me as that serpentine a thinker," Gunny said.

"Nor me," Wink said. "Smarter than he acted."

"Maybe" Jo said.

They looked at her.

"We can talk about that later," she said. "First, we fetch our quarry."

"If she's actually there," Gramps said.

"Either she is in there, or she left a noticeable amount of

her scent there," Kay said. "The smell matches that of the clothing we obtained."

Jo's own olfactories were enhanced, but even so, she couldn't keep up with Kay when it came to scent. Only so much you could do with a human nose, and the Vastalimi were still superior to the best human augmentation in that realm.

The target dome was small, no more than six meters in diameter, a camo-projector keeping it vaguely forest-colored. It was made of memory foam, probably weighed less than ten kilos, essentially half a bubble. It would be enough to keep heat or cold in or out if properly conditioned, protect occupants from rain or wind or sun, and once it was empty, activation of a simple vacuum canister the size of a small pail would suck it in for storage and transport.

Rama's, of course, was thrice the size of the others.

Not that he was going to need it anymore.

"So, what?" Gunny said. "We gonna just waltz right in and kick in the door?"

"Nope. You and Gramps will create a diversion, loud enough to draw attention, and bright enough to screw up spookeyes. Kay and Wink and I will take out the guards, grab Indira, and meet Rags. Now that he has a scooter, he'll haul her back to the hopper, we meet him there, and everybody goes home and lives happily ever after."

*Maybe . . .*

"You think it'll be that easy?" Gunny said.

"Why, of course. Isn't it always?"

They all grinned at that.

Kay whickered.

— — — — — —

Gunny looked at her chrono. "About time to get on it," she said.

"Amazing. You can tell that by looking at that itty-bitty

thing on your wrist? We use hourglasses where I come from."

"I thought you were born before there was time."

"That's true. My sister invented it. Had a bunch of sand she needed to use."

"Ah hope you don't forget the plan between here and where you are supposed to go."

"I'm sorry, who are you again? What are we talking about here?"

Gunny shook her head.

"I'll take care of the sentry," he said. "You just make sure you get the ammo bin lit properly."

"Don't you worry about me," she said.

"I mean, once it starts, you need to *leave*, and not watch the pretty shiny sparks and all."

"How did you get to be this old? Must have some bored god watchin' out for you, Ah can't imagine why somebody hasn't kilt you yet."

"They try. I'm tougher than I look."

"Pretty much have to be, just to walk around."

"Five minutes, on my mark."

Gunny held a finger over her chronometer.

"And . . . now."

Gunny triggered her timer.

Gramps moved off.

– – – – – –

Four minutes and forty seconds later:

"Heyho, Roscoe, howzu do'?"

The sentry frowned at Gramps. His transponder sig matched that of the sentry's, but still: "What are you doing here?"

"Hawkeye sent me."

"Who?"

"You know, Hawkeye, the new assistant brewmaster?

They got in a shipment of that Hemani Rum, the good, high-proof stuff? I'm supposed to give the sentries each a little bottle. The bottles are shaped like little pistols."

"Yeah? Where is it?"

"Right here, in my back pocket."

Gramps drew his pistol, slowly, no sudden moves, that was the key. By the time the sentry registered that it wasn't the small pistol-shaped bottle of liquor he was expecting to see but a real pistol, it was too late: Gramps shot him in the face.

The sentry spasmed and fell.

*That* was *pretty clever, wasn't it?*

He toggled his com: "How come I don't see you skulking toward the bin yet, Chocolatte?"

"Well, Ah could say it's because it's dark and you are old and half-blind, but the fact is, Ah am already *in* the bin, slow-eyes."

"I knew that."

"Hell you did. Hold on a second . . ."

The door slid open, and Gunny ambled out of the bin. "Probably we want to be goin', we need some distance, and slow as you are, we likely to get blown up, we don't start now."

"Yeah, well, behold my ass and elbows. Try and keep pace, Gunny."

– – – – – –

Jo glanced at her timer. "Fifteen seconds," she said.

"Fifteen seconds," Kay echoed.

There were three guards outside the target iglu, and nobody was going to do anything fancy, just dart them and hit the door, as soon as the—

*—BOOM!*

The explosion shook the ground like a mild earthquake, then there was a fireball rising behind them, casting long and flickery shadows . . .

The guards turned to look at the flare, and Jo and Kay

both shot before Wink could even squeeze his trigger—
*pap-pap-pap*—and all three were down.

But as they ran toward the iglu's door, a quad of soldiers
came into view to their left, a hundred meters away, carbines
held at low ready, jogging toward them.

Wink didn't think it was a coincidence. Must be some
kind of backup. Set to head for Indira if there was any kind
of commotion.

"I got them," Jo said. "Go get her."

Kay and Wink kept going.

Jo sprinted inhumanly fast toward the approaching four
soldiers—

— — — — — —

Jo knew what field of fire these soldiers would try, and she
was already angled out to make sure the ones on her left
would get in the way of the ones on her right.

Her faked transponder sig wasn't going to do the trick
now—

She jinked and stutter-stepped, and was within twenty
meters before the first shots in her direction, loud, dragon-
tongued muzzle flashes.

She swung her own carbine around to cover them, triggered one long AP burst sweeping from left to right, then
indexed the targets coming back from the opposite side,
squeezing off three-round bursts, not looking to see whether
she hit or not, just keeping her weapon moving—

—two of them were down from the first sweep, and she
tapped the other two in just under a second on the return—

Too easy. Four up, four down—

Whups. Not done. Here came a second quad. And, look! a
*third*—

She let go of the carbine, which wound up on its retractable sling and stuck to her chest. Banged her under
the chin as it hit. Fucking piece of shit wasn't supposed to
do that—

She pulled two grenades from her belt, right, left, thumbed the caps off, and pressed the red buttons.

*One . . . two . . . three . . .*

She threw the right one first, still running, then the left grenade.

The right one actually hit one of the soldiers square in the helmet, knocking him backward and ricocheting up two meters before it went off—

The second throw wasn't as accurate, but it was still in the air three meters in front of the lead soldier when it exploded—

Her optic filters shielded, and when her vision cleared, she saw there were only two of the eight still standing.

Grenade shadow, the shrapnel stopped by their fellow soldiers.

No time to regrip her carbine, and a waste of time to draw her pistol—it was a darter and no good against the face shields and armor they wore, so she picked up her speed. Deep into oxygen debt, even with the enhanced hemoglobin, but fast was what she had to have—

They were dazed, but coming back online—

She barreled into the first one shoulder first and knocked him sprawling, leaped at the second as he swung his weapon around to bear—

Hit him with her hip in his midsection and knocked him down, too.

She rolled, pulled her knife, lifted the second one's face shield, and stabbed him in the right eye.

The other one was on his hands and knees, trying to get up, and now she had time to get her carbine back in hand. She shot him in the back as he stood.

Twelve up. Twelve down. Now *that* was pretty good . . .

- - - - - -

Kay fired at the door's jamb, tearing the foam away and making the lock useless. Wink was slow to catch up, and she was already through the door when he got there.

Inside, a quick glance showed an armed man holding a gun at a woman's head.

"Stop, or I'll—"

Kay fired her carbine and the round went into the man's mouth. Blew the back of his head out as he spasmed away from his captive. Not as satisfying as a claw, but the best option.

"Wh-who are you?"

Wink came into the room. "That's *Kluth*fem, but you can call her 'Kay.' Your father sent us to collect you."

"Thank the gods!"

"You might spare a few prayers for Cutter Force Initiative, too," Wink said. "We sometimes do the gods' light fighting for them.

"Come on, we have to leave. We are about to be in the middle of a war zone."

— — — — — —

Cutter broke the connection with Jo. There was a shitload of chatter on all kinds of opchans, one more coded conversation wasn't going to be noticed in time to do anything about it.

He commed the Thakore's number.

"Yes?"

"This might be a really good time to throw a few rocks at Rama's forces," Cutter said. "Chances are you might get a jump on them."

"Why do you say that?"

"Rama has gone to join his ancestors. He told his people to sit tight until he got back. They'll fight if attacked, of course, but it might take 'em a few seconds to get their shit together, and your odds are not going to get better. I'm pretty sure that Rajah Ramal is about to reconsider this war in a new light. I'd guess the terms will be a lot better for an armistice."

"You found his daughter?"

"We did."

"Alive?"

"Yes."

"And Rama is dead?"

"As deep vacuum."

"Krishna and Shiva and Brahma be praised! I owe you a great debt, Colonel."

"Think nothing of it. Just doing our job."

Once the Thakore was off-line, Cutter sat alone in the dark on the scooter, waiting.

Reflecting on the new input he'd gotten from Jo.

— — — — —

Jo saw Rags standing next to the scooter right where he'd said he'd be. She and Indira arrived there.

"Colonel, this is Indira Ramal. This is Colonel Cutter."

"Nice to finally meet you," Rags said. "What say we take a little ride?" He nodded at the scooter. "We have a hopper waiting to take you back to your father."

Indira said, "Is it true? That Rama was responsible for taking me?"

Cutter shrugged. "Evidence seems to point that way."

She shook her head. "I cannot believe it. He—I never . . ." She trailed off. She looked as if she was about to cry.

Cutter and Jo exchanged quick glances.

"Best we get moving," Cutter said. "We can sort everything out once we are back at your home."

"I'll collect the others and meet you at the rendezvous," Jo said.

"Take care."

"Always do."

— — — — —

Jo jogged through the forest, fast enough to cover a lot of ground quickly, but slowly enough so she wouldn't come across nervous shooters before her senses or transponder warned her.

Wink, Gramps, Gunny, Singh, and Kay had left the camp, and she'd intersect their paths shortly. With any luck, they'd avoid further contact with elements of either army, get to the hopper, and be on their way. Thirty minutes to Mumbaiian airspace, another hour to the Rajah's, and they were done. The locals could blow each other to bits after that, with J-Corps watching and cheering. It wasn't CFI's affair. Not a done deal. Not time to relax yet.

Her strength reserves were still pretty good though she sucked down a bulb of electrolytes and carbohydrates as she moved. Good idea to charge your batteries when you could; never knew when you'd need the juice.

Not far now.

She got a hit on her transponder. Pulled up. Four of them. She took a deep breath, got ready . . . ah, wait . . .

XTJC sigs. If they weren't lying like she was.

She held her carbine ready, stopped, as the four ghosted into sight.

"Who goes there?" came the query. "As if I didn't already know."

Jo recognized the voice: Lieutenant Dodd.

Jo raised her carbine one-handed to point skyward. "Evening, Lieutenant."

Dodd moved closer. "Kind of late to be out for a walk, isn't it, Captain?"

"I have insomnia."

"Yeah, I bet."

"Sergeant Hosep here with you?"

"No, the sergeant wanted to come, but he is back at the base."

"Suffering for our little ruse, is he?"

"Yes, fem, and hating you all the more for it."

Jo chuckled. "His own damn fault."

"I know. Man is as tough as a boxcar full of boots but

not the sharpest knife in the case." She paused. "Well, we have to run. Apparently somebody is blowing things up in Rama Rajak's encampment, and we need to go see if that's appropriate and within the local rules of war and all. I'll say hello for you if I see him."

"Good luck with that part," Jo said.

Dodd looked at her.

"I don't think Rama is entertaining any more callers this evening."

# THIRTY-FIVE

Kay had the point and was out of sight.

Singh, just ahead and to her right, took the incoming round on his carbine, and while the round blew right through the gun's action, the combination of that and his armor was enough to stop the bullet from getting through to his body.

At least enough so he didn't fall down dead.

So much for the fake transponder sig.

Gunny didn't have a shot—Singh was between her and the shooter, and she looked up to see two more Pahali soldiers in front of her she had to deal with, so she swung her carbine's muzzle to the left and tapped the trigger, a pair of deuces for each—

*Pap-pap! Pap-pap!*

By the time she looked back, Singh had pulled his big knife. He charged the soldier who'd shot him.

Gunny flicked a glance at the third Pahali and saw he was fumbling with a magazine, trying to reload.

She had the shot now, but Singh was almost on top of the

guy, his knife cocked, and Gunny could see that he'd get there in another heartbeat. It was gonna be tight, and even as she lined it up, she saw she would be a hair slow, Singh would be in the line of fire again . . . *was* in it—

She eased off the trigger and lifted the muzzle, which was okay because—

Singh faked high, then skewered the guy in front of him, shoved his grandfather's knife at an angle under the man's armpit as he raised his arm to block, just over the top of his armor's cutout.

The blade went in to the hilt—

The soldier dropped his useless carbine and reached for Singh's knife with both hands

*Didn't expect to get stabbed out here, did you?*

Singh twisted the blade as he pulled it out. He thrust-kicked the wounded soldier with the heel of his right boot, hit him in the low ribs, and knocked the man sprawling.

Gunny saw the blood pumping from the fallen man's wound.

*Hit an artery—*

Singh kneeled and cut the man's throat. Still on his knees, Singh did a quick snap down and to his right and slung blood from his blade. He resheathed it. He picked up the dying man's weapon, took the magazine pouch from the man's belt, and attached it to his own. He pulled a fresh magazine out of the pouch, locked it into the carbine, and thumbed the bolt release, chambering a round. He did a 360 sweep, looking for new targets. He pulled the gun's muzzle up when he came to Gunny.

He did it all easily, matter-of-factly, as if it were a drill.

Gunny grinned. "Way to go, Singh."

She waved the advance jive. He nodded.

They continued their run through the woods.

He was gonna be okay, the kid. That was a fine combat encounter, the knife, the gun, the reload and scan. If they made it back to the transport and got back to base alive, it was gonna be a good story over drinks. And one Singh could tell to his kid someday when he passed the knife along to him or her.

She glanced back. Where the hell was Wink? He was supposed to be right behind them.

"Ease up," she said. "Wink? Where the fuck are you?"

– – – – – –

Gunny and Singh were doing okay up there clearing the forest, and Wink didn't have much to do. He heard her com.

"Two hundred meters back, Gunny. Be there in a few seconds. Don't go slow on my account, I'm just enjoying the scenery here—hello?"

Then he came across a stray picket of his own . . .

He had the advantage when he saw the Pahali soldier.

Wink knew who his friends were; the soldier, if his transponder was working, probably thought that Wink was one of his own. Since Gunny and Singh had been shooting up ahead, maybe the transponder trick wasn't working, but this guy wasn't pointing his gun at Wink.

Against the rules of war, to fake a sig that way, but this wasn't CFI's war, was it? The rules didn't apply to them— both sides would shoot them if they had a chance.

All he had to do was raise a hand and wave at the soldier in greeting. The man would automatically return the wave, and at twenty-five meters, it would be an easy shot.

That was the smartest thing to do. Also the safest.

Save for his running activity, his heart rate was relatively slow and steady, there was no bubble of adrenaline popping in him. He wasn't afraid, and given the situation, he should be at least a little bit nervous.

Again, the perils of an adrenaline junkie's habituation. You needed a little more to spark it if you went to the edge a lot, and this one soldier thinking he was a buddy wasn't gonna spike anything.

So Wink yelled: "Hey, Pahali! Welcome to Balaji!"

The soldier started as he realized what Wink had said. The transponder was wrong! This was an *enemy*!

Time seemed to slow down:

The Pahali began to raise his weapon . . .

Wink waited. *Not yet* . . .

The carbine's muzzle came up, oh, so slow . . .

*No . . . Not yet . . . not yet . . .*

*Now!*

Wink snapped his own carbine up and point shot.

The Pahali soldier's carbine went off maybe a quarter second later, and the round blew past Wink's left ear close enough for him to hear the whine and feel the wind of its passage—

Wink's shot was better. The round blew through the Pahali's armor and the man collapsed.

Wink's heartbeat went up a hair. He felt a little surge of excitement, but . . .

Not enough

"What the fuck are you doin'?" Gunny said, coming up behind him. "Why didn't you just shoot the sucker?"

"Where's the fun in that?"

"Doc, you are gonna get killed, and it will be a shame because then we'd have to break in an FNG, and that will be a pain in the ass. You need to think of us."

"Says the woman who practices her fast draw against an already-drawn gun?"

She shook her head. "Different. Let's go. The hopper is most of a klick that way—"

Then they heard Kay toggle her com and say: "Why are you here? Has the Rajah sent you?"

"What the fuck?" Gunny said. "Sent who?"

"Go see," he said. "I'll collect Gramps, be there right behind you."

– – – – –

Kay said, "Why are you here? Has the Rajah sent you?"

Ganesh grinned. "No. I am here on my own."

Kay said nothing, but she understood immediately then why he had come.

"You will not take me by surprise this time, *karāhiyat* animal!"

They seemed fond of that word here: *abomination.*

He held his knife in front of him, point facing her. Kay kept her silence as she circled slowly to her left.

The others had heard her com. They would be coming . . .

Gunny arrived and pointed her carbine at Ganesh. "Put the knife away," she said.

"This matter does not concern you!"

"On this, we agree," Kay said. She didn't look away from Ganesh. "Mine."

Gunny raised the muzzle of her weapon to point skyward. "Ah was just tryin' to do you a favor, Ganesh. It's your ass. But hurry, Kay, the clock is running, we need to get gone. Got too many soldiers roamin' around."

Wink came into the clearing, followed by Gramps. They looked at Gunny. She waved them off. "Kay's got it." Then she subvocalized into her com: "Jo? You want to see Kay dance with Ganesh? Better move."

"Thirty seconds," Jo said.

"Probably won't last that long."

Kay continued to circle. She had yet to extend her claws.

She noticed that something about Ganesh's motions seemed off. He wasn't fast, but it seemed as if he was holding back. She sniffed the air. He was downwind, but she caught a faint trace.

Ah.

Gunny also got it. "Kay, Ah b'lieve our true-believer boy Ganesh here has had some alterations done on himself."

"Yes, he has. I can smell them—even over his fear."

"Reckon that makes him calling anybody 'an abomination' kinda suspect, doesn't it?"

Ganesh edged a little to his left, seemed a little more nervous. So much for his element of surprise.

*Enhanced speed,* Kay guessed.

Jo arrived. "Did I miss anything? I—wait. Kay, he's augmented."

"She knows," Gramps said.

"No matter," Kay said. She opened her hands. Her claws snapped out inaudibly.

"Gets me every time I see that," Wink said.

Ganesh looked increasingly fretful.

"You can still walk away, Ganesh," Jo said.

"I cannot. This creature insults me."

"How? *You* jumped *her.* She kicked your ass. Ah make that *your* fault."

"She insults me by her *existence!*"

Gunny looked at Jo. "Can't say we didn't try—"

— — — — — —

Ganesh jumped, and he was a lot faster than he had been in the recording Gunny had seen of that first encounter. He led with the blade, but Kay was already moving as soon as he stepped, and she wasn't getting out of the way—she was charging at him.

He had fifty to sixty kilos on her and his reach with the knife was a lot longer than Kay's, but of a movement, she dropped lower, blocked with her left hand, and was inside Ganesh's arm, right in his face—

He tried to pull the knife back and twist away, but she raked her left claws across his knife arm and opened it from elbow to wrist; at the same time, she jammed her right claws into his throat and tore out his voice box. Then she climbed him, got her feet onto his chest, and shoved away, pushing him backward as she arced up and back, turning a high back dive into a tucked somersault, landing lightly on her toes as Ganesh collapsed onto his side like a felled tree.

Maybe three seconds, attack to ending, tops.

Kay dropped the gory part of his neck's anatomy she held as Ganesh gurgled, spasmed, went completely slack.

Gramps shook his head. "Another fucking show-off. You and Gunny could take your act out on the road."

Kay whickered.

"That was no fun at all," Wink said. "Rip-claw-thank-you-sah. I'd paid for this show, I'd want my money back—"

Jo said, "We need to go—"

Tracers blew through the clearing, and the suppressed rifles firing them became audible at the same time, *cough-cough-cough-cough—*

"Fuck!" Gunny yelled. She spun around.

Wink saw blood blossom from a wound on Gunny's un-armored upper right arm—

As he watched, her carbine retracted. She crouched, pulled a pistol with her good hand, pointed it into the woods, and started shooting—

Jo and Gramps were already hosing the forest with their carbines on full auto, spraying fifteen rounds a second waist level at the unseen shooters. Wink heard screams from the forest as he ran for Gunny, a smart dressing already in hand. He got there, peeled the trigger-stik cover off, and pressed it against Gunny's wound. The battle dressing hummed as the rudimentary computer's sensor locked the bandage down, came online, and flashed its diagnosis. He looked at the dataflux.

The shooting stopped.

The bandage whirred: fragmented round, got the arm, shoulder, broke the collarbone on that side. No big arteries hit. Could be worse—

The dressing assessed Gunny's augmentation status and added what it thought was enough painkiller to make up any difference. It also pumped coagulants and steroids and PH balancers into the wound, along with antibiotics and adrenaline.

Enough damage so that she wasn't going to be using that arm for a while—

Either the dressing gave her too much chem, or shock set in. Gunny fell.

Wink managed to catch her and lower her to the ground.

Gramps said, "Jo, you got it?"

"I got it," Jo said.

Kay had vanished into the woods, and there came another scream as she found somebody too slow to get out of her way.

Gramps spun and dropped to his knees. "Megan!" He put one hand under her head.

Wink touched the control panel on the rudcomp and the dressing gave Gunny a squirt of revivant. Her eyes fluttered open. She looked up and saw Gramps bent over her, his expression was full of worry.

"Megan?"

"Crap. Ah died and went to hell, didn't Ah? Got to be if you're here, Roy."

"You're not dead yet, Chocolatte. You don't get to do that if I can help it."

They looked at each other and had a moment . . .

Wink hated to break into it, but that was his job. "We need to get to the transport, people, and apply more than a smart Band-Aid to Gunny's injuries."

Jo used her com: "Colonel?"

"We're on board," he said. "You need to stop dicking around out there and join us."

"On the way."

"Will Ah be able to play the piano, Doc?"

"Not if you couldn't play it before."

"Heard that one already, huh?"

"No more than eighty or a hundred times. Help me get her up."

They got Gunny to her feet.

"Can you walk?"

"Nobody shot me in the leg, did they? Can't tell, all the dope."

"Legs are fine. Let's go."

Gunny looked at Ganesh. "What about him?"

"He's dead-thirty, and who gives an aardvark's ass?" Wink said.

Wink was not the kind of doctor who would shoot some-body and then hurry to fix him, especially if he had just hurt one of Wink's own. He was the kind of doctor who would shoot somebody and spit on him as he lay dying if he'd done that. Maybe kick him, too. Not a great bedside manner, but what you wanted in a fellow soldier.

"Ah do believe Ah might could go lie down for a bit. Ah'm a little tired. Long day and all."

"I'll put a mint on your pillow, Chocolatte."

They moved out.

There was a thought rattling around in Jo's head, she couldn't quite pin it down, something about Ganesh . . .

Wait. There it was:

How had he *found* them?

# THIRTY-SIX

"Hey, there," the colonel said. "You need a ride? We're going as far as Ramal, over in New Mumbai."

Jo grinned. "Well, it's pretty nice out. We could walk."

"Make up your minds," he said. "I don't have all night to chat with hitchhikers."

"Get in the hopper, Jo," Gunny said. "Ah ain't walkin' five thousand klicks with Gramps here feeling up my titty."

Gramps said, "I'm just trying to keep you from falling down. Besides, there's not much to hold on to."

Kay whickered.

They loaded in. Nancy hit the risers, and they lifted.

Nancy said. "Folks, the seat-belt sign is lit. No smoking, and if you need to pee, hold it. We are a bullet, and we ain't slowing down until we get home."

# THIRTY-SEVEN

"More tea, Colonel?"

"No, I'm good."

The Rajah smiled behind his thin beard, and once again, Cutter was taken with the notion of how complicated human beings could be. Kay had it right: Look up "devious," and there would be a picture of some sneaky-looking *Homo sapiens* next to it. Maybe one in a red turban.

Cutter shook his head.

"There seems to be something more on your mind," the Rajah said.

"Just thinking about how things turned out."

The Rajah leaned back. His form-chair shifted smoothly and silently as it adjusted to his new position. "My daughter is safe. Nothing else matters. Is the bonus payment sufficient?"

"More than generous, sir."

"But . . . ?"

Cutter looked him in the eyes. "But I hate to be lied to and used, even if I'm well compensated for it."

The Rajah could have raised an eyebrow in pretend

wonder. *Why, Colonel, whatever are you talking about?* But he only smiled a bit wider.

There was no question but that he knew *exactly* what they were talking about.

"You surprise me," he said. "I did not expect you to see past Rama."

"I'm not sure I would have, except that I have an XO who is a walking stress analyzer. She said Rama was telling the truth when he said he didn't take Indira. Although by the time I knew that, it was too late for Rama. He would have killed me."

"Ah. I keep forgetting about these unnatural things you people enjoy inserting into yourselves. We seldom indulge in such here.

"This does not automatically point at me, that Rama was not the one."

"Well. If he was telling the truth and *he* didn't do it, who did that leave? Who had the power to manipulate the situation? It would have to be somebody with major clout. The suspect list got very short when we started considering all those rich people who were involved. Who could get them to do what they did? Had to be somebody with power since they don't need the money.

"Rama had such, but if he didn't? Who else could it be? Who knew all the buttons to push? More importantly, who had inside access to all we were up to?"

The Rajah smiled and inclined his head.

"Your daughter—who I assume was never in any real danger—is back home. Was she part of it? Or did you use her as a pawn, too?"

There was a slight pause. "My daughter is an uncorrupted soul and a pearl of great value. She believes that Rama betrayed her. Eventually, he *would* have—it was his nature. She liked him, perhaps even loved him, despite the political aspect of their engagement, but he would have disappointed her. Only a matter of time.

"Women are attracted to men with a certain streak of cruelty. This is because women have that in them, too. You know the old saying, 'If you are captured in battle, don't let them give you to the women.'"

Cutter nodded. "And Rama, her cruel, ambitious, headstrong suitor, is dead, leaving his father, a weak rajah, running Pahal. A likable man, but one without strength, as you pointed out.

"How long before you install a puppet in his place?"

The Rajah shrugged. "Who can know the minds of the gods? Why do they take this one and leave that one? They are ever capricious. A healthy man falls over with a bad heart a week after his doctor told him he was fine? It happens all the time."

"So you have Mumbai, and soon, you will run Pahal. The thakoredom of Balaji is now more pliable as a result of your generous peace accord, and Rama is out of the way. There are better trade agreements favoring you, a less restrictive border, more access to their markets. And the Thakore might have an accident, too.

"Can Depal and Hem be far behind?"

"They are of lesser importance, but, yes, you are right, I cannot help but think that their governments will come to see the benefits of accepting our counsel and wisdom in the not-too-distant future.

"One way or another . . ."

"And you rule the world."

"Well, not the world; but this continent, which is, for all intents and purposes, the only part of the planet worth ruling. If, of course, the gods will it."

"And if somebody gives them a little help."

Ramal smiled. "The gods smile upon those with initiative. And I am not a despotic, cruel man—my people love and respect me, and with just cause. I have been good to them. Nothing changes, save I can be benevolent to more souls."

Cutter shook his head. "You played us like a master."

"I have been Rajah for a long time. I took especial care that the clues not be too easy to find. And that there were many leading to assorted dead ends, to delay things."

"Like the Rel?"

"I thought that one clever. One more thing for you to puzzle over. What could it mean? It must mean *some*thing, yes? Some kind of great conspiracy if it involved aliens? Wheels within wheels, as many as I thought necessary. I did underestimate you, but not all that much."

"And enough fingers were pointed at Rama so we had to think it was him. Udiva, the cloth merchant? *We* asked *you* to help us get to her—after you aimed us in her direction. Putting Indira in the middle of Rama's camp? Brilliant. How could it be anybody *but* Rama?"

The Rajah gave him a small nod, acknowledging the compliment. "I thought those particularly effective myself. Those alone were enough to sell the story, yes?"

"And if we'd captured him instead if killing him?"

The Rajah shrugged. "After you were gone, there would have been a trial. Rama would be condemned. I would be magnanimous, I would commute his death penalty to life imprisonment. A year or two or five later, Rama would have had an accident, or some sudden and fatal illness. Dead, Rama would no longer be any danger to my plans."

Cutter said, "Was the assassination attempt real?"

"Of course not. Merely a way to start you down the proper path. My daughter kidnapped, an assault on my person, which you thwarted, as I knew you would. My personal guards are completely loyal. None would have fired at me. They died accepting of their fates, honored to have been chosen, secure in the knowledge their families would be cared for. I was thus established as the focus of somebody's evil intent, you would be somewhat more invested, and at the cost of a few guards."

"You are a piece of work, aren't you?"

"But, Colonel, why should this trouble you so? You came to do a job. True, it was a sham, but you did it. It will be counted as a credit to your record, and I will be lavish in my recommendations to any who should ask. Your contract has been satisfied, payment tendered, a bonus that is, as you said, quite generous. None of your people died. You may go on about your business, richer and, dare I say, wiser? And my position is improved upon my own humble planet. A hand that might have eventually put a gun into my back has been stilled. Peace has been restored. All is well that ends well, no?"

Cutter stood. Not much he could say to that.

The Rajah stayed in his chair.

"We'll be breaking down our camp and leaving as soon as possible."

"I have disappointed you."

"I'm just a hired sword. It doesn't matter what I think."

"Ultimately, yes, that is true, Colonel. You are the blade, but I was the hand that used you. Isn't that what usually happens?"

Cutter nodded. "I guess so."

He turned and walked away.

Behind him, he could almost hear the Rajah's smile.

*The motherfucker.*

# THIRTY-EIGHT

There wasn't much left for them to do, save pack it up and lift.

Cutter had a bottle of first-rate scotch sent to Colonel Hitachi, with a note expressing his regrets that they wouldn't have a chance to sit down and touch glasses. He wanted to be off this world as soon as they could manage it, and the taste of whatever he might drink with the XTJC commander would be tinged by his bad mood.

His own fault, of course, it always was when you misstepped, but still, that didn't help, either. The Rajah had suckered him, and there wasn't anything he could do about it. Part of a standard contract was that you didn't turn your hardware on your employer for six months after the job was over. Kept you honest, that, in case somebody came up with a handsome offer to switch sides.

Not that it would take much to go that route. A bent noodle coin would be more than enough . . .

As the dingy was being loaded, Cutter looked up to see Singh marching across the yard toward him. He wasn't a happy-looking young man. He could certainly understand that: Gunny had talked to the kid and told him what the Rajah had done. Plenty for him to chew on.

Plenty enough for everybody involved to try and swallow without choking . . .

"Singh."

"Colonel. I have come to say farewell."

"You understand how I might be a little put out with you, right?"

To his credit, he didn't try to pretend that he didn't know what Cutter was talking about. "I am my Rajah's man, body and soul, Colonel. I was given my orders."

He didn't look any happier having said that, either.

"I understand your loyalty. The thought crossed our minds that when we needed a guide, the Rajah would give us one he'd told to keep his eyes and ears open. Only good tactics, and I'd have done the same in his position."

Singh said nothing.

"And when you came back later, wanting to be part of the unit for the duration of our stay here, I understand that, too. The Rajah still needed to keep tabs on us. And you thought you were helping him find his daughter by reporting on what we did.

"That's how Ganesh knew exactly where to find us on the battlefield, isn't it?"

Singh nodded. "This is so. I communicated with Ganesh."

"I'd probably be more upset, but I'm guessing that once you found out who was really responsible for Indira's kidnapping, and how he'd gone about it, your faith in the Rajah took a hit."

"I am sworn to him nonetheless."

There was a long pause. Cutter let it lie.

Finally, Singh said, "I am but a simple soldier, and unworthy to question my Rajah's motives. But . . ." He waved a hand, palm up toward the sky. "I find it hard to understand how a man of honor can justify some things."

"And you thought the Rajah a man of honor."

"Of course."

"And now?"

"It is not my place to say. But you treated me with respect and consideration, and for that I am appreciative. And sorry that I had to be less than honest with you in return."

"Tell you what, Singh. If you ever decide that the Rajah's bread is no longer to your taste, why don't you come and look us up? There's always a place for a good soldier in CFI."

Singh looked at him as if he had sprouted horns. "You would hire me after what I did? Spying on you? Betraying your confidence?"

"Sometimes it gets misplaced, but there's a premium on loyalty in our business, when it's put in the right place."

"You shame me."

"Not at all. A soldier does his duty as long as he wears the uniform. Once he takes it off? He starts over, using what he has learned. Something you might come to consider."

"I appreciate this, Colonel. In your place, I might not be so generous."

"I think you underestimate yourself, Singh. Not every man would have come here as you just did."

Cutter looked off into the distance. "We'll be leaving your world as soon as we finish loading our gear. I can't say the experience here is one I'd have chosen, but it was certainly . . . instructive."

"Gods be with you, sah."

"And you, Singh."

*Working for the Rajah, you'll need* some*body to watch your back . . .*

# THIRTY-NINE

The ship was deep into subspace, zipping soundlessly through the nether regions that couldn't really be seen as much as felt. All that emptiness had a kind of weight, at least psychologically.

Jo wandered to the infirmary. Wink stood just inside the entrance. There was but one of the medical suites occupied: Gunny, in an induced healing-trance, unconscious and scheduled to remain so for a week, as the machines pumped and shunted and applied their various chems and nanos and whatnot toward repairing her wounds. She would recover fully, Wink had told everybody, though it would be a while before her arm and shoulder were back to normal.

Sitting just inside the medical suite in a chair, leaning against the wall and asleep, was Gramps.

"He needs to get some rest," Jo said.

Wink looked at where Gramps sat. "Good luck getting him to leave."

"But she's not in any danger."

"Nope. But when she wakes up, he's bound and determined she won't do it without him there to razz her about getting shot."

Jo shook her head. "*That's* why he says he's doing it?"

"Yeah, he'd cut out his tongue before he admitted the real reason. If that was *him* in the bed? Bet your ass *she*'d be sitting in the chair waiting for him to wake up." He shook his head.

Jo smiled. "Love is grand."

"So it seems. Not that I would know."

"Never been in love, Wink?"

"Nope. Been in serious lust a time or sixty. Had a few partners I wouldn't have minded if they stuck around. But hearts and flowers and like that? No." He looked at her, saw something in her expression. "What?"

"Nothing."

"Not nothing, I'm a trained medical man here, I know a look when I see one. What?"

"I was just thinking about a reason that might be."

"Spill it."

"Maybe that living on the razor's edge keeps you from being open to that level of intimacy."

"What do you mean?"

She regarded him. "Sheeit, Wink, what do you think? You might could have fooled the Army's scryers by skirting the issue, but you aren't fooling anybody around here. That whole dance-with-death business? Doesn't leave much space for a normal relationship. Too much chance of here-today-gone-in-a-heartbeat thinking."

"Funny, coming from you."

"You're right about that. Military in general, and me specifically—I'm not the girl to be offering advice on the subject. I have my own shit to deal with. Somebody looking for something in me, there's a wall they can't get past. I put it there. That's how I know another wall when I see one."

Wink didn't say anything for a moment. Then: "Ain't we the pair? Doc the Adrenaline Junkie and Jo the Bulletproof

Woman Warrior, running pell-mell parallel with the final curtain."

She nodded. "Yep. What say we go have a drink? See what happens when we get drunk and start crying into our glasses?"

"Why don't we skip the booze and go straight to my room and screw each other's brains out instead?"

She smiled. "I thought you'd never ask."

# FORTY

After the ship dropped back into normal space, Kay found a com message waiting. She initiated the callback.

The SSC connection was bad, but good enough so Kay could see and hear her Eldest Brother, who had been three litters ahead of her own. They spoke NorVaz, the most common of the dialects on Vast, and there was no frippery, he got right to it.

It didn't take long, the conversation, and when it was over, Kay sat for a moment, pondering her course of action.

No question what she had to do; only how best to go about it.

She left her quarters and went to find Wink Doctor.

He was in the infirmary, working on his computer.

"Kay," he said. "How are you?"

"I am well personally; however, I have spoke to my Eldest Brother, *Droc*masc, on Vast, via SSC. There is a medical problem on the homeworld with which he needs my assistance."

"Anything I can do to help, I will."

"Thank you, Doctor."

He furrowed his brow. "Just curious, why did your Eldest Brother call you?"

"Before I left Vast and joined Cutter Force Initiative, I was a Healer."

He blinked at her. "You were a physician?"

"Yes."

He shook his head. "Why didn't I know that?"

"I had no need to mention it before now."

"Son of a bitch. Like calling home to talk to my mother— only way to find out anything is to ask a specific question; otherwise, she doesn't bring it up, just says everything is fine." He looked at her again. "So what is your brother's problem, medically speaking, if I might ask?"

"He is also well; however, several score Vastalimi have died recently. Our Healers have not been able to discover the cause."

"And he thinks you can?"

"I was considered an Adept Healer when I practiced. And I have the advantage of having been exposed to extraspecies medicine. My brother thinks I might bring a new perspective to the problem."

"What can I do?"

"I will shortly have test results from our Healers. I thought perhaps you might see something in these they missed."

"Sure."

"I will be taking leave to space to Vast as soon as we make planetfall. Perhaps with information that I can apply to the situation."

"You could just send it to them."

"No. Among the sufferers are my parents and a number of my siblings. I need to go home and help them. A matter of personal responsibility."

"Okay. Let's see what we can find out."

# FORTY-ONE

Cutter was not a natural time-binder. He'd learned early in his career that he had to track dates; it was necessary to slice the calendar into months, weeks, days, hours, even seconds, to achieve military goals with the necessary precision. When he remembered big events, though, they were seldom linked to a number. Sometimes, even a year or season weren't readily available. But there were a few dates that stuck.

Midnight bringing one of the most memorable ones was upon him.

As he sat behind his desk, staring through the wall and into the past, sipping at a fine bourbon whiskey over ice, he couldn't forget what this day's date meant.

Radé would have been nineteen today, had he survived.

He didn't spend much time looking backward, there was no joy in that. Sure, you had to learn from history, or be condemned to repeat it; and yes, there were good memories that brought smiles. But in this universe, time's arrow flew in one direction, and you couldn't go back. Were that possible, he'd give everything he had, or would ever have, to be able to step in front of the bastard who killed Radé. And, if he could manage it, put a bullet into Melinne's head on his way down. The universe would be better off.

Now and then when he was out of sorts, he considered hunting her down and doing that part. She was still out there, somewhere, and, unless there had been some kind of miracle, still fucking up everything she touched.

Her fault their son was dead.

He sipped at the bourbon. It was Hirsch Reserve, the last of the current bottle. Five hundred ND each—and that only if you bought a case at a time. It was aged for twenty-six years, first in charred French oak, then in isotet barrels, and sold to a select clientele. Cutter was on that list because he had done a big favor for the maker. He had five cases left, stashed in two different storage units on Earth, guaranteed to be safe from fire, flood, earthquake or other natural disasters. He allowed himself one glass a day, and he drank it slowly, though not so much so that the ice had a chance to melt too much and water it down. Normally, it was the highlight of his day, to sit quietly and drink his single glass of fine bourbon.

Not on what would have been his son's nineteenth birthday, though. The taste was great, but the experience was tinged with too much regret.

*Can't fix something? Let it go.*

He told himself that every year, but it didn't really help.

He lifted the glass in salute: "Here's to you, son. Wherever you might be."

# EPILOGUE

The team was on Saturn Main, and gearing up to do another TotalMart run. This one would be dealing with dirty-tricks-harriers working for one of TM's biggest competitors, Masbülc. It was way the hell and gone away, on Far Bundaloh.

It was a long-standing and ongoing problem, no emergency, so there was no hurry to burn aether and get there. It had become enough of an irritant that TM wanted it dealt with, but a few weeks more or less? Not that big a deal. And another easy caper, in theory.

Gramps read the news dataflik, idly skimming the galactic feed.

It was a long trip to the Veldt System, even in n-space. Maybe he could catch up on his Chapman Stick, he hadn't practiced nearly as much as he should have recently. There was that Bach concerto he never seemed to get quite right.

Gunny was working to improve her fast draw. She said she was still a hair slow, though he couldn't tell. She was diligent. The arm and shoulder were almost completely well, Wink had told her. Once the biology was right, Formentara would tweak the augs. Be as good as it was, which in Gramps's estimation was as good as anybody he'd ever seen. Looked like a magic trick: Pistol in holster. *Blur.* Pistol on target. Woman was a walking death-machine with anything that went bang or twang.

She said, "Any word from Kay and Wink?"

Gramps said, "Nope. On their way to Vast, they'll call when they get there."

"Sounds like a bad situation, her people dyin' like that."

He shrugged. "Between the two of them, I wouldn't be surprised if they figure out a cure."

Maybe Wink and Kay would make it back before they had to leave.

There was a pause. He blinked. *Ho!* "Well, well, would you looky here," he said.

Gunny glanced over at the projection floating above his computer. "What?"

"News of the galaxy. You remember our recent visit to Ananda?"

"Ah haven't gone completely senile like you. Ah remember it every time Ah move my fucking arm."

"You'll like this: It seems that our recent employer, the Rajah? He died suddenly."

"No shit?"

"Yesterday. Reviewing a parade, fell over, dead as a stone statue. Heart failure, it says."

"Huh. Couldn't happen to a more devious asshole."

"Says too that his daughter, Indira, has become the Rani—that's apparently the female version of 'Rajah,' and is now running the place."

"Good for her." *Blur.* Reholster. *Blur.* Reholster. She chuckled.

"Something funny, Chocolatte?"

"Just before we left, after Rags went to see the Rajah? He had a little talk with Indira."

Gramps grinned. "Really? You don't think he let on that

her father was behind her kidnapping and the death of her fiancé?"

"Well, you know, they could have been talking about the weather. But Ah saw her after they chatted, and the woman had steam coming out her ears, she was madder than a kicked spitcat."

"Oh, my." Irony practically dripped from those two words.

"Remember what Rags said, about how the Rajah told him all was well that ended well?"

Gramps nodded. "And about not letting them give you to the women."

"Looks like he was right."

*Blur.* Her pistol appeared in her hand, pointed at an invisible enemy.

Gramps nodded.

Sometimes it did end well.

**Want to connect with fellow science fiction and fantasy fans?**

For news on all your favorite Ace and Roc authors, sneak peeks into the newest releases, book giveaways, and much more—

**"Like" Ace and Roc Books on Facebook!**

**facebook.com/AceRocBooks**

M988JV1011

Step into another
world with

DESTINATION
ELSEWHERE

A new
community
dedicated
to the best
Science Fiction
and Fantasy.

Visit
 /DestinationElsewhere

M1160G0712